THE LADY OF THE NIGHT WIND

THE NIGHT WIND SAGA, VOLUME IV

BY

VARICK VANARDY

Edited by Christopher R. Yates
Foreword by J. Randolph Cox

THE BORGO PRESS

An Imprint of Wildside Press LLC

MMIX

CONTENTS

ILLUSTRATION

DEDICATION

This edition of *The Lady of the Night Wind* is dedicated to Maude Wayne, born March 26, 1895, died October 10, 1983. Ms. Wayne portrayed "Lady Kate," aka Katherine Maxwell in the silent movie *Alias "The Night Wind,"* a five-installment serial by Fox Studios in 1923 based on the first of the Night Wind novels by Frederic Van Rensselaer Dey. Ms. Wayne had a distinguished Hollywood career spanning at least a decade (1917-1927). She appeared in movies starring Rudolph Valentino, Gloria Swanson, and Roscoe 'Fatty' Arbuckle. In 1923, in the film *Hollywood*, she made a cameo appearance, as herself, along with Douglas Fairbanks Sr., Will Rogers and Charles Chaplin, among others. The undated photograph of Ms. Wayne, above, is reproduced here courtesy of the Academy of Motion Picture Arts and Sciences.

A NOTE ON THE TEXT

ACKNOWLEDGMENTS

This project would not be possible without the cooperation of the Old Worthington Library, Worthington, Ohio and the interlibrary loan service that made it possible for me to acquire the original text of *The Lady of the Night Wind* from the Public Library of Cincinnati and Hamilton County, Ohio. I am grateful to Kristine Krueger from the Academy of Motion Picture Arts and Sciences, Beverly Hills, California for her kind guidance through the process of securing the wonderful photograph of Maude Wayne displayed in the Dedication portion of this book. My sincere thanks go to Steve Miller for the original cover scan that graces this book, and to Bill Thom and Phil Stephenson-Payne for introductions to Mr. Miller. This cover is a digital copy of the cover of *All-Story Weekly* magazine, October 5, 1918, wherein the first installment of *The Lady of the Night Wind* originally appeared.

FOREWORD

The Lady of the Night Wind is the fourth of the novels about Bingham Harvard by Frederic Van Rensselaer Dey, writing as Varick Vanardy, a pseudonym created in part from his own name: Van R Dy. As the title suggests, this is the story of Katherine Maxwilton, also known as Kate Maxwell and Lady Kate of the Police and now the wife of Bingham Harvard, alias The Night Wind. It is so much her story that her husband spends very little time on stage compared to the first two books. There is really no room for him.

When Katherine observes Conrad Belknap cheating at cards she decides to deal with the possible scandal herself and not risk arousing the wrath of her husband. Had she not made that decision this novel might have been half as long, but by now she is used to protecting others from her husband's temper. The outcome of this resolution and what we learn about Katherine's own background should interest any reader able to appreciate fiction written in the early 20th century.

Those who have read the Foreword to *Alias "The Night Wind"* in the Wildside Press edition know that the creator of these characters did not live for many years after writing about them. In the early morning of April 26, 1922, Frederic Van Rensselaer Dey took his own life in the Hotel Broztell, on East Twenty-Seventh Street, in New York City. His death might have attracted little attention in the press but for the fact that he was recognized as having been the leading writer of the famous Nick Carter detective stories. He was not the creator of the character, though the *New York Times* credited him with that achievement in its front-page obituary. A few of his pseudonyms were mentioned, but the fact that with the death of Frederic Dey, Varick Vanardy also died went unnoticed.

Frederic Merrill Van Rensselaer Dey, born February 10, 1861, was a graduate of Columbia University Law School (1883) and a practicing attorney for a brief period. In 1881, when he was twenty years old, he sent a story to Beadle and Adams, a leading publisher

The Man Who Made Nick Carter.

The elder DUMAS boasted to NAPOLEON III, that he had written 1,200 volumes of fiction, but this huge total included the novels he wrote in collaboration and the stuff he bought from others and touched up. In point of actual personal production it is unlikely that DUMAS approached the number of words written by FREDERICK VAN RENSSELAER DEY, whose death was announced yesterday.

Beginning in 1890, DEY wrote one Nick Carter dime novel every week, with few exceptions, for twenty years. The name of the famous detective did not originate with DEY; one book about Nick had appeared before DEY took up the task of providing the weekly feast for the multitude of devourers of inexpensive tales of crime and adventure. The publishers who had copyrighted the hero's name handed it over to DEY with a contract for one thriller a week and it was DEY who made Nick's reputation.

Under the guidance of DEY Nick became a detective so lively, so resourceful, so modern in his methods that most of the older set of fiction detectives retired from the field. Before Nick's time there had been Old Sleuth, Cap Collier, Old King Brady and Old Rafferty. Men who are now gray haired golfers knew these celebrities well in the days when their adventures tiptoed through the pages of the *Family Story Paper* and the hebdomadal "libraries." They had pistols, handcuffs and dark lanterns galore, but none of them was as ingenious as Nick.

CONAN DOYLE introduced Sherlock Holmes to the world in 1887, two years before Nick Carter made his bow; but DEY always vigorously insisted that the powers of deduction with which he invested Nick were borrowed direct from POE and not from the author of "A Study in Scarlet." Not that deduction mattered much to the followers of Nick; they were keener for the grim chase of criminals, the wonderful disguise and the amazing strength of DEY's protagonist.

Yet DEY was more wonderful in real life than Nick was in fiction. He worked five days a week and each day turned out between 5,000 and 6,000 words—nearly three-quarters of a newspaper page. To perform such a feat it was necessary to have all possible ease of body and mind. DEY sat in a Morris chair and drew close to him a typing machine fastened to a platform which rested on the arms of the chair. Then he lay back, physically at rest, and drummed out page after page of "copy." He planned no plots; it would have been too much of a burden to follow them. The talent of DEY for the dime novel was so great that he could start a story with three minutes' thought. In came Nick before the second page was typed, and after that Carter and his associates, Chick and Patsy.

WRITER OF NICK CARTER STORIES WHO KILLED

FREDERICK VAN RENSSELAER DE

New York Herald editorial excerpt on the passing of Frederic Van Rensselaer Dey, dated April 27, 1922.

of dime novels. That first long story "Captain Ironnerve, The Counterfeiter Chief; or, The Gipsy Queen's Legacy" appeared in *Beadle's Dime Library*. His work for Beadle was not extensive and they did not publish another of his stories for eight years. He may have received encouragement for his writing if not immediate publication for he soon abandoned his law practice for a career as a writer.

His first detective novel for Street and Smith Publications, *Muertalma; or, The Poisoned Pin*, appeared late in 1890 under the pseudonym Marmaduke Dey, the name he had used on his work for Beadle. It attracted the attention of Ormond G. Smith, the president of the firm so that in 1891, at the age of thirty, Dey signed a contract to produce a weekly novelette of 20,000 words for a new publication devoted to the adventures of a detective named Nick Carter. The character had been created in 1886 by John Russell Coryell, a cousin of Ormond Smith, and the three novels he had written about Nick Carter had sold well enough for the publisher to decide to follow them with a regular series. Dey wrote a story a week for the *Nick Carter Detective Library* (later known as just the *Nick Carter Library)* until the end of the year when he was asked to add a weekly serial installment of six thousand words about Nick Carter for *Street and Smith's New York Weekly*, a popular story paper, to his schedule.

Dey paid little attention to the Nick Carter of John Coryell's novels. The new Nick Carter was slightly shorter than average and his strength was as great as that which he later assigned to Bingham Harvard. Thus, his nickname, The Little Giant, was appropriate. Where Coryell's hero had been trained in the detective arts by his father, old Sim Carter, Dey's Nick Carter was already mature and streetwise. He relied on his wits as well as his fists, but he had an arsenal of devices to aid him—lockpicks he had invented and revolvers hidden up his sleeves that dropped into his grasp when he pressed a spring. In common with other dime novel detectives he was a master of disguise and maintained a separate residence or office in the name of each of his alter egos. The tools of his trade included the usual wigs, beards, paints and dyes, but he could also alter his appearance with a twist of his facial muscles. Only a trusted few ever saw his real appearance.

Nick Carter often received assignments from the official police, sometimes from the famous inspector Thomas Byrnes himself, thus adding a touch of reality to the cases. Sometimes Nick worked for the government or for someone who was in trouble, but he might take a case for the sheer pleasure of tracking down a notorious smuggler or a swindler. His staff numbered three or four regular assistants: Chick, Patsy, or Ida Jones, whom he trained as his father had trained him. Other assistants came and went over the years.

He worked out of a mansion on New York's Madison Avenue where his wife, Ethel, assisted by Peter, the butler--later replaced by Joseph--kept house for him. Ethel was one of the few characters that Dey borrowed from Coryell. Nick met and married her in the course of working on his first case, the murder of his father.

Nick was victorious over many criminal masterminds in his long career, but the most popular one was the wily Dr. Quartz. Dey wrote nineteen stories about Nick's encounters with Dr. Quartz.

Young boys devoured the five-cent weeklies. When the stories were combined into paperbooks (Street and Smith's own term) businessmen tucked them into their coat pockets and read them on the way home from work. Dey helped develop the publishing "triplet" that Street and Smith employed extensively in which a story arc would be designed to last for three or more weeks so the parts could be edited later to form a single novel of 200 or 300 pages.

Dey constructed his fiction like other dime novels: stories that sometimes rambled, swift scene changes with multiple plots told in single sentence paragraphs and dialogue developed by writers paid by the line. Ideas came from everywhere and he admitted later that he made everything up as he went along and never knew how the story would end. This method extended to his later fiction as well. He wasted no space on descriptions of locations; if Nick went to Paris the reader had to accept that it was really Paris. Current events from the real world did not intrude into the imaginary world where Nick Carter lived. Characters spoke laconically. Repetition was common and no question was answered immediately. In addition, Nick and Chick would often discuss the outcome of a case over cigars.

In 1892, Dey found the routine of writing a fresh story every week difficult to maintain and other Street and Smith staff writers were assigned to fill in the gaps between his manuscripts. Years later, Dey claimed he recruited some of the substitute writers himself to allow him more time for the story paper serials. On some occasions, however, he took credit for writing all of the stories himself and completely dismissed Coryell's contributions. According to the publisher's records he suspended work on the novelettes entirely, but continued with the serials until the end of 1894. The publisher alternated the novelettes of other writers with reprints of Dey's earlier stories.

In 1893 he wrote a series of short stories about Alexander S. Williams of the New York police force and sent them to Beadle where they appeared under his own name Frederic M. Dey on a weekly basis from May to August in *The Banner Weekly*.

He appears to have published no fiction for the next four years and when he surfaced again on the literary front it was with a series of patriotic stories about the Spanish-American War for Frank A. Munsey's periodicals. The material appeared in *The Argosy* and *Munsey's Magazine*, most of it under his own name and this is where the name Frederic Van Rensselaer Dey first appeared in print. For one serial he adopted the equally flamboyant pseudonym Col. Aaron Ainsworth Burr.

With the end of the war, Dey turned to other topics for his *Argosy* serials and expanded his market to include newspapers that published fiction. In 1900 *Success Magazine* published his fantasy "The Magic Story." This guide to self-reliance for which he was paid $50 sold phenomenally well in book form and remains available today in its original form as well as revised and updated.

In 1904 he returned to work for Street and Smith and resumed writing novelettes for the *Nick Carter Weekly*, the colored cover successor to the old black and white cover *Nick Carter Library*. Other writers had kept the series going for the decade the original author was absent. The new stories were imaginative and his writing more polished. He brought back villains from the past and created new ones for Nick to battle. Followers of Nick Carter consider this period to be the Golden Age of the series. The pattern established before was soon repeated as staff writers filled in the gaps between Dey's contributions. He managed to write more than 300 novelettes before he finally quit in 1912. It was probably the most dependable employment he ever had.

Frederic Dey appears to have led the life of the quintessential dime novelist, living beyond his means and constantly in need of an advance from his publishers. When he moved into a new home in Westport, Connecticut, in 1905 he wrote Street and Smith for money to pay his bills since he had only enough on hand to pay for mailing them his next story. In 1909, a year in which he supplied only half the weekly novelettes issued, and perhaps to augment his finances, he recycled his old *Argosy* serials in clothbound novels, one under his own name and the others under pseudonyms. Each had a new title to disguise its origin.

12

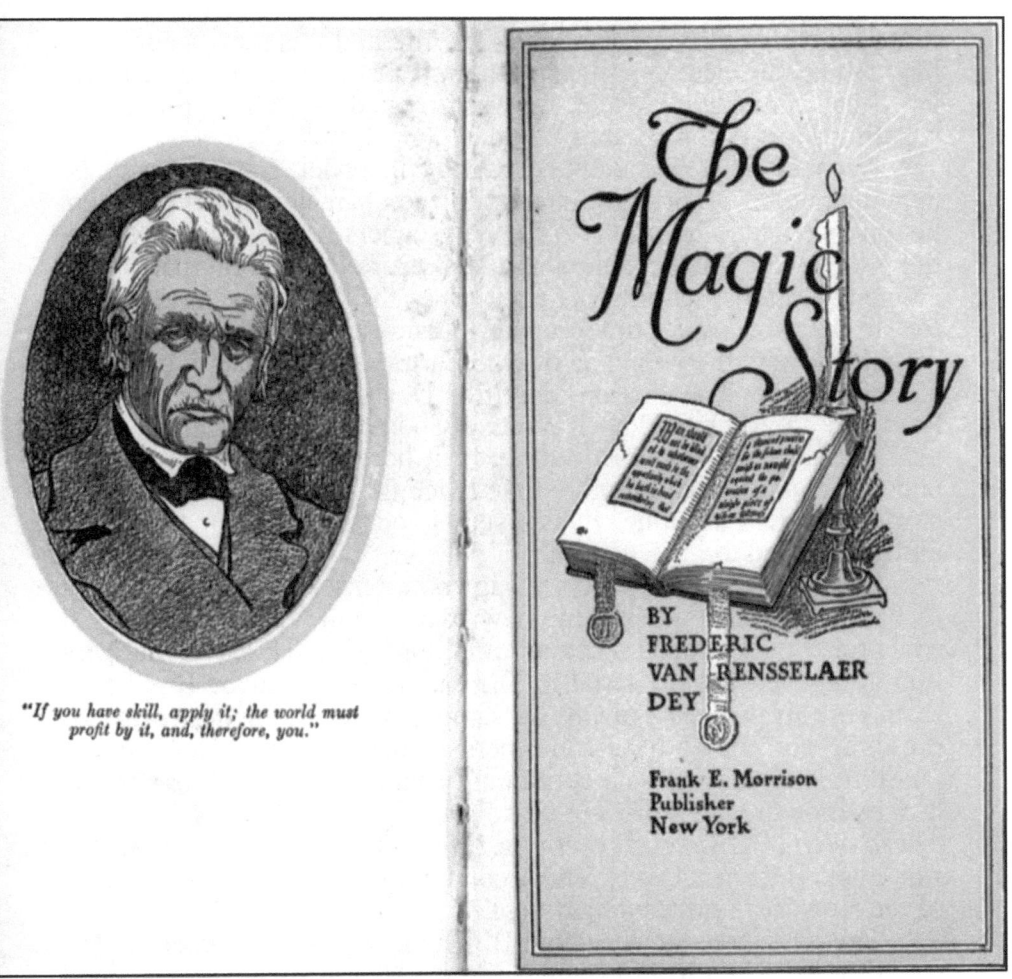

"If you have skill, apply it; the world must profit by it, and, therefore, you."

Frontispiece from the 1914, Frank E. Morrison, Publisher, 6th edition of Dey's most popular book, "The Magic Story" that originally appeared in *Success Magazine* in 1900.

Little is known of his personal life. Married twice, the father of three children, he had an older brother who survived him. He suffered from alcoholism for much of his life and this may account for his inability to meet deadlines. A newspaper account from 1913 relates that, while intoxicated, he was arrested in Denver for impersonating a law enforcement official.

Even after he had stopped writing the Nick Carter stories he demonstrated a proprietary interest in the character. Interviews that he gave or letters he wrote to the newspapers if they printed something he deemed misleading about Nick Carter were only part of his active role in maintaining his position as the great detective's mentor. In 1914 he was photographed outside the Hudson Theatre in New York with the young actor who portrayed boy detective Barney Cook on stage. The caption identified Dey as Nick Carter. In 1920 he wrote an article, "How I Wrote a Thousand 'Nick Carter' Novels," for *The American Magazine*. In it he enhanced his reputation and laid claim to writing more than twice the number of Nick Carter stories that he had done. It was very good publicity for the writer and only added to his legend.

Shortly after he stopped writing about Nick Carter he went back to work for Munsey using his new pseudonym Varick Vanardy. It was probably the encouragement of editor Robert H. Davis that kept him going. A two-part serial in *The Cavalier* introduced Birge Moreau, portrait painter, and Crewe, saloon-owner and underworld figure, who are one and the same person. It was Davis who saw the possibilities in Crewe as a continuing character and Dey returned to him in enough later stories to be collected in two volumes *The Two-Faced Man* (1918) and *Something Doing* (1919). Dey dedicated the first book to Robert Davis. The second book he dedicated to the men of the New York police department.

The first three stories about Bingham Harvard appeared in *The Cavalier* in 1913 and 1914 and it is likely that was all Dey intended writing in the Night Wind series. When the third story, *The Night Wind's Promise*, was published as a book it was both advertised and reviewed in *The New York Times* as the final work about the character. Dey may have felt he'd said all he could about Bingham and Katherine Harvard and he devoted the next four years to writing fiction for *All-Story Weekly* (which had merged with *The Cavalier*), *Argosy* and Street and Smith's new *Detective Story Magazine*. In many of these he demonstrated a style that could be considered a prototype for the hard-boiled style made so famous later in *Black Mask*.

Why did he return to the Night Wind after that? Did either the readers or the publisher ask for more? We may never know. The new story appeared in six parts in *All-Story Weekly* in 1918. When *The Lady of the Night Wind* appeared in book form publisher Macaulay syndicated it to newspapers like *The Atlanta Constitution* where installments appeared on a daily basis for nearly a month in 1919. (Dillingham, the publisher of the first three Night Wind novels went bankrupt in 1916 and Dey switched to Macaulay.) In many respects the story is just a recycling of elements from *The Night Wind's Promise*, but it must have appealed to readers though *The New York Times* found the book "somewhat cheap and dime novelish."

Dey published little magazine fiction that year: one story as Varick Vanardy and a second as Ross Beeckman, a name he had used earlier. In 1920 Macaulay published his final novel *Up Against It*, originally serialized in *Argosy* as "Odds and the Man." It is an adventure novel set in Canada about railroad magnates and devious doings in the great outdoors. There is an irony in the title of that last novel. During the following years he became convinced he had no prospects for the future and didn't want to be a burden to anyone. His hero, Dan Randall, came "up against it" and succeeded where his creator could not. In the end Dey had forgotten the precepts outlined in his most popular book *The Magic Story*.

Newspaper accounts vary as to the details, but the basic story is that he registered in the Hotel Broztell as "J. W. Dayer, of Nyack, New York," then wrote and mailed three letters, each of which indicated that he could see no way out; the newspapers disagree as to the recipients. One of them went to the hotel to look for him and found his body. Did he hope someone would arrive in time to rescue him? It would have been a feat worthy of his greatest character Nick Carter, and one equally worthy of Bingham Harvard.

—J. Randolph Cox
Northfield, MN
October 2007

J. Randolph Cox is a professor emeritus at St. Olaf College in Northfield, Minnesota and the editor of *Dime Novel Round-Up* – "A magazine devoted to the collecting, preservation and study of old-time dime and nickel novels, popular story papers, series books, and pulp magazines."

He has published widely in diverse periodicals. Professor Cox is the compiler for *Dashing Diamond Dick and Other Classic Dime Novels* (Penguin Classics, 2007), co-author, with David S. Siegel, of *Flashgun Casey, Crime Photographer: From the Pulps to Radio And Beyond* (Book Hunter Press, 2005), and author of *The Dime Novel Companion: A Source Book* (Greenwood Press, 2000).

Professor Cox played various roles in a string of publications in the late 1980s as well; among them are author of *Man of Magic and Mystery: A Guide to the Work of Walter B. Gibson* (Scarecrow Press, 1989), with William J. Scheick, he compiled *H.G. Wells: A Reference Guide* (G.K. Hall, 1988), and editor of a collection of essays in honor of the twentieth anniversary of *The Armchair Detective*, called *Tad-Schrift* (Brownstone Books, 1987).

Professor Cox is a contributor to the *Dictionary of Literary Biography, Twentieth Century Crime and Mystery Writers, The Oxford Companion to Crime and Mystery Writing,* and the *Encyclopedia of Mystery and Detection*. He is a recognized authority on the Nick Carter detective stories for dime novels, pulps and paperbacks. Other authorities in the field have been heard to say that "J. Randolph Cox has read more Nick Carter stories than any decent man should acknowledge."

CHAPTER I

BETWEEN THE PORTIÈRES

Katherine Harvard parted the curtains ever so little and peeped—the word is used advisedly—into the smaller room, and—the thing that she discovered was so amazing, so astounding, so paralyzing in its effect upon her that for an interval she stood perfectly still, without moving, barely breathing; indeed, it seemed to her as if her heart had stopped beating.

Her impulse in approaching the curtains and parting them thus silently had been one of playful mischief only. The thought that she might see something forbidden, something not meant for her or anybody to see, had not remotely occurred to her.

She knew that five of her guests were playing cards in that little room off of her husband's den—bridge, she had assumed—and had decided that it was high time for them to forego their game and join with the others on the veranda and the lawn; and so she had sought them.

There had been no sound of her approach, although she had not intended it to be silent or stealthy. She had ascended the stairs swiftly, passed through the open doorway into the den, crossed it to the curtains, parted them—and had come upon that stupefying knowledge—that hideously unthinkable monstrosity—a cheat. A cheat at a gentleman's game of cards. A cheat—a swindler! for the man could be nothing else—and he was one of her accepted guests.

She was herself not seen; her nearness was not suspected; each man of the five was, at the moment, busily intent upon his cards. Even the three who, by a mere lifting of their eyes would have discovered her, looked only upon their respective holdings. The backs of the remaining two were toward her; one of them obliquely; the other one directly. She stood at the parting of the curtains, immediately behind him, where she could look down over his shoulder upon the hand he held—where she could plainly see what he did and what he was doing.

Very gently indeed she permitted the curtains to fall together. She moved backward, away from them, exerting the utmost care to avoid the slightest sound that might betray her presence. She retreated to the doorway and halted at the threshold. From there, after a moment, she called aloud, using the given name of one of the players—her intimate friend, and Bingham's.

"Tom! Oh, Tom!" she said. "Are you men still playing cards—spoiling the afternoon for the others by your selfishness?"

Then, while at least three of the five responded, she crossed to the curtains and drew them wide open.

Tom Clancy was already on his feet.

"All through, Lady Kate," he announced, with the easy formality of an old and intimate friend. "Lucky thing, too. I'd have been a bankrupt in—" He stopped shame-facedly, and grinned.

Katherine shook a finger at him, half playfully, yet reprovingly, pretending not to notice the perfectly apparent evidences of high play that were all about her, in the expressions of the faces of the five men, and upon the table.

"You have been breaking my rule, Tom, haven't you?" she asked; and plainly did not expect an answer. Then she turned to the man whose back had been directly toward her when she parted the curtains the first time, and said smilingly—even ingenuously:

"You are almost a stranger, Mr. Belknap, so, of course, you could not have known that I strongly object to gambling, particularly among my guests at Myquest. But the others, all of them, did know—so, I will suggest"—she turned a smiling face toward the others, permitting her glance to rest upon each one of them for an instant at a time—"that the winner, or winners, make restitution to the losers. Of course you will all agree to that, to please me? However, I did not come here to chide you. I want you to come down to the veranda at once; really; as soon as the winners have made good to the losers. And, please, no more gambling."

She left them then still smiling, leaving behind her the impression that she had no idea that they might not obey her suggestion, which had, in fact, amounted to a mandate.

Four of the erstwhile players made no comment whatever after Katherine had gone. The fifth—Mr. Conrad Belknap, so called—smiled coldly, a slow, half-sneering smile that was not pleasant to see, and which might have been ingratiating, submissive to circumstance, or insulting, according as one wished to take it.

"Of course," he said, shrugging his shoulders significantly, "if you gentlemen wish to take advantage of Mrs. Harvard's dictum and—er—receive back what you have lost, I will obey her, and re-turn—"

"Don't be an ass, Belknap," Clancy interrupted sharply. "Come on, all of you. We're wanted below and out on the lawn. We will write our checks for you a little later, Belknap; and if, in the mean-time, Mrs. H. should ask questions, which she is not likely to do, it can truthfully be said that not a dollar in money has changed hands. Get me? Now, let's join the others downstairs."

The five descended the stairs together, and separated as they came out upon the veranda. Belknap dropped upon a vacant chair beside Betty Clancy, Tom's wife, who was chatting with the small group of ladies around her and painstakingly manipulating silk floss, needle, bodkin, and embroidery-frame with abundant skill at the same time. Archer, Sears, and Demming wandered with apparent aimlessness toward the tennis courts while they began to talk ear-nestly together; and Tom, after hesitating at the top of the steps to light a fresh cigar, felt a soft arm slipped beneath his own, and heard Katherine's voice remark, so that the others might hear her:

"Walk around to the kennels with me, Tom. I want to show you—"

When they had turned a bend in the path, and were lost to view from the veranda, Katherine asked abruptly:

"Tom, just who is Mr. Conrad Belknap?"

"Search me!" Clancy replied. "You ought to know better than I. Doesn't Bing know him? Where is Bing, anyhow?"

"He was detained in town and will be out later; about five or six o'clock, he said, over the telephone...No; Bing doesn't know Mr. Belknap. Neither of us ever saw him or heard his name before yes-terday. The Archers brought him with them yesterday afternoon. He is staying at their house—quite unexpectedly, Belle told me, when she telephoned to ask if she could bring him along. I thought, per-haps, you might have met him in town—that you might know some-thing about him."

"He certainly is some poker player if anybody should ask you," Clancy remarked with a wry smile.

"Poker! when you know that I disapprove! Really, Tom, I am surprised at you," Katherine returned with a half-mock show of in-dignation.

"Oh, well, I'm sorry. It shall not occur again; that I promise you."

19

"No," she said, as if that were a foregone conclusion.

"We were playing bridge—Demming, Archer, Sears, and I—when Belknap joined us. We had just finished a game. Five can't play at bridge, you know. Somebody suggested a small game of poker—just a few hands, and—"

"Who suggested it, Tom?"

"Blest if I remember; probably I did; I'm always doing the asinine thing, you know."

"It was not—really—what you would call a small game, was it?"

"Hardly."

"But"—Katherine stopped and stood facing him in the pathway, and there was an unmistakable twinkle in her eyes when she continued—"it is all right now, isn't it? Of course you all did as I suggested about the winnings and losses?"

Tom Clancy laughed aloud; then he chuckled; then he grinned, broadly.

"If I weren't entirely respectful to my hostess I might reply as I did to Belknap when he suggested it after you had—"

"Did he suggest it, Tom?"

"Yes—with a nice, new, super dreadnaught anchor chain welded onto it. You're much too good a sport, Katherine, to expect that we could accept—of course we couldn't welch on our losses. You know that."

She nodded.

"I understand," she said. "Was Mr. Belknap the only winner, Tom?"

"Practically. Harry Archer was a few dollars ahead, I believe, but—" Clancy stopped speaking. Then, quite seriously, he asked: "What are you trying to get at, Lady Kate? The game was perfectly fair, if that is what you're driving at. Belknap played in phenomenal luck, that's all, and so far as its having been a stiff game is concerned, that part of it was really my own fault."

"How was that? Please tell me."

"Oh, I happened to catch a pretty good hand—cold. See? I made the remark that if it were only 'table-stakes'—and so forth; you know the rest. Everybody was willing, and I won the pot. After that—well, the sky was the limit. We just drifted into it."

"I see; I understand," Katherine replied absently. "Shall we go back? There isn't a thing at the kennels to show you; you know the dogs as well as I do. Suppose we try a foursome. You take Belle Archer, and I'll ask Harry to play; they both love it."

"Look here, Katherine, if you expect that I'm going to quiz Belle about her gues—"

"My, my, my! I had forgotten all about him. He really is unusually good-looking, don't you think?"

"Who? Belknap? Uh-uh. I suppose so."

Later, when the tennis had been played, and Katherine and Harry Archer had seated themselves for a moment to rest beneath the spreading shade of a box-elder, she remarked, casually, and apropos of nothing in particular:

"Is Mr. Belknap quite an old acquaintance of yours, Harry? He is a handsome man, and such an interesting talker. Have you known him a very long time?"

"Never saw him in my life until day before yesterday—Thursday, you know," was the indifferent response of the always blunt and outspoken Archer, whose inheritance had been a comfortably large fortune, a great and never-varying good nature, and only a nominal supply of wit and brains. "He blew in to see me at the office, you know; brought a letter of introduction from Beekman Storrs—Beeky 'n' I were chums at Old Eli, y' know—so I asked him down to Ledgewood. Belle gave me the devil for it, too; said I'd no call to do it when I knew we were comin' here for the week-end, 'n' I told her to fetch him along. She phoned to you, didn't she?"

"Oh, yes, and it was perfectly all right. It always is, Harry, to bring your guests with you, if you have any. They are calling us. Shall we go in?"

Katherine was no longer in a dilemma.

Until she had satisfied herself that Conrad Belknap was really nothing more than a passing acquaintance of the Archers, she had not known what course to take after her discovery of the true character of the unbidden guest; but, after the short conversation with Harry, her duty seemed extraordinarily clear.

She went about it, too, with her customary directness, having determined that she would indulge in no confidences whatsoever, concerning what she had seen; she decided that she would not even confide in her husband—until after their guests had departed, Sunday evening, and Monday morning.

Harvard arrived in time to dress for dinner. After it they all went again to the wide veranda, for the month was June, and the evening an unusually warm one, even for that time of year.

Presently, when another half-hour had passed, Katherine left her chair, paused at the top of the steps, and said to Belknap, who was seated there:

"Will you take a walk in the grounds with me, Mr. Belknap? Myquest is beautiful in the moonlight, viewed from a short distance."

He was beside her instantly, and with ill-concealed eagerness; and he talked much and well, while Katherine directed their steps toward a summer-house a few hundred feet away.

She was silent meanwhile, replying to him only in monosyllables—until she stopped and turned, confronting him in the moonlight, directly in front of it.

"Mr. Belknap," she began, without preface, "I had a distinct purpose in asking you to walk with me just now. I have a most unpleasant duty to perform; but it is a duty, and it must be done. Please do not interrupt me; there will be no need for you to speak at all. It is my duty to tell you that I was at the curtains and looked between them this afternoon while you were dealing the cards for that last hand at poker. What I saw then you know, without the need of telling. I have brought you out here to suggest that if you can find it convenient to receive a message, by telephone or telegraph, that will necessitate your return to the city to-night—at once—no other person than ourselves will need to know the true reason for your sudden departure. But you must go, to-night."

If Katherine had anticipated the infliction of a shock upon the swindler, she was disappointed. He only stared at her; and then—

He laughed aloud.

CHAPTER II

THE INSOLENCE OF BELKNAP

"Brave talk, Mrs. Harvard; but"—Belknap shrugged his shoulders and grimaced a smile that was plainly intended for insolence as well as amused tolerance—"just talk. Nothing more. You order me from your home—to leave Myquest?" He shrugged again and smiled the more. "Very well, madam, I shall—*not*—go."

For a brief moment Katherine stared at the man, too astounded, and vastly too indignant to reply. His attitude was as amazing as it was intolerable; and the fact that he offered no attempt to deny the imputation she had made against him was inexplicable—save only that he doubtless comprehended the uselessness of denial.

Argument with him was out of the question. She had taken him to the summer-house beyond the lawn to tell him quietly of what she had seen believing that he would slink away afterward, crestfallen and beaten. Instead, he faced her; he laughed at her threat; he sneered at and ignored the charge she had made; he received her ultimatum with contempt; by inference, he defied her. He! the cheat! the card-sharp! the swindler whom she had detected in the act! He, whose attitude and manner were confessions twofold, even if she had not seen his act with her own eyes.

Katherine swung upon her heel. She started swiftly away, took two steps, and halted. Over her shoulder she threw back at him:

"There is a train for the city at ten-forty. One of our cars will take you to the station. If you do not make use of it, I will denounce you in the presence of the four men you swindled, and my husband. There will be no question about your going then."

She started on again, her head held high, the light of righteous anger in her eyes.

Belknap made no attempt to stop her, but he laughed chuckingly, and with so much of self-assurance and contemptuous indifference to her threat, that she swung half round to face him again.

The man was regarding her coolly, quizzically, unperturbed.

Whatever Katherine's impulse might have been when she made the half turn to face the man a second time, she controlled it—and herself.

There was something about Belknap's demeanor that infused a sudden, although indefinable, sense of fear into her consciousness. He appeared so utterly indifferent concerning the ethics of his position; so contemptuous of what she might or might not do in the premises; so cocksure of himself and of some power over her that he was holding in reserve, to use whenever the need to use it—or the will to do so—should arise.

Yes, that was it, she determined swiftly, even though she was barely conscious of such a foregone conclusion. He believed that he had some unsuspected hold upon her. She would not have had such a thought had she been conscious of it; she would not, could not, have admitted even to herself that there did exist a circumstance of the past that was the father of that unadmitted, but still existent fear.

The thing—or rather the succession of incidents that made up the whole—was so far in the past that it had long been buried.

It was not forgotten—such experiences never are quite that—but it might have been said to be unremembered.

Even while she was remotely conscious of the sudden misgiving within her as she faced Belknap in that brief interval, the skeleton in the closet of her memory did not rattle its bones with enough emphasis to cause her a second thought about it. The memory was merely there, in the back of her mind, like an indistinct shape that one can just discern through a fog, but which does not assume enough of an outline to be recognizable.

She had parted her lips to speak, but she closed them and stood facing the man whose coldly cynical smile was an epitome of all insolence.

Everything about him suggested the self-assurance of conscious power over her; and yet—and yet—

Never had the sound of Bingham Harvard's voice been more welcome than it was at that moment when she heard him calling her name from the concreted pathway, close at hand; he came upon them the next instant.

"I was sent to take you back," Harvard told her. "They are planning something for to-morrow, I believe, and your approval is needed, it seems, although I assured them to the contrary."

If Katherine had been for a moment obsessed by the vaguest of fantoms of the past, the ghost was instantly laid with the appearance of her husband on the scene. She replied quite coolly, and with a directness which was meant to leave no room for doubt in Belknap's mind that her ultimatum had been spoken. She said:

"We were on the point of returning, Bingham. Mr. Belknap has just told me that he is compelled to go back to the city to-night by the ten-forty—within a little more than an hour. Will you tell Julius to take him to the train?"

She had slipped one of her arms within Bingham's, and already they were retracing their steps toward the house, Belknap having fallen in beside them so that Katherine was placed between the two men.

"I am sorry to hear that, Mr. Belknap," Harvard commented heartily. "It is too bad, really. We haven't had an opportunity to get acquainted—barely. Somewhat sudden, isn't it?"

"Quite so," Belknap drawled slowly, with a suggestiveness in his manner of speech that only Katherine could detect. "So sudden, in fact, that I am strongly inclined to resent it, and—ignore it."

"Good!" Harvard rejoined earnestly. He was the most hospitable of hosts. "By all means ignore it, if you can. If the call isn't really imperative, you know—if you can substitute the telephone for your personal appearance in town, why, do so, and stay on."

"Thank you. I think, now, that I will do so," was the cold reply.

A flame of hot anger surged from Katherine's heart to her brain.

The man was insufferable; his effrontery was beyond belief.

"Does he suppose," she thought swiftly, "that I will hesitate to expose him, as I threatened to do?"

She stopped in her tracks, bringing the other to a halt beside her, and her impulse was to make the disclosure of Belknap's infamy to her husband then and there.

"Bingham," she began hotly and stopped. She controlled the impulse, and, before there was an appreciable hesitation in her speech, continued—not because of any delicacy of feeling toward Belknap, but because she feared a flaring-out of Bing Harvard's hot temper upon the instant that he should learn the truth.

"Bingham"—she moved forward again, and her repetition of the name was much softer, and this time held a pleading note—"I don't think you ought to urge Mr. Belknap to stay over. I have been made

25

to understand that his reason for going is imperative; that it is of the gravest importance; that, in short, it is a matter in which his honor is at stake, if I understood correctly; so, dear, don't you see you must not put an obstacle in the way of his going? We ought not ever to *permit* him to remain at Myquest under such circumstances."

That time Belknap did not offer to reply, and while Harvard murmured something entirely conventional, Katherine shot a covert glance from the corner of her eyes at her unwelcome guest.

He was smiling with a complacency that was utterly amazing to her, and she understood in that instant that he was as decided as ever that he would not go.

More than ever she was as determined that he should.

CHAPTER III

A VOICE ON THE WIRE

It so happened that Harry Archer and his wife were standing to-gether at the top of the veranda steps, and that Julius—Katherine's black servant and trusted chauffeur, who had been with her since her childhood—appeared at that moment in the doorway, so she seized upon the double opportunity.

"Julius," she called calmly, and when the black came nearer, added: "Mr. Belknap will want you to take him to the ten-forty train." Then, with barely a pause in her speech, and this time ad-dressing the Archers: "Such unpleasant news, Belle. Mr. Belknap has just told me that he must leave us to-night. Isn't it too bad?"

There were expressions of surprise from every direction, for the entire company had heard the announcement. Those who were seated bent forward in their chairs as if to utter a word or two of pro-test. Tom Clancy and Danford Demming, who were standing, moved nearer to the group on the steps; and Belknap, at the bottom of them, smiling, unperturbed, shrugged his shoulders and drawled with deliberate distinctiveness:

"Really, I had no idea that I was so popular. You know, I felt ra-ther like an outsider—being such a stranger among you—and prob-ably I put too much emphasis upon the summons that I received, to go to the city to-night. But—er—now that both Mr. and Mrs. Har-vard have urged me to stay, and—well, I have changed my mind. I won't go. I couldn't think of it under the circumstances. Julius, I won't need you after all; you need not bring the car around. Har-vard, if I may, I will use your telephone."

He nodded genially, and without awaiting permission, ascended the steps and went into the house.

While the others were variously expressing their approvals of Belknap's change of mind, Katherine turned her back to them, pinching her under lip between her teeth and tapping one foot impatiently upon the concrete walk; then, with a quickly spoken word of excuse she turned away and passed from sight around one corner of the house.

She was suddenly convinced that it might be important to know to whom Conrad Belknap desired to talk by telephone—if, indeed, he intended to make use of the wire at all; for, of course, she knew that there was no necessity for him to do so in order to stay on at Myquest. Still, if there was somebody who was available to him by telephone in such an emergency, it was up to her to know who the person might be—and because the man was a card-sharper, a swindler, and—she had no doubt at all—a crook, any method that she might employ in contesting his effrontery and insolence would be fair.

Katherine's former experiences as a police-headquarters' detective stood for her just then; she had not been called "Lady Kate of the Police" in the days of "Alias the Night Wind" for nothing.

She judged from Belknap's manner that he really did intend to telephone to New York to somebody; and for her to know who that "somebody" might be, would supply one item, at least, in discovering his identity—for she was thoroughly convinced that he was not what he had made himself appear to be, at Myquest.

There were several telephones in the house, and Katherine assumed that Belknap would seek the one in her husband's den, because of its seclusion. She certainly hoped that he would do so, because that instrument happened to be on the same wire that communicated with her own private sitting-room.

When at Myquest, Katherine was in the habit of making as much use of Bing's den, and the little room off from it where the card-playing had been indulged in, as of her own boudoir, and for the sake of convenience the two telephones had been connected as one, the instrument in the den being the extension.

The instant she turned the corner of the house she quickened her pace, ran up the steps at a side entrance, ascended the servants' stairway to the second floor, and entered her own suite, where she closed and locked the door after her.

Very gently, so that there might be no warning click upon the wire, she lifted the receiver from the hook and pressed it against her ear. Then she smiled, breathlessly, for she had hurried greatly, and she was there in time to hear a voice say "...three-two-oh." She listened-in at just the moment when the operator was repeating the last of the number asked for. (Harvard entertained so many guests at Myquest who quite frequently made such constant use of the telephones that connected through the two-trunk switch-board in the butler's-room that, for his own convenience, he had long ago put in an extra direct wire from the exchange for his own and Katherine's uses.)

She heard the unmistakable voice of Conrad Belknap reply: "Right!"

There was a short wait after that. Then the voice of a woman—a voice, too, of unusual melody and sweetness—called: "Yes? Who is it, please?"

"C. B. is talking," Belknap replied, speaking in a low tone. "No names, please. Do you get me?"

"Yes," came the monosyllabic response—and it was remarkable how the voice of the woman had altered in that brief interval, to one that was coldly formal, and which somehow suggested hardness and defiance, as well as dislike and repugnance.

"Very good. Pay attention now. I am not at Ledgewood. My present address is at Myquest, as I told you it would be; you know the rest of it; also the telephone call—if the necessity should arise to make use of either one."

"Very well, I understand. Is that all?"

"No. I shall be here all through the coming week, at least. You must be prepared at any moment to carry out the plan I made for you. To-morrow I will write; you will get my letter Monday morning. It will contain full instructions. That is all. Good-by."

"But—" the voice of the woman began in an expostulating tone; but the click of the instrument in Belknap's hands as he hung up cut her off.

Instantly Katherine acted upon one of those impulses which works before one has opportunity to take a second thought. She spoke through the transmitter before she realized what she did.

"Please!" she said. "Hold the wire! Wait a moment."

Something that sounded like a gasp came to her ears through the telephone, and dead silence followed it. But there was no warning click of disconnection. Katherine knew that the woman of the melodious voice, and who either disliked or feared Conrad Belknap, was still at the telephone listening.

But Katherine did not know what to say, now that she had secured the woman's attention. Why had she done it? Why, with her experience, had she permitted herself to do such a manifestly fool-thing as that? Undoubtedly the woman was a creature of Belk-nap's—a tool—or a confederate; certainly she was more or less in the card-sharper's confidence. His manner of speaking over the wire had assured Katherine of that much.

While she hesitated the unknown woman became either impatient or curious. She spoke again, in the same hard, metallic color-less voice in which she had replied to Belknap, and at once Katherine's ingenuity came to her aid; she determined upon a subterfuge.

"What do you want? And—who are you?" the woman asked; and then, before a reply was possible, she asked a third question. It was: "Are you with—with him? With C. B.?"

"No, no, no!" Katherine replied quickly. "There is nobody with me. Please listen to me; *please*, madam! I am in terrible trouble. I—I—I—" and she ended by uttering a perfect imitation of a gasping sob.

But even so, before the woman at the opposite end of the wire could speak, Katherine continued rapidly, and brokenly, as if she were in great mental distress:

"Please tell me how I can call you on the telephone; please, please, please do! I cannot talk now. I dare not. I am likely to be interrupted at any moment. But oh, I do so need a friend—a woman friend. Won't you help me? Oh, something tells me that you will. It was your voice, I think."

"But, my dear young lady—" the voice began.

"Oh, you mustn't ask questions, now. You can't imagine what might happen if I should be caught, and then I would never have another chance to use the phone. Please be kind and help me. I am in terrible trouble and distress. Let me call you up some time, won't you, please?"

There was a hesitating silence at the other end of the wire. Then:

"Very well. Ganesvoort five-four-three-two-oh; but never before midnight, and not later than a half-hour after it. And you must understand—"

"Oh, somebody is coming!" Katherine interrupted. "Thank you. Oh, you can't know how much good—" She hung up.

Then, with a deep sigh, which was also accompanied by a smile of satisfied approval of her own act, she leaned back in the chair and wrinkled her brows in thought.

It had been imperatively essential that she should not say too much—nor too little—just then; but the point, the great point at which she had sought to arrive, was achieved.

She had succeeded in arresting the woman's attention and in securing her sympathy, without arousing her suspicion—the woman who, all too evidently, was an accomplice of Conrad Belknap in whatever felonious designs he might have upon the house of Harvard.

Katherine had made it appear that she was in great distress, that she was deeply in need of a woman's aid and sympathy; and, knowing, because of the short conversation she had overheard, that the strange woman would be suspiciously alert by reason of her presence on the wire, she had succeeded in conveying the impression that she had heard nothing.

Also, the woman could have no idea whence Katherine had spoken. She would get the impression of crossed wires, so-called. She might, at the next opportunity, question Belknap about the circumstance covertly; but he, having already hung up the receiver and gone, would have nothing to impart.

Altogether, Katherine felt that she was to be congratulated upon the achievement of a point in the battle of wits between herself and Belknap, for already she was convinced that the contest between them had reached that point. Had he not coolly informed the woman accomplice of his intention to remain at Myquest "through the coming week, at the least"?

Oh, yes, Katherine was determined that she would talk with the voice again; but not too soon; no, not too soon. There must be time to think and plan in the meanwhile. She would have to be wary, well poised, and provided with a plausible story to unfold.

All of the time while Katherine sat there turning the incident over in her mind, she was convinced of two pleasing and helpful, although minor, considerations: One, that the woman accomplice both disliked and feared Conrad Belknap; the other, that the possessor of such a throaty, richly melodious, sympathetic voice must be good and kind at heart, no matter what might be the condition and circumstance that bound her to such a knave as Belknap had already proven himself to be. She went out of the room presently, strangely exhilarated—either because she was conscious of the eve of battle between her wit and her unbidden guest's; or, because of an intuition that the unknown woman with the sweet voice would some day develop into a friend in need, to serve as a foil against Belknap. At the top of the stairway, she met him face to face.

CHAPTER IV

THE THREAT

"Well met, Mrs. Harvard," was Belknap's greeting.

His teeth gleamed at her beneath the close-cropped black mustache, and his oddly brilliant eyes glistened with a suggested menace as he smiled upon her coolly, for all the world as if he knew himself to be thoroughly master of the situation.

It was with difficulty that Katherine repressed a visible shudder.

The man had become utterly hateful to her, and strangely menacing. It was as if he held a physical threat over her head. She controlled herself with difficulty, and compelled her voice to calmness while she replied, with entire remoteness, with the air and attitude of addressing an entire stranger:

"That is as you elect to regard it, Mr. Belknap—if that is your name. I am going, now, to ask my husband, and the four gentlemen with whom you played poker, to go with me to the library. It is my purpose to tell them, plainly and unequivocally, everything that I saw when I looked between the portières, and to describe your conduct since then also—unless you choose to change your mind again and leave Myquest now, at once."

He made no attempt to interrupt her. He permitted her to finish what she had to say without changing his attitude or altering his demeanor; nor did the wolfish smile leave his face. If anything, the glitter in his eyes became more mocking and insolent—and threatening.

"Brave words, Mrs. Harvard," he responded coldly, retaining the inscrutable smile as he quoted the words he had spoken to her a half-hour earlier at the summer-house on the edge of the lawn. Then, with a barely perceptible pause, he added, with menacing meaning: "I shall not change my mind about going away; I shall not go. You will change *your* mind about what you have just threatened to do, for—you will think better of it."

He had been standing thus far between her and the stairway, but with the close of his statement he stepped aside, leaving her ample room to pass him if she wished.

"Go ahead," he said calmly, "if you have the courage to take the bit in your teeth, and run; but let me beg that you will not forget that I hold the reins, that a curb is generally regarded as an instrument of torture and—that I am a merciless driver when I encounter fractiousness. Go ahead, if you like. Call your husband and the others to the library. Speak your little piece." He shrugged his shoulders and permitted himself a low chuckle before he added: "But unless you are fully prepared to face the consequences of such a proceeding, I strongly advise you not to do so."

Katherine should have taken him at his word, and gone; but she did not. She should have carried out her threat to the end; but she hesitated. She would have passed him by without another word; but—she temporized. Even she, who was not given to temporizing.

She still faced him unflinchingly, it is true; but she stayed. There was about her not one outward sign of fear or misgiving; but Belknap knew that both were present in her heart and brain, else she would have left him.

Could she have suspected, even remotely, how greatly the game he was playing depended upon his success in instilling in her that nameless dread of something intangible, but threatening—could she have guessed that three-fourths of his insolent effrontery was pure bluff that he had feared she might not "fall for," she would have passed him then, with head held high, would have summoned her husband and her friends, and denounced Conrad Belknap for what he was. Instead—

"What do you mean?" she demanded. "Am I to understand that you dare to threaten me?"

"Precisely that, Mrs. Harvard. You have threatened me; I give you back threat for threat. I am threatening you—with the consequences of what you might still very foolishly do."

"You threaten me—with what?"

He shrugged again, took out his cigarette-case, selected one from it, and answered:

"I have just told you; with the consequences of an extremely foolish whim that you still entertain, although not so strongly now."

"You are"—she hesitated—"insufferable!" she ended.

33

"I am—I," he retorted, showing his teeth in another wolfish smile.

It seemed then, for the briefest instant, as if she would indeed leave him. Her lithe body swayed slightly forward in the beginning of the act to do so, but neither of her daintily shod feet moved under her. She stood quite still.

Belknap chuckled again. He restored the cigarette-case to his pocket, brought out a gold match-safe, and coolly lighted up.

She knew that he did it all purposely to test her; to defy her; to dare her to carry out her threat. She knew that she ought to do so, and bandy no more words with him. But she could not do it.

She knew that he was conquering her spirit by the mere power of his will, and that for some miserably unknown reason which she could not define at all, she dare not defy him.

She knew that she was frightened, but she did not know what it was that she feared; and in that moment she hated herself for temporizing with the man whom she honestly believed to be a real denizen of the underworld—a crook.

Having lighted his cigarette, properly inhaled the smoke, and expelled it, he said, with cold and careful selection of each word he uttered:

"We all have pasts, Mrs. Harvard; some of them are made by ourselves; some of us have them manufactured for us by others. But—they are none the less *our* pasts, whether they happen to be self-made, or otherwise. Sometimes we try to outlive them and forget them, and we deceive ourselves into the belief that we have succeeded; but they live—and they rise up to confront us when we least expect it. I have my past, and—it is not *all* pleasant, although it was self-made. You have *your* past, and, although *you* did not make it yourself, and are not responsible for it, it is none the less ugly. If you should go now and carry out what you threatened to do, I could see over your shoulders while you were thus engaged, the white, set features of a person we both knew, gazing yearningly upon us—upon you particularly—from between the iron bars of a narrow prison window. Can you guess, Mrs. Harvard, to whom I refer?"

It seemed to Katherine as if fingers of ice clutched at her heart-strings then.

In that instant she understood the reason for that vague dread and fear that she had sensed since the moment when she had faced this man in the moonlight at the summer-house steps. She comprehended the undefined terror with which he had imbued her, by reason of his wolfish, crafty smile, which had informed her, if she had only believed it at the time, that he held something in reserve, some knowledge of the past, which emboldened him to defy her and her threats to expose him to her husband and her guests for the cheat and swindler that he was; and the last part of his statement, as if in letters of fire that burned and seared into her brain, recurred to her.

"...the white, set features of a person we both know, gazing yearningly upon us—upon you particularly—from between the iron bars of a narrow prison window. Can you guess, Mrs. Harvard, to whom I refer?"

Thus was a ghost of the past resurrected!

Thus was Katherine Harvard brought face to face with a condition which she dare not, could not, *must not*, avoid.

She knew, while Belknap slowly and incisively voiced the threat, that she must surrender, or, at least, must appear to do so. She knew that she must temporize; that she must seem, for the time being, to condone the perfidy of the man who faced her so coolly, and who dared her to do her worst against him.

She realized that she was compelled to surrender; that was the terrible thing.

Not because she sought to spare herself any consequences of the revelation that Belknap threatened; let us not deceive ourselves by any thought that Katherine harbored one grain of cowardice, one faintest streak of yellow, in her heart or soul. Let it not be supposed that it was any consideration for herself that compelled her to wave a flag of truce to the scoundrel in front of her.

Her courage was never so great as in that moment when she understood and acted upon the necessity that confronted her.

As one will think quickly in moments of extremity, so it occurred to her in one wild impulse, to defy Belknap even then, and to seek her husband and confide everything to him; but a second thought, as quickly uppermost as the first one, made her realize that *she did not dare to do that*—made her understand that she was mortally afraid to tell Bing Harvard about this man who faced her, and his threats.

Again we must not misunderstand.

It was not that she feared to inform her husband fully about the secret of the past which Belknap threatened to expose. Not that. No, no; not that.

The condition that frightened her was Bingham Harvard himself, and what she perfectly well knew that he would do to Conrad Belknap upon the instant that he was made to understand thoroughly the situation. It was Bingham Harvard's temper that she feared—the tremendous, the superhuman, the awful strength, and the uncontrollable temper when once roused, of the man who had once borne the *alias*, The Night Wind.

She knew, just as well as she knew that it was a despicable scoundrel who threatened her at the moment, that Harvard, the instant he was made to understand the situation, would become transformed into a silent and implacable fury; that he would seek Belknap in a rage which nothing could stay or hinder, and that with his great strength like unto that of Samson of old, he would seize the man with his hands and rend him limb from limb.

In a word, Katherine knew that if she should tell her husband that this man had dared to threaten her, his wife, Bing would kill him—kill him with his hands—crush the life out of him.

We ask—you and I—why not?

Such a killing would be justifiable under the circumstances; the world would be well rid of such a contemptible person; justice, when the facts were known, would deal gently with him who did the killing. Ah! Therein was the rub—to say nothing of the shuddering horror that Katherine felt when she considered such a possibility—the killing of this man by the hand of her husband.

But, the facts behind such an extremity *could not be made known*; not even to that intangible, that inchoate thing called justice. Then, too, she realized, with still another inward shuddering, that even then—even with Belknap silenced forever (if such a dread possibility were to be considered), the fact might not stay the consequences of the exposure that he had threatened to make; the white, set features of a person she knew, might still be made to stare between the bars of a narrow prison window.

Furthermore, with the approach of evening of the succeeding day, former U.S. Senator Maxwilton, with Mrs. Maxwilton—Katherine's father and mother—would arrive at Myquest, from their home in Kentucky. That was the hardest rub of all, for this exposure that Conrad Belknap threatened to make would stab both of them to the heart, would bow with withering shame the tall and stately form of that proud old man, and would crush, even into the grave, the stately, yet delicately sweet mother whom Katherine adored with a devotion and love that was beyond words.

For the white, set features that would be made to stare between the bars of a prison window belonged to Katherine Harvard's brother; her brother—Roderick—the first-born of her parents—their son whom they had once so profoundly loved, who had begun so bravely and so proudly, and who had ended so miserably—*their only son, whom both believed to be dead, and whose mistakes and failures had been forgotten in the memories of his childhood and promise.*

The mere suggestion that either of them should ever be made to know that their son Roderick Maxwilton was still among the living, and that he might be, or would be, called upon at any moment to pass into another death—a living one—behind prison bars, was not to be considered, no matter what sacrifice should be fixed as the price of avoidance of such a calamity.

Katherine had believed that she alone knew that her brother was alive. She had, up to the very instant of Belknap's uttered threat, had no thought that another person in all the world harbored any doubt of Roderick Maxwilton's death. There was a grave within the family inclosure on the Kentucky estate wherein he was supposed to be at rest, and above it there was a stone that bore his name and the date of...

Katherine knew as well as if Belknap had spoken the name, that he had referred to her brother Roderick.

Those flash-light thoughts continued to dart in and out of her understanding during the brief space of her silence while she faced the card-sharper; those, and others, coming and going with the swiftness of thought itself, yet consuming no appreciable time; and among them were the natural questions—"Who, then, is this man who confronts me?" and "When and how could he have known Roderick?"—questions for which, alas, she had no answer.

So swiftly did her mind work that there was no appreciable interval between Belknap's last utterance and Katherine's response to it.

She could not reply in words; she had none to use, just then. But—

With a haughty uplift of her shapely head, with a gesture of utter repugnance for the man, she went past him down the stairs.

Belknap, with that inscrutable smile of defiance, derision, and conscious power over her, still upon his lips and in his eyes, stepped deferentially aside. He bowed, mockingly. He seemed to know, without her admitting it in words, that he had won out in that first actual passage at arms. He made no attempt to detain her.

Thus was Katherine Harvard's wit matched against the wit of Conrad Belknap.

Thus was the battle of wits begun.

Thus the match—which might well have been named: The Crook *versus* Lady Kate of the police.

CHAPTER V

LADY OF THE NIGHT WIND

Katherine slept but little that night.

She was torn by a conflict of emotions, and chiefest among them all was the passionate longing to confide everything to her husband, which she knew to be impossible even while she considered it; impossible because she knew what he would do. She could not tell Bingham about her brother, now, at this late date, without disclosing her reason for the telling—without denouncing Belknap; and if she did that, the tempest would be let loose, the long-stilled Night Wind would be unleashed.

That was the consequence that she dreaded greatly, although almost as terrible in its effect would be discovery by her father and mother that Roderick's body did not rest in the grave that was marked by his name, at their Kentucky home. Years had come and gone since that grave was made; and now, to exhume the living from it—Such a circumstance was not to be thought of.

During the day that followed—it was Sunday—she avoided Belknap as much as possible without the appearance of it. She did so manage that she was never alone with him for an instant. With twilight her father and mother came, and Bingham went with her to the station to meet them.

It happened just before bedtime that Katherine, longing for a moment of solitude, stepped through an open window to the veranda and glided noiselessly and swiftly down the side steps and along a secluded pathway toward a rustic bench that was half hidden beneath a bower of climbing crimson-rambler.

She passed inside of it before she discovered that the place was already occupied; that Belknap, whom she supposed had gone to his room, was there, exactly as if he were awaiting her. Yet, she knew differently, because he could not have known that the rose bower was a favorite retreat of hers.

He stood up and bowed, coolly polite; insolently sure of himself.

"I was waiting for you," he said.

"But—" she began, and stopped.

"Oh, I did not know that you would come here, of course." He smiled provokingly. "It did not occur to me that you would seek me, Mrs. Harvard." He was mocking her, she knew. "I did think that you might wish for a moment of solitude, so—I came here. You see, I could watch you through the window from this point of vantage—and—I have been calling you; mentally, of course. Will you be seated?"

"No."

He produced his cigarettes and lighted one leisurely.

"I did not know that Senator and Mrs. Maxwilton were expected," he said when he had extinguished the match.

Katherine made no reply. He continued as if casually:

"Their coming rather strengthens my position, doesn't it." It was a statement, with a period, not an interrogation. Again she was silent.

"They do not suspect that a certain grave in Kentucky contains the bones of an unknown, and not the remains of him whose name is on the headstone," he went on. "It would be a shock to them—such knowledge—would it not, Lady Kate?"

She started backward a step, white to the lips.

"You dare—" she began, and stopped because of sheer inability to speak on, so greatly was she outraged by his insolent familiarity. Then, controlling herself, compelling herself to speak calmly, she continued: "Let me advise you to beware lest you drive me too far, Mr. Belknap. It is true that it would be a shock to—to them—to know the truth, now, so late, but—do not deceive yourself into the notion that I have refrained from exposing you solely for that reason. There is another one—even a more important one. You do not know it; you may not believe it when you are told. It is this: if I should tell Bingham Harvard of the things that you have said and done to me, he would pluck you from your hold upon life like that"—she reached out and pulled a cluster of roses from their stems—"he would rend you and tear you apart like that"—she crushed the roses in her fingers and tore them into a pulpy mass—"and when he loosed his grip upon you, as I loose mine now upon these rose leaves, you would be as they are, crushed, lifeless, dead! I have kept silent thus far, not so much to spare my father and mother the knowledge that you threaten to disclose, as to spare your worthless, contemptible life."

Belknap tossed the cigarette from him into the pathway. He bent nearer to her, smilingly unmoved. Not a tone of his voice was changed when he spoke.

"To spare my life?" he questioned. "Oh, no. Say, rather, to keep *two* persons instead of one, outside of a prison house. To save *me*? What folly to suggest that! But to save Bing Harvard from the commission of a crime. Oh, yes. Quite so. And you will continue to do that very thing, believe *me*! That, my dear lady, is why I hold the whip hand—and it is why I will keep on holding it to the end; because you are afraid, if you speak, that your husband will go to the electric chair as a murderer. Did you expect to frighten me, Lady Kate? Yes, I will call you that if I choose. Nonsense; utter nonsense! I was never afraid in my life, so do not think that you can scare me. You can't."

"You are right," she returned as coolly as he had spoken. "I have kept silent only to spare my husband the commission of a crime. I could look upon your features, crushed, and dead, with unmixed pleasure; and if you, by word or deed, by innuendo or gesture, betray what you know to either of my parents, I will loose the Night Wind upon you, no matter what the consequences may be."

She turned to leave him. She stepped into the moonlight on the path. There she halted, and turned, and faced him again. He was in the shadow beneath the rose bower; she stood in the light outside of it—and at that instant Bingham Harvard from the veranda, where he had gone to seek her, saw her; saw her and thought nothing of it, then.

"Why do you insist upon remaining here?" she demanded of Belknap. "What do you want at Myquest? Or of me? Is it blackmail? If so, name your—"

He laughed aloud, gleefully, interrupting her.

"My price, sweet lady," he said mockingly, "cannot be paid with money. I seek for something better—something far dearer to you than that—something, too, that I will compel you to pay."

* * * * * * *

Week-end gatherings like that one at Myquest sometimes develops into established house-parties.

That Sunday evening just past had ended by a somewhat general understanding that several of the guests were to stay on for the week, and the week-end to close it. Betty Clancy decided that she would fill out the week with Katherine, and so Belle Archer—whose home at Ledgewood was not ten miles away—elected to remain also. Her husband, Harry, who never had known more strenuous duties than clipping coupons, was just as willing to loaf and do nothing at Myquest as at his home, so he stayed—after he had "persuaded" their own guest, Belknap, to do likewise. His decision, however, was not known until Monday morning, when Julius brought the big car to the door preparatory to driving Harvard and Clancy into the city.

Danford Demming and Horton Sears pretended to a consuming desire to return to town, and Demming went so far as to order out his roadster (the two had gone down to Myquest together in it), but as neither one was in business, and could be as contented in one place as another, both were easily persuaded to stay. As a matter of fact, Katherine very greatly preferred that they should remain, because—well, there might still be occasion for her to denounce Belknap to all four of the men whom he had cheated at cards.

There were several others—"just girls," Tom Clancy would have called them—who were induced to stay on, for there were tennis, and golf, and motoring, and horseback riding to be indulged, and bridge to be played—and the possibility of harmless and pleasing flirtatious interludes with Sears and Demming and "that handsome and fascinating Mr. Conrad Belknap," whose covert references to mines and ranches in Arizona, and whose frank, but evidently insincere declarations that he was a confirmed bachelor, were not the least of his attractions.

And Katherine permitted him to stay. She did not denounce him. For the time being, at least, he had conquered.

She had not forgotten what she had heard over the telephone, nor the short conversation that followed it between her and the woman accomplice. Katherine intended, that very night—that Monday at midnight—to take advantage of the permission that had been given her, to call up Ganesvoort 54320.

Also, she had watched for that letter that Belknap had promised to write and post to the woman; she had even searched the mail-bag for it late Sunday night, intending, if she found it, to—she did not know quite what she would have done in that case.

But she did not find it, and so was spared a temptation to commit an act which, according to police headquarters ethics, would have been entirely justifiable.

41

However, she had no doubt that Belknap had written it, and sent it—by one of the grooms, possibly, or he had carried it himself across the golf-links to the post-office when he had walked away alone late Sunday afternoon.

Throughout the day, Monday, Katherine devoted herself to her father and mother; and Belknap, obligingly or with intention, kept himself aloof from her.

She knew that he, with the three other men who had stayed on for the week—Demming, Sears, and Archer—played bridge together all of Monday afternoon in the billiard-room, but she consoled herself with the thought that if they were mere lambs to be sheared by the first card-sharper who appeared, they not only deserved the operation, but each one could well afford his losses.

Harvard and Clancy returned shortly after five, and the evening that followed was entirely uneventful, although Katherine could not overcome the feeling of impending disaster. To her the very atmosphere seemed to be charged with calamity; every hour was full of menacing portentousness.

During the evening Belknap devoted himself first to one and then another of the married and unmarried women of the party; at something after eleven o'clock all of the guests retired to their respective rooms, and at a quarter to twelve she and Harvard sought their own double suite in the easterly wing of their home.

Katherine stood with her husband for a moment in his dressing-room, with her hands resting gently upon his arms. She was looking into his eyes, longing to uncover, to his great and indulgent devotion to her, everything that troubled her.

She passionately wanted to throw her arms around his neck, to force him down upon a chair, to sit on his knee, and to confide all her perplexities to him; but—she was afraid. She dared not do it.

Gazing down upon her, he saw the vague shadows—or sensed them; and he folded her into his embrace, and held her so for a long minute.

"What is it, sweetheart?" he asked softly. "What is troubling you?"

Instantly she was alert again, and pulled herself slowly out of his embrace, smiled into his eyes, kissed his lips gently, and replied:

"I am tired, I suppose; that is all, dear. I will go to my room, and to bed."

So they said good night and parted.

CHAPTER VI

GANESVOORT 54320

In her own room, with the door closed, she at once dismissed the maid who awaited her, glanced at the little clock, and saw that it was five minutes to midnight; and composed herself to wait five minutes more before she would ask the telephone operator to connect her with Ganesvoort 54320.

But she seated herself beside the instrument, and before one of the five minutes had elapsed she lifted the receiver from the hook, very, very softly—not because she had any idea that the extension to Bingham's den might be in use, but solely for the reason that she was conscious of doing something stealthily.

Instantly she was all alertness, for at once she heard the voice of Conrad Belknap.

The fact told her much upon the instant, even while she listened intently to what was being said: it told her that Belknap had made the discovery that a direct wire from the telephone exchange, not connected with the switchboard in the butler's quarters, led into Harvard's private library, or den, and that the man had gone to it from his own room after he supposed that all others in the house had retired, to make use of it—and what she heard presently confirmed that assumption; as also the fact that Belknap had *no* suspicion that her own telephone was likewise on that direct wire.

She was aware, too, that she was to hear *all* that Belknap was to say to the unknown, as well as the woman's replies, for the first words that came to her in Belknap's voice were:

"...been here for the last fifteen minutes, but I waited, to be sure that you were there to answer me."

"Well?" the voice of the woman answered, and there was that same quality of repulsion, dislike, and fear in it that Katherine had detected Saturday evening. "What do you want to say?"

"You received my letter?"

"Yes. Wait a moment. Do you think you are wise to use that telephone? When you did so, Saturday, there was a crossed wire from another house near there, and—well, I could hear a woman's voice upon it after you hung up."

"Crossed wires happen sometimes, but not as a rule. It is late now; everybody here is in bed. This 'phone is not connected with the switchboard downstairs; it is a direct wire from the exchange. Anyhow, there is nothing much to be said—nothing that anybody but ourselves could understand. Have you made your arrangements to carry out the directions in my letter?"

"Yes."

"Well?"

"There is nothing more to be said about it, is there, save that you may look for me at the appointed time? I will not disappoint you."

Katherine supposed that that would be all, and was on the point of returning the receiver to its switch, when the woman spoke again after Belknap had agreed with her that nothing more need be said.

"Wait a moment," she asked him. "Are you quite positive about that direct wire?"

"Yes; but all the same we need not discuss things too plainly," he replied.

"I know. It isn't that; it's this: I want you to come into the city to see me before I go there. You know why. There are some questions that I wish to ask. I want to know—certain things that I cannot ask you over a telephone-wire."

He replied to her angrily: "What nonsense is—"

She interrupted him.

"It isn't nonsense, C. B.," she said coldly, and with an added ring of hardness in her voice that rendered it almost unrecognizable. "You may as well understand that I am not going to thrust my head into a lion's jaws, as you want me to do, until I am well assured that they won't close up on me, and that you won't be the one to press the spring that does the closing. Don't interrupt me! You're quite capable of doing that very thing, provided that you are reasonably sure of not getting bitten yourself. So—you see—and you thoroughly understand, too—that I won't make a move or do a thing about what you want done, until I am convinced on that point, and you have got to *see me first*, to convince me."

"Look here, Berta—"

"None of that, C. B. I know you, going and coming, across from both sides, and down the middle. You are just a little bit afraid of me, C. B., although I reckon that I'm about the only thing in the world that you do fear. You'd like nothing better than to be jolly well rid of me, and you know it; so—come across."

"What do you mean by that—'come across'?"

"I mean that you'd better blow into town between now and Saturday, and look me up, if you want me to do my part. That's all, Good-by."

"Wait— Look here, Berta, can't you wait till you get here? I will—"

"Good-by, C. B. I don't think you'd best do any more telephoning from that house to me. Goo—"

"Wait, I tell you!"

"I won't wait. I have said my say. I'm through. Good-*by*—and if you don't show up in town between now and Saturday, *good* NIGHT."

The woman hung up; and after a moment, evidently of indecision on Belknap's part about asking for a renewal of the connection, Katherine knew he had returned the receiver to its hook.

She replaced her own, then stole to the door, opened it softly, and only a very little, and waited, for she knew that Belknap, in returning to his room, must pass a point at the end of the corridor where she would be able to catch a glimpse of him.

Presently she saw him, and she closed her door with a sigh of relief, and locked it. Then she went softly into her dressing-room, and listened at the door to Bingham's suite to assure herself that he had gone to bed. Being satisfied, she went back to the telephone, hesitated for a time to determine exactly her course of procedure, and asked for the Ganesvoort connection.

The response came quickly.

"Yes?" the sweetly melodious voice that had so charmed her the first time she heard it, answered, and, without pause, added: "Is it my young friend of Saturday evening—the young woman who seemed to be in trouble?"

"Of course it is," Katherine replied in the most girlish manner she could assume. "I have been on pins and needles waiting for midnight, to call you up. And I can't tell you how kind you are to let me do it."

"Have you, indeed? It is long past midnight now; half an hour, at least."

"Really? I wonder if my clock is slow."

"Very likely—if you have been watching it impatiently."

"You can't think, madam, how kind it is of you to let me talk to you; and—do you know that your voice is just beautiful? It makes me simply crazy to know you. Won't you please tell me your name, and where you live, and let me go to see you the next time I am permitted to go to the city?"

A low ripple of laughter sounded through the telephone.

"Dear me, what a lot of questions," the woman said. "Have you quite forgotten why I gave you permission to telephone to me? It was not to ask questions, surely."

"No, no," Katherine replied hastily. "Please forgive me."

"You said that you were distressed, and in trouble, and that I could help you; but, my dear—You are quite young, are you not? I have assumed that much about you."

"Y-yes," was the faltering response; purposely faltering. Then: "Perhaps you are young, too. Your voice makes me think that you are, although I don't know whether you are seventeen or seventy."

"I suspect that you are the one who is seventeen, my dear. But I? I am very, very old. I am ages—epochs—cycles old. I have attained the great age of twenty-seven. It is wonderful, isn't it? Just to think of it! To have lived a thousand years in twenty-seven." The ring of utter bitterness in the unknown woman's voice when she said that, was unmistakable. But she went on quickly: "Tell me about your troubles, and how I can help you."

Katherine had prepared herself for that question, and was ready with her reply.

"You see," she said slowly, "I was probably more frightened than anything else. When I spoke to you Saturday evening, I was locked in my room, and badly frightened, though the word 'rattled' expresses it better. I wanted to ask somebody to help me, only I did not know whom to ask. Why, I even thought of the police—which was silly, of course. Then, when I took up the receiver, I heard your voice—you were saying 'Good-by' to some one, and it attracted me. You know the rest."

"Am I to understand that your troubles are past, and that you no longer have need of me?" the woman's voice asked, with another touch of bitterness—perhaps of regret—in it.

"Oh, it was all about a man who insists upon imposing himself on me—and—and—I really don't suppose it amounted to half as much as I feared it did. But, *please*, won't you tell me your name? Just so that I may feel as if I knew you, really?"

46

"My name? Will Roberta suffice? It is my first name. What is yours, my dear?"

"My father and mother and brother, and my girl and boy friends used to call me Kitten. Do you like that?"

"It doubtless fits you perfectly. Mine used to call me Bobby."

"Won't you tell me your last name, and where you live, and let me write to you?" Katherine insisted.

"No—not now—I will think about it. Perhaps some day—" She stopped speaking, and Katherine said:

"Perhaps you will consent to write to me first. I *wish* you *would*. Send it to Greendale, Long Island—the last name is Maxwell. I will get it from the post-office myself, and I will look for a letter from you every day until I get one—and you *must* tell me how to answer, *won't* you? And—"

"There, there, Miss Kitten. I must go. Good-night."

Click went the instrument.

Katherine kept the receiver at her ear, listening. After an interval she began to move the switch slowly down and up; and then:

"Central," she said, when the response came, "this is Mrs. Harvard, of Myquest, speaking. Please ask the other exchange for the street address of the telephone with which I was just now connected. I neglected to take it down. Yes; it was Ganesvoort 54320."

Thus presently Katherine was in possession of the address of the woman accomplice of Conrad Belknap—as she believed.

It had not occurred to her that "the voice" might not live at that address.

CHAPTER VII

BEWARE OF THE STRANGER

Two items stood out prominently visualized in Katherine's thoughts while she prepared for bed: One was that Belknap intended to stay on at Myquest, indefinitely, unless a means could be found to drive him away; the other was that the woman accomplice—she Roberta—was to appear at Myquest presently under some guise which would enable her to be properly received, and which, it would appear, had already been arranged. What form that guise, impersonation, character, or pretense might take could not be foreseen.

Meanwhile Bingham Harvard—once *alias* the Night Wind— had not gone to sleep immediately after Katherine's departure to her own room.

He went to bed at once, to be sure, but he was wakeful without being restless—and somewhat concerned and irritated—without being in the least troubled—because of an annoying incident of the preceding day.

He had received an anonymous communication of nine type-written words: "Beware of the stranger that is within thy gates." It had been mailed at the general post-office in Eighth Avenue at noon that Monday. The envelope and single sheet of paper had borne the imprint of one of the leading hotels of the city, and any person wandering through its corridors might have used the hotel stationary; but he had to acknowledge to himself at once that the typewriter that had been used for conveying the message had quite evidently been sought for elsewhere.

He had been in bed a short time when he arose for a drink of water. In returning he paused for an instant at Katherine's door— and he knew at once that she was using the telephone, although he caught no word of what was said, and did not think of attempting to hear.

However, when he returned to his bed he found—more than ever to his intense annoyance—that he was willfully reminded of several incidents that had occurred since there had been a stranger within his gates, so to speak.

There was the incident of the summer-house, when there had been talk of Belknap's immediate departure Saturday night—and Belknap's attitude and remarks on the subject—and Katherine's somewhat remarkable insistence upon the importance of his going. Nevertheless he had remained.

There was Katherine's avoidance of Belknap throughout the day, Sunday—although Bingham insisted to himself that that was entirely his own imagining; yet the fact remained that he *had* "imagined" it.

There was Tom Clancy's covert though constant attitude of watching Belknap as if he were studying the man—and again Bing attributed the thought of it to his own imagination.

There was the double episode of the rose bower: the still burning cigarette that he had seen tossed from it—Katherine's appearance, coming from it a moment or two later—her strained and somewhat tense attitude when she did it, and her manner of turning about when in the pathway, to add to something that she had been saying. Harvard knew Katherine's every gesture and mannerism as intimately as one knows the way to one's own mouth with a fork or spoon; and he had seen defiance, dislike, and impotent rebellion in her manner then—and he knew mighty well that his imagination had played no part in that opinion.

There was the shadow that he had felt, rather than seen, hovering over her while she was bidding him good night, and the intuitive belief that had been in his mind at the time, that she was on the point of confiding something to him, and had decided not to.

Then, after she had gone to her room with the expressed determination of retiring at once, there was the fact that more than half an hour later she was at the telephone in conversation with somebody.

The following morning, while he and Tom Clancy were riding into town together, Harvard inquired of his friend, as if casually:

"How do you like Belknap? I don't seem to have had a chance to get acquainted with him yet."

"Do you want the answer straight from the shoulder, Bing, without even so much as an honest fool-reason to back it up?" Tom asked bluntly; and added, before Harvard could reply to the question: "I don't like him a little bit. I think he's a rotter, from Rottersville; and that, if he stays on at Myquest—oh, it's just a case of 'I do not like you, Dr. Fell, the reason why I cannot tell.'"

"You must have some reason for such an emphatic opinion, Tom."

"Huh! I don't like the shape of his nose, the color of his hair, the cut of his coat, the size shoe he wears, and the way he walks. In other words, I don't like the soil he stands on, and I'd like to pick a fight with him and have it out."

Harvard laughed aloud, and changed the subject. There was never any accounting for Tom Clancy's likes and dislikes, and they were as often prejudiced as otherwise, so far as the reason for them was concerned.

* * * * * * *

Immediately after luncheon that day Katherine invited Betty to a ride with her in her own roadster, which she always drove herself, and, telling her other guests that she would leave them to their own devices for an hour or two while she and Mrs. Clancy tore a hole in the atmosphere, she drove her car directly to the city.

Betty always had shopping to do. Tom's ample bank account did not prevent her from being an inveterate bargain-hunter, and Katherine very easily found the means to leave her friend long enough to drive past the address that the telephone operator had given her the preceding night.

She sought merely to locate it, because it happened to be in a street with which she was unfamiliar—a street in the Greenwich Village section.

She knew the fringes of that neighborhood well enough, for she had, in the police days, lived in West Eleventh Street for a time; but the mazes of Greenwich Village—and to a stranger the locality is something of a labyrinth—were unknown to her.

She found the address readily enough, and drove on past it without stopping, for she was intensely disappointed, and not a little disgusted. It was plain enough that "Roberta" did not live there— although it was not so plain how the woman could make use of a telephone from that address at midnight and after.

The place was a combination stationery, toy, and cigar store and news-stand, and moreover, it was only one story high, being a makeshift little building thrust in between two taller ones.

Katherine stopped her car at the next corner, got down, and walked slowly back to the address.

50

She occupied a moment or two in peering in at the window to select something to purchase, and then went inside. She saw at once that the building was as shallow as it was low, that there was only a very small room at the rear into which the doorway was wide open, and that the frowsy-headed woman with the cracked and beery voice, who waited upon her, quite evidently cooked and ate and slept in the tiny quarters. But there was a telephone of the drop-in-a-nickel type in the store, and its number was the one she had sought.

Katherine, having returned to her car, summed up the incident thus:

"Roberta lives in the neighborhood. She fees that old woman liberally for the use of the telephone, and she either carries a key to the store or rouses the woman to admit her whenever it pleases her to go there. The only way to trace her by that means would be to watch and wait just before midnight—which isn't worth while, since Roberta is due to arrive at Myquest shortly; only, if I were back at headquarters, I think that I would do it just the same. I wonder," she mused silently just before she came to a stop in front of the store where she had left Betty, "if it would not be a good idea to send for Rodney Rushton and ask him to help me. He could trace that woman for me; he could find out all about Conrad Belknap, and he—"

Betty appeared on the scene and interrupted her train of thought.

CHAPTER VIII

THE BEAUTIFUL PIANISTE

Cards? Oh, yes, every day—and sometimes the greater part of one—with the billiard-room for scenery, bridge for the vehicle, and Archer, Sears, and Demming for the goats.

Katherine chose to ignore the fact of the gambling—which she perfectly well knew took place—and left the players severely alone. She noticed that always the games were brought to a conclusion before the hour of Harvard's and Clancy's arrival from business in the city.

The four concerned in it never spoke of their play, save on the rare occasions when Belknap had lost (presumably only a small percentage of what he had theretofore gained), when, as a rule, they twitted him more or less, with some small indications of temporary exultation. It was plain to Katherine, however, that the man was a loser only when he deemed it to be politic.

Throughout the days and evenings that followed upon the (to Katherine) memorable Sunday and Monday, Belknap was consistently considerate of everybody, gracious to all, and—he played the gentleman as thoroughly well as he played cards, which is high praise.

It was Wednesday evening when an incident happened which, although carefully planned by its instigators, had every earmark of casuality. A Mme. Savage arrived at Myquest. She possessed the several qualifications for a welcome at Harvard's home, of being a large stockholder in his bank, a lifelong friend of the former president of it, Chester, who was the only father that Bing had ever known, and she was one of those rare and lovable old ladies whose thought remains as young as ever it was, at eighty.

She came, she saw, and was seen, and before the evening was finished she conquered—in the fact that she succeeded in persuading

Katherine to engage for the approaching week-end, to play for them, the services of one whom she described as being the most wonderful pianiste she had ever heard perform. Katherine was not given to employing hired talent for the entertainment of her guests, but when there was a chorus of approval of the idea from one group—of which Belknap, by the way, was the center—and when Bingham suggested, "Why not have her down, Katherine?" she assented.

"My goodness, no," Mme. Savage said in reply to a question, "I have never met her personally. I have heard her play three or four times—maybe not so many—but I never saw her nearer than across a crowded room; and my eyesight isn't as good as it was once. Just the same I have been told that she is very beautiful—the Spanish type, you know—and—er—all that sort of thing. She does play magnificently, believe me! Do have her down, Katherine, for a change, if you want entertainment; she isn't expensive, so I've been informed. You see, she probably has been told that I have heard her play, for she wrote to me—let me see, last week it was—and asked me if I would recommend her to my friends as an entertainer; and I told my secretary to send her word that of course I would—so—well—you see"—the old lady turned toward Harvard—"you can charge it to me, Bing Harvard, if you don't like her. Of course I've got her address; I made a note of it on my tablets before I started. Here it is now—*Señorita* Cervantez, care of the Bannister Entertainment Bureau, Metropolitan Building. There you are, folks."

Katherine sent off a letter that night, requesting the services of the señorita from Friday until Monday, unless she was otherwise engaged.

Friday, at two in the afternoon, she arrived—two hours before she was expected.

The consequence of that fact was that nobody met her at the Greendale station, and, whether she made inquiries and was directed how to find Myquest, or did not, the fact remained that she walked the distance of a little more than a mile across the golf-links, and so arrived unheralded and unannounced.

She approached the house by way of the tennis-courts, where some of the ladies were playing a four-some, and where Katherine was seated beside Betty, looking on.

It was Katherine who saw her first, and at once guessed her identity. Indeed, there could have been no mistaking the Spanish type of beauty that was hers, and to which Mme. Savage had referred.

53

She walked moderately fast, with a graceful, swinging gait (daintily, like a gazelle, Tom Clancy said afterward), like one who had spent much time in the open and among the wilds, who had scaled mountains, perhaps.

Katherine left her chair and hurried to meet the señorita, with both hands outstretched in greeting, and she exclaimed, while they were yet some distance apart:

"It is Señorita Cervantez, isn't it? I am so sorry that nobody was at the station to meet you, but really, I understand that you were to arrive at four, and you must have come on the one-twenty."

Katherine saw an expression of utter amazement flashed into the eyes of Señorita Cervantez; and it was only a flash, being gone again with the instant of its appearance, like the distant lightning of a summer night. Katherine was not even sure that it had expressed amazement; it might have been—anything.

And then Katherine met with a surprise; an astonishing one.

Señorita Cervantez did not reply.

She smiled—and it was a beautiful smile that lighted up her countenance wonderfully—thus indicating that she had perfectly understood all that Katherine had said. A quick and emphatic nod of her perfectly poised head accompanied the smile. The fingers of her left hand, exquisitely gloved, were lifted to her lips, and touched them, while she shook her head slowly, still smiling; and then, for a brief instant, she accepted both of Katherine's extended hands.

But she dropped them at once, and bent forward over the small black satchel she had been carrying, which she had put down as Katherine approached her.

She opened it, she thrust a hand inside, into a pocket of it, and brought forth a fountain pen and a small pad of paper; and then, to Katherine's utter amazement—even to her consternation and dismay—the *señorita*, began to write upon it.

The tennis game was momentarily discontinued. The players were grouped together, close to the net. Betty left her chair and moved slowly toward Katherine and the new arrival—and the *señorita*, with never a word or a lifting of her great, dark eyes, continued to write while Katherine awaited the dénouement, whatever it was to be, with many emotions. When the topmost sheet of the pad had been half filled with written words, the *señorita* lifted a pair of smiling eyes and passed it to her bewildered hostess.

It read as follows:

I regret that I cannot speak these words to acknowledge your gracious welcome. Once I thought I was to be a great singer, but on the eve of success my voice was taken from me utterly. Sometimes—not always—it is possible for me to converse in a faint whisper, although it is an effort to do so. I hear perfectly. Forgive me, and please be patient. My fingers shall talk to you, in this manner, and—still better upon the keys of a piano.

"Oh, I am *so* sorry!" Katherine exclaimed, and with an impulse she did not seek to control she put her hands upon the stranger's shoulders and kissed her on the cheek—and it was a glowing, olive-and-rose-tinted cheek that anybody might have been glad to kiss.

Katherine, by a gesture, summoned the others around her. She presented the *señorita*. She explained the situation, almost with tears in her eyes, for she felt instantly and mysteriously drawn to the woman who was so strangely bereft of the power of speech. The *señorita* was undoubtedly beautiful, with face and features and glowing eyes as young as Katherine Harvard's or Betty Clancy's, and yet whose hair, once of midnight hue, was thickly interwoven with gray. She was tall—as tall as Katherine—and straight, and willowy, and as graceful in every motion she made as a fawn.

Katherine took the little bag, to which the pen and pad had been returned, and led the pianiste toward the house.

Bridge, in the billiard-room, had been discontinued somewhat earlier than usual that day, and thus it happened that Conrad Belknap sauntered through the wide doorway at the moment when Katherine and the *señorita* arrived at the top of the veranda steps.

He came to a sudden stop at the threshold when he discovered them.

It seemed to Katherine—vaguely then, although she recalled the circumstance later—as if he had the impulse to turn about and escape. Instead, he moved forward, and with the expression in his eyes of one who expects to be introduced.

Katherine presented him to the *señorita* in a few cool and well-chosen words, to which she added, as briefly as possible, an explanation of the *señorita's* infirmity.

A look of wonderment—or was it genuine amazement?—appeared upon the features of the gentlemanly card-sharp. For a brief moment it appeared as if he likewise was speechless. Then, as if he had suddenly recalled the last words of Katherine's explanation to the effect that Señorita Cervantez could hear perfectly well, he uttered a few well-selected words about the pleasure of making her acquaintance, bowed low over her extended hand (another indication of her Spanish type, by the way), and went past them down the steps.

But he turned around and stood staring at the doorway after they had passed into the house and disappeared.

There was an unmistakable grin of amused annoyance upon his face. He bore the attitude of one who is asking himself many unanswerable questions, although he uttered no word, and his lips did not move. Presently he shrugged, and threw out his hands with the palms upward, like a pawnbroker who is remarking, "Vell, how much did you expect, anyhow?" and continued on his way to the tennis-courts.

To Betty, by whose side he seated himself, he appeared strangely preoccupied; so much so, indeed, that she spoke about it.

"I was thinking," he explained smilingly, "what a pity it is that one so exquisitely lovely as that piano-player should be speechless. By every rule of fair-play, you know, she ought to possess a beautiful voice; one expects it of her. I—er—I experienced something very much like a shock, Mrs. Clancy, when I was told that she is dumb."

"You met them, and Katherine presented you? Isn't it too bad?"

"Too bad! Why, if you knew what a voice she—I am getting twisted. If one stops to realize what a voice she ought to have, to match such a face—" He stopped again, and a grimace which might have expressed regret, disappointment, admiration, or resentment, and which, in fact suggested all four, found expression in his features.

"To think of *her* being a *dummy*!" he added, *sotto voce*, but with emphasis.

"That is distinctly an unkind expression, Mr. Belknap," Betty exclaimed indignantly: "She is not a dummy. She lost her voice while she was taking singing lessons—strained it studying for the opera. She was to be a very great star, but—her voice left her. Her hearing is perfectly good; sometimes she can speak, in a very slow whisper, although it is a very great effort for her to do it, and nobody ought to ask it of her. Always she can talk with her fingers on the piano-keys. She—"

"You surprise me, Mrs. Clancy. I am not aware that you knew the lady. I had been led to believe that she was a stranger to all of us," Belknap said quietly. "Have you—er—met her before somewhere—or heard her play?"

"No. I don't know her at all, although I feel as though I should. She is—" Betty stopped.

"She is—what?" Belknap asked with repressed eagerness to hear the answer.

Betty tossed her head and laughed aloud as she started from her chair to her feet.

"I started to say that twice," she remarked, with mischief in her eyes, "but just because you seem so anxious to know the rest of it, I won't finish it. I am afraid, Mr. Belknap, that you are considering the practicability of a serious flirtation with a speechless woman, so—I shall keep half an eye on you."

"Are you leaving me so quickly?" he asked, with a show of regret in his eyes.

"Yes, M. Pathétique—for you are pathetic in your pathos over the beautiful pianiste—I am going in, to the telephone, to speak to my husband. Tom is so impressionable that I really think he should be warned beforehand of the presence of one so surpassingly beautiful as Señorita Cervantez. Alle-ka-zam, Mr. Belknap," she finished mockingly, and ran away, laughing.

Without in the least realizing it, she left the man writhing.

Betty had done nothing more than banter him, without forethought or objective; but in both her words and her manner he read—it was pure fancy, of course—a threat. She had conveyed the idea, without intention to do so, that she had seen, or heard, or known Señorita Cervantez before that day, and that for some undisclosed reason she preferred to keep others in ignorance of that fact.

If Betty had sought with studied deliberation to stick a poisoned pin into the only vulnerable part of Belknap's anatomy, she could not have accomplished it so well as by those carelessly and mischievously chosen words.

He stared after her, wondering what could be behind what she had said, for he was strangely puzzled, oddly disturbed, and actually worried by the developments that had followed upon the arrival of Señorita Cervantez; and he was asking himself over and over again:

"What the devil does she mean by playing dumb? What's her game in being speechless? Has this confounded Betty Clancy ever seen her, or heard her play, or—*heard her speak*? And if so, does she know that the dummy act is a lie? Has Betty Clancy seen me before, too? Has she seen Berta and me together somewhere? She is from the South; it might be so. And what the devil is she telephoning to New York about, right off the bat after this happens?"

Those were the questions that flew into Belknap's mind when Betty left him, but the most puzzling one of the lot was the first one:

"What in the world does Berta mean—what is her game—what does she hope to accomplish by playing dumb?"

CHAPTER IX

LADY KATE GETS WISE

Betty, having Tom on the telephone, announced the arrival of the *señorita*, described her beauty and her infirmity, expressed the hope that he would be out early, asked a lot of immaterial questions, and finally came to the real purpose of calling him up.

"I want you, please, to stop at the house on your way out to-night, and bring to me that old morocco case with the strap around it, that used to belong to my grandmother. You remember it, don't you? It's in the safe where the silver is kept. Uh-uh. Yes, dear. There are some old daguerreotypes in it, you remember? They were made about a thousand years ago, but all the same, Tom, this Señorita Española is a dead ringer for one of those old daguerreotypes, unless I am very greatly mistaken. When she first appeared I couldn't for the life of me think where it was that I had seen her before, and then I remembered that old portrait in grandmother's morocco portfolio-case. Of course, dear. It may be just a fool-notion of mine, but I'd like to see for myself, so you needn't look at it; you wouldn't know, anyhow, because you haven't seen her. A beauty? Oh, my dear! I should say so! Mr. Belknap has lost his heart to her already. Anyhow, I would just like to show her that old picture, if it does look like her. Uh-uh. Yes, dear, of course. Now, listen."

She finished by making a sound in imitation of a noisy kiss, and hung up.

* * * * * * *

Katherine, having attended to the wants of her beautiful enter-tainer, and asked her to join the guests on the veranda as soon as she was inclined to do so, and having directed that the *señorita's* small trunk be brought from the station, went out of the house by the side

59

door, and, without previous intention, but because she found it pleasant to be alone for a moment, dropped upon the sheltered rustic seat
beneath the rose bower which had been the scene of one of her ver-
bal contests with Belknap.

One could see out from its secluded recess much better than into
it from without, and from where she sat, through the interstices between climbing rose-stems and interlaced boughs of foliage, she
caught glimpses of the figures around the tennis-courts, and of those
upon the veranda.

She saw Betty leave the side of Belknap and go into the house,
laughing; she saw Belknap, presently, rise and stroll about the
grounds with apparent aimlessness, although—and she found that
she was watching him intently, without having realized it—each
turn that he made carried him nearer to that same side entrance from
which she had just come.

She saw, too, that when he had passed behind the partial screen
of the nearer gardens, he glanced, furtively, this way and that, as if
to discover if notice was being taken of his movements.

Then, of a sudden, he started into quicker motions, approached
the steps to the side entrance, sprang up them, and darted inside.

It was then that Katherine's police training—in other words, *the
habit of suspicion*—proved its value.

As palpably as if the words of it had been spoken into her ears,
the truth about Señorita Cervantez was betrayed to her.

Señorita Cervantez was not Señorita Cervantez at all—or, if she
were that—if Cervantez happened to be really her true name, then
her other one, her first one, the given name that belonged to her and
that had not been mentioned, was *Roberta*.

She was the woman with the voice!

She was the female accomplice of Conrad Belknap, whose arrival at Myquest she had been anticipating.

Katherine was dazed by the shock of the intelligence, and she
sat very still, indeed, in her rose bower.

She had not dreamed of such a possibility—although she realized that she might well have done so, for was not the time at hand
when the accomplice was to be expected to arrive at Myquest? Such
a thought would not have occurred to her in wildest imaginings if
she had not seen and watched Belknap's actions just then; but was
not the time at hand for the fulfillment of the "arrangements," for the
appearance at Myquest of the accomplice, as revealed by the voices
in the telephone?

"Assuredly," she told herself inaudibly, "there can be no mistake."

She recalled also the meeting between the two on the veranda, when she was taking the *señorita* into the house—Belknap's apparent amazement because of the pianiste's infirmity, which had been natural enough at the time, but which took on an entirely new aspect in the list of the later revelation.

He had not anticipated that; he had not expected it; it had amazed him out if his studied reserve and calm—*because he had not been told to expect it.*

"But why, *why, why* was he not told?" Katherine demanded of herself voicelessly; and immediately a great light fell upon her.

"Why, indeed?" Katherine did not give voice to her thoughts, but they were perfectly worded for all of that; and she replied to the self-asked query:

"Because she did not know it herself until, upon that instant when she heard my voice speaking to her in welcome, and recognized it, she knew that she would betray herself to me on the spot, if she uttered a word. That's why. And, oh, what wit! What splendid presence of mind! What superlative mental preparedness for emergencies! And she never once batted an eye."

It would be difficult to describe the precise effect upon Katherine Harvard of that suddenly acquired knowledge—for, be it said with all emphasis, it was knowledge absolute, even though it had not been so much as suggested to her mind until that moment of complete conviction of its truth.

It stunned her for the moment.

The face, the manner, the personality of the *señorita*, had impressed Katherine as favorably as had the woman's voice when she had first heard it upon the telephone wire. She had been drawn to the entertainer, strangely, oddly, psychologically, intuitively—perhaps inexplicably is a better word than any of them—and the fact remained, the puzzling fact, too, that it had been a rare event, indeed, in Katherine's experiences, when her intuitions had been at fault.

Yet, present in her own home, was the beautiful woman who was a declared enemy; a woman who must, perforce, also have knowledge of Katherine's secret, and who had come there to act as an accomplice and an assistant to Belknap in the threat to divulge it, unless—unless what? That was the puzzle. What—what could it be that Belknap and this beautiful woman were after at Myquest?

And in her was no mean adversary.

In her was a foeman worthy of all of Katherine's skill; as subtle, as resourceful, as ready of wit, and as courageous as Katherine herself.

Like the war-horse that scents the distant battle, like the cavalry steed that hears the bugle's peal to "boots and saddles," Katherine lifted her head, and with partly distended nostrils, started to her feet beneath the rose bower, with the light of battle shining in her eyes, with defiance in her heart and brain, and with the glory of successful conquest for her accepted goal.

"So be it," she murmured, and stepped from the bower into the pathway, moving swiftly along it toward the side entrance through which Belknap had disappeared.

She believed that he had gone in to seek an interview with the *señorita*, and she hoped that she might find them and surprise them in the act of conversing together, thus exposing the *señorita's* subterfuge.

Such was Katherine's intention when she started forward, for she was filled with resentment at the deception that had been so deftly practiced upon her; but by the time she passed the doorway a second thought convinced her of the impracticability of such an act.

"Better, much better, to make them both believe that I am ignorant of the deception," she told herself, "and to watch—and wait—and to keep on watching and waiting."

She came upon them silently herself unobserved, where they faced one another in the embrasure of a window in the drawing-room.

Señorita Cervantez, pianiste, undoubted accomplice of Conrad Belknap—voiceless, and yet, if the truth were known, the possessor of the most attractive speaking-voice that Katherine had ever heard—proved herself to be far too capable and shrewd to expose herself through carelessness at the very beginning of her stay at Myquest.

She was standing in the embrasure of the drawing-room window, with Belknap, it is true, when Katherine noiselessly approached them through the music-room; *but*—a little sheaf of ivory tablets and a tiny gold pencil (not unlike the same convenience that was affected by Mme. Savage), dropped from her fingers at the moment when Katherine discovered them, and it would have been apparent to anybody that she had been using both, to converse with her companion. The articles were, seemingly, a part of her regular apparel, and were attached to a fine gold chain that encircled her neck, as an older woman might have carried a lorgnette.

There was not a circumstance connected with her expression or demeanor to betray her to the sharpest observer, and the sole satisfaction that Katherine could glean by reason of her stealthy approach, was in Belknap's attitude.

He was plainly annoyed, palpably frustrated, and flustered. It was evident to Katherine that he had demanded an explanation, and that it had been denied to him. If she had been aware of the last communication that was written on one of the ivory tablets, and as speedily erased, she would have comprehended better the reason for the exasperation that gripped him.

"One more such remark from you will send me back to where I came from. I will take no risks. R.'s sister is shrewder than you think for. If you don't play up to me, thoroughly, I will go away, and you will have to play a lone hand; that is final," was what the *señorita* had written—and Katherine had not arrived on the scene soon enough to overhear the remark that had induced it.

Having expressed herself, the *señorita* was ready to end the interview.

Even as Katherine crossed the music-room toward them and saw the ivory tablets drop from Roberta's fingers, she stepped through the open window to the veranda, and Belknap, perforce, followed.

So did Katherine, in effect, although she passed out by way of the door.

Belknap joined the society buds at the end of the veranda, who like to coquette with him, and Roberta (it was thus that Katherine mentally named her, now) was standing beside a chair occupied by Mme. Savage, and was writing rapidly upon one of the tablets when Katherine went outside.

"Dear me! You don't say! How sorry I am!" Mme. Savage was exclaiming while she read what was written for her. "And to think that I was never told about it. Oh, well, I suppose I *was* told, and paid no attention; it's just like me; I'm often told things that I don't hear."

Then, with amazing suddenness, the old lady changed her speech into Spanish, taking it for granted that it was the native tongue of Señorita Cervantez—and Katherine, watching and listening, saw Roberta smile and nod her head, and have recourse to her tablets again, evidently responding in the language of Castile.

So she was quite prepared in that way, too, and was not to be surprised off guard.

Katherine went to them, and Roberta wrote:

"Please go with me to the piano, and let me play for you, first; but ask the others not to follow us. I wish to play, now, to you, alone."

So Katherine made the announcement—and then, as they went toward the doorway side by side, she felt one of Roberta's arms passed softly around her, and heard the faintest of whispers in her ear, saying:

"May I, please?" And, when Katherine nodded her head in reply, and they had passed the portal, that far-away, almost indistinct whispering continued: "You are so sweet and lovely to me, Mrs. Harvard. Forgive me if I seem too familiar."

Then, to Katherine's utter amazement, Roberta kissed her on the cheek.

Was the strange woman a saint in the toils of Satan, compelled against her will to become Belknap's accomplice in dishonor and crime? Was she, also, a victim of the effrontery and threats of Belknap, because of some secret of hers that the man possessed? Or, was she just a willing tool, an unmoral creature, a beautiful vampire, and, with it all, a perfect, a superb actress?

Katherine shuddered involuntarily even while she returned Roberta's embrace. She was repelled and attracted. The woman frightened her, and charmed her. She wanted to strike her and hurt her because of her association with Belknap, and she longed to embrace her and make a friend and confidante of her, because of the magnetism and the fascination that she exerted.

Roberta played.

Katherine had dropped upon a chair with her elbow on the arm of it and her chin in her hand.

Never, never, had she listened to such music as she heard then.

Señorita Cervantez had written truly upon her tablet when she asserted that she could talk with her fingers.

Such fingers and hands, such messages as they sent out, such music as they produced! It was wonderful—impromptu, also, Katherine believed.

It began with brilliance, as if portraying the fullness of life's contentment; it glided into the rhythm of quiet harmony, as if two, who were all the world to one another, were alone together, and dwelt in happiness; it rumbled into distant storms and the threatenings of gathering clouds; it crashed into violence, and upheaval, and strife, and terror; it minored into pathos and sorrows, and into the shadows of regret and remorse; it rose again into a tarantella of recklessness and abandon, of license and irresponsibility; it subsided, slowly, into the humdrum of mingled storm and clearing; it died away, gradually, in major and minor minglings of uncertainties and doubts, mitigated by the offerings of promises and hopes—and at last it tinkled away into silence, at high treble, followed by a single, distant note of bass, uncannily giving the impression of a double interrogation at the end.

Truly the woman could talk with her fingers.

Katherine had the indefinable sensation of having viewed, as in a dream, the pictured story of Roberta's past—of having seen a vague, unshaped vision of it, with its hopes, and promises, its passions and emotions, its mistakes and their penalties, its regrets and yearnings; and, at the end, it had seemed like a whispered, inarticulate prayer for uplift and aid to an opportunity for atonement by good deeds.

Roberta left the piano and went to Katherine where she sat in silent and motionless absorption. She bent down close to her beautiful young hostess—as beautiful in a different type as herself—and with her lips touching Katherine's ear, whispered, so faintly that it was an impression rather than a sound that escaped her:

"Dear Mrs. Harvard, did I say truly when I wrote that I could talk with my fingers? I have tried to tell you something about myself—something of the past." She seemed to hesitate, then, for an instant, and added—the whispered words being fainter than before: "I want—oh, how much I do want to have you try to love me."

Katherine, startled by the passionate longing that was conveyed, even by so faint a whisper, looked up quickly, but already Roberta had pulled herself erect, had turned away, and was gliding swiftly out of the room.

Truly was she a woman of mystery; aye, truly!

Then it was that Katherine saw something more; she saw Belknap as he stepped partly into view from behind an easel in the drawing-room; she saw him thrust out an arm and hand, and seize upon one of Roberta's wrists; she saw him draw her forcibly after him as he retreated again behind the easel; and she saw a frown between his eyes and the sneering snarl of his wolfish smile baring his glistening teeth. Also, having studied it and been trained to it, she could not hear them—but, if Katherine had needed confirmation of her suspicions, she received it.

"You she-devil!" were the words he used. "What do you—"

Then they both passed beyond her view.

CHAPTER X

THE OLD DAGUERREOTYPE

Tom and Betty Clancy, in the privacy of their own suite at My-quest, were differently employed, and yet the investigations of both were tending toward the same consequence—if either had but known it.

It was Saturday midnight; that is to say, the night of the day following upon the arrival of Señorita Cervantez, and Betty's absorption by her occupation was due to the fact that Tom, the preceding day, had entirely forgotten her telephonic order about the morocco portfolio-case that had belonged to her grandmother. He had not been neglectful a second time (after Betty had expressed her opinion of his indifference to her wishes), you may be sure; and so, she was studiously examining the daguerreotype likenesses of a collection of individuals who had lived generations before she was born.

Tom, on the other hand, had taken a sealed envelope from the coat he had worn into the city that day, and was poring over a couple of typewritten pages that it had contained.

Both had preferred to wait until they had gone to their rooms for the night to perform their separate tasks, for, although not a word had passed between them in regard to their designs, each wished to discuss with the other the facts—or the suggestions—which might accrue.

We already know what Betty searched for. As for Tom—well, we need only recall to mind a conversation between him and Bing when they were on their way to town the preceding Tuesday, and when the latter had sought Tom's opinion of Belknap, and Tom had so frankly expressed it.

Neither of them had said much on the subject at the time, but both had continued to "think" about it afterward—and Tom had done some "acting" as well as thinking.

He had no sooner attended to his mail and finished his regular morning dictation, that day, than he swung the bracketed telephone beside his desk into use, and called up the Rodney Rushton Detective Bureau. His instructions to ex-Lieutenant Rushton, formerly of the police headquarters detective staff, were characteristic, and are worth repeating.

"Hello, Rushton," he said. "This is Clancy. Sure. I'm always well. Say! take your pencil and jot down a few of the items that I'm going to mention, and that you will want to remember. All ready? There's a guy down at Myquest—Mr. Harvard's place on Long Island, you know—by the name of Conrad Belknap. Got that? I don't suppose it's his right name, but it's the only one I know. He had a letter of introduction to the Harry Archers, and they took him to Myquest. I don't like him, Rushton. No; there is no particular reason why I don't; I just do not. He plays cards just as if he knew how, and he's got a grin on him exactly like the cat's after it swallowed the canary. Get me? I want his *dossier*. I want you to find out where he came from, what brought him to New York, what he is here for, who his acquaintances and friends are, what he eats and where he sleeps when he isn't leeching on somebody, and—you get me, don't you? All right, Rushton. Have some sort of report ready for me by noon, Saturday. No; send it to my office. I'll take it down to Myquest with me, and look it over, and Monday morning I will telephone for you to come down here to see me."

It was the report that he had received from Rodney Rushton that Tom was reading while Betty was searching among the daguerreotypes.

Betty completed her investigations first.

She started eagerly, and her lips parted to speak to Tom, when, perceiving that he was closely occupied, she waited; then, after another interval, he broke the silence between them—rather queerly, too, she thought.

"Look here, Betty," he said, "what is your opinion of that chap Belknap? You're rather clever about such things, and I'd like to hear it."

"Mr. Belknap? Oh, he's good looking, rather distinguished in appearance, and—"

"That isn't *your* opinion; it's the verdict of the bunch. I want yours—flat-footed."

"I think he's horrid—if you must know."

"Oh, do you?" Tom laughed. "I'd have bet a thousand on your answer. Now, tell me why?"

"Oh, I don't know. I couldn't put my finger on a thing that he's done, or failed to do, for that matter. He's—just horrid—kinda snaky. I always have the feeling when I am near to him, that he ought to smell bad; only he doesn't; or, at least if he does, I have never noticed it. He's—er—repulsive to me; and—I ought not to say this, but I'm going to, just the same—I can't get the notion out of my head that Kitten is afraid of him."

"What-*a-at*?" Tom, in his astonishment, turned around in his chair and stared.

Bessie nodded her head with emphasis. Then she replied, slowly:

"I've seen her start, and shiver, and contract her lips and her eyelids when he has spoken suddenly to her—not so that anybody but I would notice it—not so that I would, if we hadn't been almost like twin sisters ever since we were born. I—I feel it, rather than see it. Katherine is afraid of him or I miss my reckon-so. And, say, Tom, dear, have you ever watched a cat that was playing with a mouse that wasn't much hurt? Just pretending not to see it, but watching all the time with a sort of satisfied smirk around its jowl, and with one of its velvet-padded paws ready to shoot out and plant their needle-pointed claws into Mr. Mouse's tender skin? Well, that's exactly the way that Conrad Belknap looks to me when he's anywhere near to Katherine. Now, if you can make head and tail to that, you're welcome."

"That isn't a polite way to speak of one of her guests, is it?" Tom bantered.

"He isn't her guest; he's Harry Archer's—and Harry doesn't know him from Adam. Kitten told me so. I asked her, and she had to tell me. What are you questioning me about him for?"

"Because I don't like him any more than you do, Betty."

"I thought so."

"So I put Rushton on his trail."

"What does *he* say about him?"

"That is what I've just been reading. He doesn't say anything—and he uses two sheets of letter-paper to do it. The gist of it all is that Belknap showed up in town about three weeks ago; brought letters of introduction to a lot of good people; has been 'put up' at half a dozen clubs; lives, when he's in town, at the Hotel Colossal; is always well supplied with money; poses as the owner of mines and ranches in the Southwest, and is probably trying to promote them; registered as from Phoenix, Arizona, but is supposed, in Arizona, to be from New Orleans—and the chief of police in New Orleans never heard of him and doesn't know anything about him. Rushton's report closes with the two words, 'more later.'"

"Are you through with Mr. Belknap for the moment, Tom?"

"Yes. Why?"

"Come over here and take a peep at this picture, and tell me who it looks like."

Clancy did so. He leaned over Betty's shoulder, and because of the reflected light, could not see the daguerreotype distinctly. He took it in his hand and presently got it into a position so that the picture was visible.

"Great Scott!" he exclaimed, staring at it. Then he turned it over in his hand, satisfying himself that it really was an ancient daguerreotype, case and all. Next, he covered the lower part of the picture with one of his hands and put a thumb over the top of it, concealing the hair; and after a moment, with entire conviction, he said:

"Betty, if it weren't for the style of dress, and the way the hair is done—if I could see nothing but the features, I'd be willing to take the witness-stand and swear that the beautiful dummy who played for us so wonderfully to-night—Señorita Cervantez, is her name, isn't it?—sat for this picture. Whose picture is it, anyhow?"

"She was my great-grandmother, Tom. Also, she was Katherine's great-great-aunt, because her brother was Katherine's great-grandfather. But that isn't the point; this is it; who is Señorita Cervantez—who can she be—that she is a perfect facial reproduction of my great-grandmother and Kitten's great-great-aunt when she was twenty years old—in the year 1845, seventy-two years ago? *Who is the beautiful señorita, Tom? Who can she be?*"

There were other restless spirits and preoccupied mentalities at Myquest that Saturday night.

The guests had begun to seek their several quarters earlier than customary, ostensibly to make ready for a planned excursion for the morrow, so that by eleven o'clock Tom and Betty Clancy, the Archers, Demming, and Coraline Crane—who were rapidly approaching the beatific state whereby an engagement is announced—Diana Loring and Belknap, who seemed to find mutual delight in one another's society, and the *señorita* with Bing and Lady Kate, were all that remained below stairs.

It was shortly after eleven when Demming and Miss Crane wandered down a path into the shrubbery for their last good-nights, to reappear shortly, and part, and disappear toward their separate ways. Then the *señorita* rose abruptly, murmured a collective good-night to all of them, and glided swiftly away, thus anticipating by a hair the departure of Miss Loring—and making it seem to the ever-observant Katherine that Roberta had been watching them for the very purpose of rising and going at the moment when she would best be able to avoid Belknap; and Katherine was sure that she caught a glint in Belknap's eyes that manifested chagrin because Roberta had avoided him.

However, she did escape without giving Belknap an opportunity for a word with her, and without a glance in his direction, although he did rise from the swinging piazza-chair, as if to approach her.

The Archers were next to leave; then the Clancys; and as they passed into the house Belknap lighted a fresh cigarette, crossed to the top of the steps, and remarked:

"The night is much too fine to turn in yet. I think I'll take a stroll."

He disappeared down one of the paths, thus leaving Harvard and his wife alone.

"Go to bed if you like, Katherine," Bing remarked. "I'll sit here a while longer—possibly I'll wait for Belknap. I don't feel like going in just yet."

Katherine, who had risen at the beginning of his speech, started a trifle as she bent forward to kiss her husband good-night—and then assuming that his remark about waiting for Belknap had been merely a casual one, an excuse rather than a purpose, she went inside.

Bing Harvard did not alter his reclining position upon the chair he occupied for several moments after Katherine had gone; but, then, he got upon his feet, passed down the length of the veranda, turned and descended by the side steps to the path.

Instantly, when he had gained the shaded walk, he was all alertness.

The instinctive dislike that he felt toward Belknap had crystallized into a settled one during the week just past—and he had not a reason in the world that he could call by name to account for it.

But the fact troubled him; also it had made him hypersensitive to every surrounding condition, and super-watchful of the little things that happened—and he had made up his mind to be the last one in the house to go to bed that night, with no reason whatever for the decision.

Nor did he become alert because of any accountable reason when he entered the shadows of the grounds; rather, it was the alertness of habit, inculcated during the Night Wind days, and never quite abandoned since then.

70

Like every other member of the household, he was conscious of the charm of Señorita Cervantez, and under the spell of her marvelous skill upon the piano; also, like the others, although a little more so because more sensitive in that respect, he resented the unkindness of the fate that had deprived her of the power of speech. It seemed monstrous to him—unbelievably preposterous—a travesty; and he had found it difficult to keep his eyes away from her.

Thus, while studying her with no other incentives than sympathy and admiration, but nevertheless watching her covertly, he had seen—well, other things that he had not sought; little, nameless, unimportant trivialities, chiefest among which was the impression he received of her suppressed—but to him apparent—consciousness of Belknap.

Outwardly she seemed almost to ignore him—to be less aware of him than of any other gentleman in the party; and yet Bing felt, rather than was conscious of it, that the man did not utter a word that Señorita Cervantez did not hear and register—that the man did not make a move, however natural, simple, or unimportant, that Señorita Cervantez did not, by some occult sensitiveness, anticipate.

Perhaps it was partly because Bing was also covertly watchful of Belknap, although unconscious of it, that he saw and took account of such happenings—if there were such; and he was by no means sure on that point.

He did not go around to the side steps of the veranda and descend to the path for the definite purpose of watching Belknap; in reality he had no thought of such a purpose when he started.

Nevertheless, it was his purpose, just the same—and before he returned to the house and sought his bed, he had found a reason for more puzzling surmises anent the true character and calling, and the undeveloped purposes, of Mr. Conrad Belknap.

Katherine was restless also.

She did not retire when she had prepared herself for bed. Instead, after a moment of pondering, she put on a daintily embroidered negligée over her night dress, extinguished the lights in her room, and stepped through the open French window to her private balcony.

She had at the moment no other thought than to sit, quiescent, in the starlit night and think upon her perplexities; but, with the instant of stepping outside, with the black background of the darkened window behind her, and the starlight and waning moonbeams upon the gardenlike grounds of Myquest beneath her, she too, became alert and watchful.

CHAPTER XI

MIDNIGHT—AND AFTER

She saw the figure of a man standing without motion just within the deep shadow cast by a thick-boughed balsam that grew near to one of the paths, and a spark of light that wavered close to him told her that it was probably Belknap. Harvard did not smoke.

He stood like a statue, and nothing about him, save the spark of fire, moved. He seemed to be watching and waiting, and Katherine remembered that the tree which sheltered him was located about midway of the distance between the little balcony beneath her own window, and another one like it at one of the windows of the room that Roberta occupied—which, as she discovered by one swift glance in that direction, was still lighted.

Katherine was puzzled and disturbed.

It did not occur to her that Belknap might be watching her own window—or that she was visible from the grounds below. She did at once assume that he was waiting beneath the *señorita's* window for some sort of signal—and that she desired very much indeed to see whatever might happen.

However, there were eyes in the shadows below that did discover her; eyes that did not belong to Conrad Belknap; eyes that had seen him standing in the shadow of the balsam as if waiting, that had then sought the windows of Katherine's room in time to see the light extinguished behind them; eyes that glowed and burned in the darkness because of what they had seen, and were seeing; Bingham Harvard's eyes.

Katherine had no thought that Bing might be somewhere down there. He was the last person in the world to watch or spy upon another; and there was no reason that she could be aware of why he should watch Belknap.

If she had thought of her husband at all at that moment, which she did not, she would have believed him still seated on the veranda or gone to his room and to bed.

It did not occur to her to have a care lest Belknap discover her, but she reflected that the pink of her negligée would be like black in the shadow where she stood, and therefore practically invisible; nevertheless, she drew the balcony-chair closer beside her, and was on the point of seating herself upon it when an upward glance discovered the sudden extinguishment of the light in the *señorita's* room.

She remained in an upright posture a moment longer to see the better. In her eagerness to observe closely she leaned upon the balcony-rail, bending over it and peering—believing, and at the same time fearing, that Roberta would come out of her window to keep, from her balcony, some sort of a tryst with Belknap, and hoping and praying at the same time that she was mistaken.

All unknown to her as she bent over the rail, her handkerchief slipped from beneath her sash where she had tucked it, and fluttered to the ground; and being white it attracted the attention of *two* pairs of eyes—with a widely different effect upon them.

Belknap had not seen her until that happened, and in another moment he would have betrayed his purpose in being there, and therefore would have informed Bing of the fact of his somewhat intimate acquaintance with the *señorita*—for it had been his intention to call her to her window at the least.

As it was, he abandoned his first intention for another that instantly occurred to him.

He stepped out from the shadow of the tree precisely as if the dropped handkerchief had been a preconcerted signal upon which he might act. Within a second he stood directly beneath Katherine's balcony, and with both arms outstretched as if beseechingly he called softly:

"Lady Kate! Katherine!"

He did it, let us say, only to annoy her, to trouble her, to anger her, and to give her an added proof of his power. Perhaps there was even a deeper motive, but that, if there was one, has not yet appeared.

But—he did it; and other ears than Katherine's heard him.

For an interval too short to measure by ordinary standards—an interval, nevertheless, in which Bingham Harvard fought desperately to control himself, and succeeded—Conrad Belknap was never so near to death as then, and doubtless never would be again until he met it.

Yet Harvard never once moved a muscle of his Herculean strength.

He stood like a statue in stone, and as hard and frozen.

He saw Belknap's uplifted arms, as if the man were expecting Katherine to leap from the balcony into them. He heard Katherine gasp—and utterly misunderstood the meaning of it. He saw her grasp the rail with both hands and for just an instant bend her body across it, as if to speak or gesture. He saw another white thing, like an envelope, drop into Belknap's clutching fingers, and he heard Belknap speak the same two names again.

"Katherine! Lady Kate! Don't go away. Wait. I will tell you—"

But she was gone by the time he had got that far and had disappeared into the room behind her.

Harvard saw it all and misunderstood it all. Who would not?

The simple truth of the matter was that Katherine, in her consternation and fright at being discovered by Belknap, was so startled that as she attempted to escape into the house she tripped upon the leg of the chair that she had drawn forward to sit on.

Two things happened as a natural consequence.

She seized the rail of the balcony to save herself from falling; and a book that had been left on the chair that afternoon was dislodged and fell, and an old letter that had served for a bookmark dropped out of it into Belknap's hands.

Katherine escaped into her bedroom.

Belknap's teeth shone and glittered with his wolfish smile.

Bingham Harvard, *alias* the Night Wind, waited among the shadows.

That night—and after—seemed to be replete with surprises for everybody.

Belknap's wolfish smile still lingered upon his face, and he was in the act of turning away, unaware that a grim, silent, implacable man of superhuman strength awaited him amid the deeper shadows when, sibilant and sharp upon the night air, he heard a call:

"C. B.! Ce-e Be-e!" the call sounded the enunciation of it being no more than a whisper, although the sibilance of the utterance gave it a penetrating force that carried it over to the ears of Harvard, where he stood, twenty or thirty yards away, waiting.

The sound of it startled him and relieved the tension of his attitude.

His instant thought was that Katherine had returned to the balcony, but one swift upward glance assured him differently, and at the same time he saw Belknap start and turn and glance upward at another window.

Now, Harvard had no notion regarding the location of Señorita Cervantez's room. That was a household detail to which he paid no attention—the rooming of his guests—and in the darkness he had not the least idea of the identity of the second individual to appear that night in another balcony scene.

He knew, or sensed, or believed, that it was a woman who had called to Belknap—little reckoning that in doing so she had perhaps spared his miserable life—not that Harvard had formed the intention of killing him actually; but he had been awaiting the man and—

Belknap, with one hasty glance at Katherine's window, went swiftly toward the person who had summoned him, and Harvard, profoundly mystified—and possibly more than ever angered because such happenings should be undertaken at Myquest—was torn by a thousand conflicting emotions.

Nevertheless, he did not change his position, nor attempt to approach nearer to the woman on the balcony and the man beneath it. The idea of listening to their clandestine interview did not occur to him, for in point of fact his mind still dwelt upon the preceding scene which had culminated in the dropping of a message into Belknap's outstretched hands.

Nor—notwithstanding what he had seen—was he suspicious of Katherine. He had no thought of willful wrongdoing of any character on Katherine's part. The suggestion of such a thing was not in his thought—but the scene he had witnessed was no less strange, and all the more incomprehensible.

While he thought, and he thought rapidly, his eyes followed every act of this second balcony scene; he saw Belknap stop beneath it, and heard his voice speaking, although he could not distinguish the words. He saw the woman bend across the rail and put the fingers of one hand to her lips, while with the other one she extended and dropped—precisely as Katherine had done, Bingham thought—something white, which, no doubt, was also a message. He saw, rather than heard, the man speak again; but the woman—who could she be, he wondered—shook her head in a decided negative, turned abruptly away, and disappeared into the darkened room behind her.

Again he heard Belknap's voice and the utterances as well—although it was spoken in a very low and guarded tone.

"Berta! Berta!" he called twice; but the window remained closed; and after another moment of waiting the man of such mysterious actions retreated slowly to the shadow of the same tree that had sheltered him before.

Harvard, still watching in utter silence and as motionless as a statue in stone, saw the flash of a pocket-electric and then a faint glow, as if Belknap was endeavoring to conceal the light while he read his messages by it.

His messages!

One of them and its contents did not concern Harvard in the least, but the other one did, and he determined then and there to possess himself of it—of both, in fact, since he would have no method of differentiating between them in the darkness.

It was then that he began to move stealthily nearer to Belknap with the slow, relentless, absolutely noiseless advance of a leopard that creeps without sound upon its prey.

The sod beside the pathway was as soft as velvet. Harvard's footfalls were as light and transient as a globe of drifting thistle-down, and Belknap, absorbed in his occupation, had no suspicion of the presence of another person near him.

Bingham Harvard's superhuman muscular strength as compared to that of the ordinary man, might be likened to the average man's strength as compared to that of a little child; certain it was that Conrad Belknap felt like a child in the grasp of the hands that seized upon him without warning, as if they had reached out of the black shades of night and clutched him.

His arms were pinioned behind him so suddenly that the articles, three in all, that he had held in his hands, fell to the ground: an open sheet of paper covered with writing in pencil, an envelope that had passed through the mail and that contained something within it, and a small pocket flashlight.

He attempted to struggle and instantly realized the futility of it.

The person who had seized him uttered no sound whatever; everything that was done was carried out in utter silence.

Belknap's arms, drawn quickly and forcibly behind him, were held together at the wrists by the grasping fingers of one hand of his captor, while his own handkerchief was taken from his coat-pocket and used to bind his wrists together.

Once, when he made an effort to turn his head to discover the identity of the man who had attacked him, a hand flew to his throat and seized it, and he was so powerfully choked for a moment that he made no further effort of that sort. When his wrists were securely bound, he was lifted from his feet and lain, face downward, on the ground, and held there by the pressure of a knee against the small of his back while a second handkerchief was tied over his eyes.

Up to then Belknap had entertained no doubt that the man who attacked him was Bingham Harvard—and for once in his life he was frightened, realizing his danger if Harvard had witnessed the two scenes in which he had so lately been concerned.

The next act of his assailant amazed him—and it convinced him, also, that the man was not Harvard but a footpad or a yegg, who had caught him unawares while wandering in the shrubbery— which was, be it said, precisely what Harvard wanted him to think, and exactly why Harvard carefully and expeditiously relieved him of everything of value that his pockets contained.

Watch, pocketbook, loose change, stickpin—Harvard took everything from Belknap that was worth taking exactly as a footpad or a disappointed yegg might have done it, and Belknap was the more readily deceived because he had never seriously believed the occasional reference he had heard to Harvard's wonderful strength of muscle.

Then, as silently as the robber had approached, he went away.

Belknap had no knowledge of his going until he realized that he was alone.

Alone, prone upon the ground, face downward, blindfolded, and with his wrists tied behind his back!

But his feet and legs were free, and by dint of great effort he managed to struggle to his feet, and a moment later he started blindly forward in search of the path by which he hoped to find his way back to the house.

But he made turns in the wrong direction; he collided with trees; thorns penetrated his flesh and scratched his face; he tripped in the soft loam of a flower-bed and fell—and got to is feet again and went on.

Harvard, in the meantime, had resumed his chair on the veranda, and was waiting.

CHAPTER XII

HARVARD'S STRATEGY

Bingham Harvard did some serious thinking while he awaited the coming of Conrad Belknap whom he had just attacked. He did not doubt that the man would be able to find his way to the house without much difficulty, blindfolded and with his hands tied behind his back though he was.

Although the time was short until Belknap staggered gropingly into view, Harvard was able to review the several details that had happened during the past ten days to disturb and annoy him.

He recalled again the scene at the summer-house when Belknap was supposed to have received a message summoning him to the city; Katherine's avoidance and dislike of the man which Harvard believed that he saw or felt plainly; Tom Clancy's confessed repugnance of him, and the ill-concealed covert watchfulness with which Tom regarded him; the short scene at the rose bower—nothing at all of itself, yet which might have a distinct meaning in its relation to other incidents—when the burning cigarette was tossed from it, when Katherine stepped out from it and turned in the path to speak again to the man inside it—and her all-too-evident perturbation at the time; her very plain repression of something that she wanted to confide to her husband that night, and which she refrained from doing; her midnight, and therefore secret, talk over the telephone that same night; the atmosphere of restraint and portending disaster that seemed to pervade the whole place since the coming of Belknap; the anonymous letter; and, last, more disturbing and confounding than all of the other incidents put together, the utterly amazing and astounding incidents that he had just witnessed.

Throughout all of it not one thought of doubt about Katherine's motive entered Harvard's mind; not once did it occur to him to question *her* conduct or to condemn it, save only in so far as the apparent fact that she had *not* deemed it best to confide in him; and even for that—when he thought of it—he was certain that she must be following the dictates of her own best judgment.

It was not until he saw—and heard also—Belknap's approach that he remembered that he carried in one of his coat-pockets at that moment, the electric flashlight and the two written messages that he had seen fall from the balconies into Belknap's hands, and that they might, and doubtless would, disclose some of the mystery.

But there was no time to examine them just then.

Belknap had found the path and was stumbling along it toward the veranda where Harvard was seated, awaiting him.

Bing had himself thoroughly in hand by that time; not one whit of the blind fury that had gripped him while he had waited for Belknap under the trees remained. He was prepared for Belknap's approach, and he received it as naturally as if it had been in fact a surprise.

He started from the chair to his feet, shoving it away from him so that it scraped noisily.

"Hello, there!" he called out, and ran forward and down the steps to the path, and so met the sorry-looking victim of his controlled rage and strength. "What in the world—why! is it you, Belknap? What has happened?" he demanded, with exactly the right degree of stupefied amazement; and without waiting a reply he began at once to remove the handkerchief that covered Belknap's eyes. (It was his own, it may be recalled, and although there was no mark upon it, it would be, nevertheless, readily identified, so he thrust it into one of his own pockets.) Then he untied the other one, releasing Belknap's hands—and retained possession of that one also, so that it might not appear that he had kept only one of them.

He seized Belknap by the arm and led him swiftly forward, up the steps into the house, and up the stairs to Belknap's own quarters, saying sharply as he did so:

"Don't talk now. Something has happened to you, and we must do nothing to startle the people in the house. Wait."

The man was a sorry-looking one, indeed, under the glare of light in his own lavatory, whither Bing piloted him; his face was scratched and bleeding in several places from contact with the thorns of rose-bushes; his nose was plastered with loam where it had plowed into the flower-bed; one of his trouser-legs was badly torn at the knee; his collar had been ripped open, and his tie was twisted around so that the knot was under one of his ears; several of the buttons had been torn from his white vest, which was terribly bedraggled and soiled.

"You look as if you had been through a threshing machine, Belknap," Harvard remarked, secretly enjoying the evidences of his own handiwork and its consequences. "What happened to you?"

Belknap had done some thinking also while so precariously making his way back to the house; and so, while he washed away the marks of his adventure, he told his story—which Harvard naturally accepted as literal truth, and was proportionately sympathetic. He told it in jerks as follows:

"Standing under a tree, smoking—fellows, chaps, footpads, something of the sort came up behind me—didn't hear a sound—they jumped me and had me down—before I knew it—two of them; maybe three—tied me up as you found me—went through me, too—took everything—watch, money, stickpin—By Jove!" He came to a sudden pause.

"What's the matter?" Harvard asked quietly.

"H-m! Just remembered that I had a letter; important one, too. I must have dropped it. I say, old chap, wait here, will you, while I go back and look for it? I—er—couldn't afford to lose that; and they wouldn't have taken it."

He was gone before Bing could reply, but the latter called after him:

"I'll go to bed, Belknap. You're all right now. See you in the morning. Good night."

Thus, while Belknap returned to the scene of the attack upon him, to recover the two objects that had been dropped to him from two balconies, Harvard sought his own room, carrying them with him in his coat-pocket.

So many things happened at Myquest that night, and happened so nearly at the same time, that it is difficult to keep them in mind as being of approximate simultaneousness.

Betty was occupied with the daguerreotype, and Tom was engaged upon Rushton's report, while Katherine was preparing for bed, and Belknap was taking his stroll in the grounds, to be followed presently by his host. Señorita Cervantez, also restless, was at the same time arriving at the decision that she must have an interview with Belknap without delay, and so wrote a hasty note to him as soon as she got to her room—to be surreptitiously delivered at the first opportunity that offered; and having done that she turned off her light and stepped out upon the balcony from her window.

She did not do that quite soon enough to discover Katherine, who had the instant before disappeared into the darkness of her own room, after tripping upon the chair and so—without knowing it—dislodging the book which caused the old and forgotten letter to drop down to Belknap; but she did see Belknap beneath Katherine's balcony, and she surmised that he had mistaken it for her own; so she darted back, secured the message she had written, hurried outside again and called to him in that sibilant whisper.

So Katherine did not discover her, and she did not see Katherine; and she was much too wary to risk the use of her voice even then.

Having dropped her written message to Belknap, she retreated with almost the same haste that Katherine had employed, with the difference that while Katherine pulled down the shades and snapped on the lights, Roberta came to a stop just inside of her window and, concealed by the darkness, peered outward, watching Belknap.

Thus she made several interesting discoveries—and was separately and severally alarmed by each of them.

She saw the light flare into being in Katherine's room behind the white but opaque shades, remembered that Belknap had stopped beneath that balcony instead of her own—and asked herself if, after all, he had made a mistake, as she had at first supposed.

She saw the flash of Belknap's electric, and watched him—and then she saw the light disappear, and discovered the figure of another man struggling with him; and she caught her breath, frightened, although she made no move whatever.

Roberta could see very little of what happened in that deep shadow beside the thick balsam. She had no idea as to who Belknap's assailant might be, or why he had been attacked; but she was conscious of an insane joy because he was in danger, and if she had known that his life was at stake, she would not have lifted so much as a finger to save him. After a time she saw one of the shadowy figures glide swiftly away, and the other presently get to its feet and lurch into the moonlight.

She recognized Belknap and saw that he was blindfolded and had his hands tied behind him—and she laughed; not loudly, but with intense amusement at the chagrin she knew him to be experiencing; and then she became grave again, for she remembered that the person who had attracted him must have seen him beneath her window and have witnessed the dropping of the written message from her balcony.

That suggested a complication that might prove portentous—if, as she began to fear, the unknown happened to be an inmate of the house; and then she started violently and clasped her hands together as she breathed tensely the words:

"Bingham Harvard himself! The Night Wind! Was it he? Could it have been—I wonder!"

It was not of herself that she thought then, but of Katherine.

If the man were Harvard, he must have seen Belknap beneath his wife's window, and—what might not be his conclusions? "Yet," she mused on, unconsciously uttering the words aloud: "C. B. still lives; he is alive—so—it could not have been the Night Wind. *He* would have crushed C. B. into a pulp; he would have torn him apart piecemeal if he had caught him beneath Katherine Harvard's bedroom window at this hour of the night."

She looked out into the darkness again.

Both of the men had gone, and she stepped out upon the balcony.

The light was still glowing in Katherine's window and for a moment Roberta wished that there were a way to pass from one balcony to the other. She would have gone to Katherine's room and peered into it had it been possible; and then she remembered that she was still dressed, having seated herself to write the note as soon as she got to her room.

"Why not?" she asked herself, meditating upon boldly seeking Katherine's room into which she had already several times penetrated by invitation and tapping on the door. "I will—yes, I will pretend that I saw a man prowling in the gardens below, and am frightened, and perhaps—that is, possibly—she will talk."

So without turning on her own lights she went out and glided like a spirit toward the door to Katherine's bedroom.

She had reached it, she had lifted her hand to rap upon the panel, when that indefinable sixth sense which, without conscious sound, warns us of the nearness of another person, made her withhold her hand; and with the same impulse she sprang away from the door and crouched, hiding behind the solid back of one of the big chairs that flanked Katherine's doorway at either side.

Then she held her breath in startled, half-frightened uncertainty.

Approaching swiftly along the wide hall, arrayed in negligée and with slippered feet, and with something grasped tightly in one of her hands, came Betty; and Betty's errand she knew was probably the same as her own—to make a midnight call on Katherine.

Betty, she well knew, had a habit of seeing things; there was little that escaped her.

Discovery was almost certain, and yet—

CHAPTER XIII

NIGHT-TIME COMPLICATIONS

Intent as the *señorita* was upon observing the approach and preparing herself for the encounter, she was not aware that a third person had appeared upon the scene until she saw Betty stop, hesitate, dart aside, seize the knob of the door that was nearest to her, open the door swiftly, and disappear beyond it. (Betty, it must be borne in mind, was almost as much at home in that house, and quite as familiar with its interior, as was Katherine herself. She knew what rooms were occupied and what were not.)

At the instant when Betty passed out of sight, the *señorita* became aware of the third person, and she crouched still lower behind the high-backed chair in the dimly lighted hall.

Belknap—for it was he—was walking swiftly, but stealthily.

It was apparent that he had a definite purpose, and the watching *señorita* could not doubt what that purpose was—an interview with herself.

Was the man mad to attempt such a thing? To dare to approach her door in the middle of the night and summon her to it? To risk the betrayal of both—of their complicity?

She could see, when he went past her hiding-place without discovering her, the marks upon his face where thorns had scratched it, and she noted the absence of collar and tie and his general disheveled appearance—and also she believed that Betty was watching him through a crack of the doorway of the room in which she had hidden herself.

Betty, of course, could see the man go to Señorita Cervantez's door and—no matter what was destined to happen after that—would form her own conclusions.

Something had to be done, and done at once to offset them. There was not a moment—not an instant—to be wasted, and so—

The *señorita* darted from her hiding-place as soon as Belknap had passed her. She seized the opportunity when Betty would be absorbed in watching Belknap and moved the chair ever so little, and so was directly at Katherine's door. She pressed her body closely against it, thankful that the embrasure of it was almost deep enough to conceal her unless an observer stood well out into the hall.

Then—not too loudly; not with force enough, she hoped, to attract the attention of Betty, who was concealed behind a door that was nearly tight-closed, or of Belknap, whose own motion and footfalls might prevent him from hearing—she tapped against the panel.

The door was opened instantly, so that, pressing against it as she had been, the *señorita* literally stumbled into the room and against Katherine, who had been passing it at the moment of the summons and had pulled it open quickly.

The *señorita* was really startled into the appearance of fright. She had meant to play the part, but she did not need to, because she looked it; and yet she was none the less cool, resourceful and competent.

She gasped—in that whispering manner of one who is without voice; she turned like a flash, seized the door, closed it, turned the key in the lock, and leaned against the barrier with every appearance of one who is on the point of utter collapse. Thus she succeeded in frightening Katherine momentarily, which she had meant to do.

"Why, *señorita*! What—"

Katherine got no farther, for Roberta seized her by both arms and clasped her tightly; she put her lips close to Katherine's ear; she exclaimed, in that breathlessly faint whisper of her adoption:

"Burglars! Oh, Mrs. Harvard! Burglars! Thieves! The house is being robbed!"

Now, Katherine was—Katherine.

She had no more terror of prospective burglars than of crawling bugs and worms in the paths outside; and literally she did not believe that burglars had entered the house. She only thought that the *señorita* had been unduly frightened, so she acted in a perfectly rational manner: she put Roberta aside, unlocked the door and pulled it open—and came face to face with Betty Clancy, who had just at that instant lifted a hand to rap against it.

Betty was looking frightened, too, and Katherine began to believe that there *were* burglars in the house—and Betty, meanwhile, could not see Roberta, who was concealed from her by the opened door.

Betty was holding her fingers at her lips to enjoin silence. She did not attempt to enter the room; instead, she grasped Katherine by one arm and pulled her partly into the wide hall—and she whispered in a tone that was as nearly inaudible as the *señorita's* had been:

"Look!"—and she pointed down the hall. "Do you see him? He is at the door of Señorita Cervantez's room. He is rapping upon it. Do you see him, Kitten? It's Belknap—Conrad Belknap, I tell you? What—"

Katherine had stepped farther into the hall, and at that instant the door of her room behind her slammed shut with a loud noise.

A draft of air from the open windows might have caused it—but it didn't; Roberta, the resourceful, did it. She did it to warn Belknap—to make a sound that would let him know that he was seen and watched—perhaps, or possibly, to prevent him from proceeding farther with his prowlings. She remembered that her own door was not locked, and she knew that it would be quite like him, when he received no response to his rapping, to turn the knob and open it.

Indeed, he had done that very thing when the door somewhere behind him slammed and warned him.

It startled him so that he left the door in front of him wide ajar. A turn of his head apprised him of the fact that he was seen. The two figures outside the door to Katherine's room were apparent.

Belknap knew that he was caught and that it would require every whit of his wit and skill and effrontery to get him out of the dilemma.

Katherine had, in her turn, taken Betty by the arm. She had moved a step forward down the hall toward Belknap, and Betty was holding back a little, reluctant to follow. Both were astounded, but for different reasons; for Katherine knew what Betty did not: that Belknap and the *señorita* were confederates.

Just then both of them were amazed anew by Belknap's actions.

He seemed to be groping with searching hands along the wall. He moved away from the door at which he had been rapping and drew nearer to them; and although they were by then plainly in view, he seemed not to see them.

They both stood very still watching him. The door behind them opened by a crack, and Roberta peered into the hall, but neither of them knew it.

Belknap came nearer and nearer to them gropingly, feeling with his uplifted hands along the wall. His eyes were wide open and staring, and he acted like one who is in a trance, or who walks in one's sleep; and Betty, pressing her lips close against Katherine's ear, whispered:

"Kitten! He's walking in his sleep! And look at him! He has had a fall. His face is scratched and—"

Katherine disengaged herself from Betty's grasp and went swiftly to Belknap.

She was not deceived, although she believed that Betty was.

She seized him and shook him, and he came "awake" with a shudder and a half-inarticulate cry. It was surprisingly well done—amazingly well acted; and *he* believed that he had fooled both of them.

Katherine was astounded by his condition, his torn clothing, his scratched and blood-marked face, the absence of collar and tie, his soil-stained garments, his torn trouser-leg. He had been immaculate at dinner and throughout the evening; he had seemed to be so still when she had seen him beneath her balcony; but since then something untoward had happened to the man.

For a moment she was almost deceived into the belief that he *had* wandered into that part of the house without knowing what he was doing; she might have been entirely deceived about it if he had been wise enough to continue his play-acting instead of "coming awake" as he did when she grasped him and shook him.

"Great Caesar!" he half gasped. "Where am I? What has happened? What—"

"You had better go to your room, Mr. Belknap," Katherine said coldly, interrupting. "You are disturbing the household by wandering in the halls and rapping at doors. Come, Betty."

"Wait," said Belknap. "I want to—"

"Good night, Mr. Belknap," Katherine interrupted again. She was already at her door.

She opened it, drew Betty into the room with her, and closed it, and so left Belknap standing alone in the hall with his sleep-walking act half done, with his suddenly assumed subterfuge of doubtful success.

Meanwhile Betty was encountering another surprise, for inside of Katherine's room, huddled in the depths of a big arm-chair and apparently trembling with fright, was the *señorita*, who, the moment they appeared, sprang out of it and faced them timorously.

Her lips formed words. She seemed to try to speak—and to fail; but she managed to make them both understand that she was trying to ask Betty if *she* had also heard and seen the burglars.

Betty, by the way, still clutched the old-fashioned case that contained the daguerreotype picture of her great-grandmother, and the presence of the *señorita* in Katherine's room brought to mind her own reason for being there.

While Katherine was reassuring the *señorita* and explaining that the supposed burglar was nothing more than one of the guests walking in his sleep, Betty hesitated; then, with an impulse born of the moment, she extended the three-generations-old likeness toward its living replica and said quietly:

"Look, *señorita*, and see what I have found, then tell me if you can guess who it resembles. I had intended to show it to Katherine first, but—it would seem to be your privilege—don't you think?"

CHAPTER XIV

A SCREAM—AND THREE SHOTS

Bear in mind the fact that the *señorita* was still dressed exactly as she had been throughout the evening; Betty and Katherine were the only ones at that impromptu gathering in negligée, and Betty explained even while she passed the daguerreotype to the pianiste, that she had sought Katherine's room at that late hour only on impulse, and with the thought that the latter might not yet have extinguished her lights.

Roberta received the closed and hooked gutta-percha case into her hand wonderingly; but ever on the alert, she prepared herself instantly for whatever disclosure was to follow; and she knew that there must be one of some sort, else Betty Clancy would not have sought Katherine's room at that hour of the night to show her the daguerreotype.

Nevertheless, she could not hide her amazement when she opened the case and looked upon the picture of a young woman so exactly like herself save in the fashion of coiffure and style of dress that, barring the lapse of approximately three-quarters of a century since it was made, she herself might have "sat for it."

Roberta could not have concealed her astonishment had she tried, and she made no attempt to do so. Curiosity, intense and absorbing, outweighed discretion had there been need for it; but she did not forget to remain speechless.

She seized upon her tablets and wrote:

"Wonderful! Who was she? Please tell me all that you know about her."

Katherine, who had been peering over the *señorita's* shoulder, exclaimed enigmatically before Betty could reply to the written words.

"How strange! Yes, and wonderful. I understand now, *señorita*, why, ever since you came to Myquest, your face has reminded me of another one which I could not bring to mind; but I know now. Betty, my father has an old daguerreotype portrait of that same face. It was made, I think, some years later than this one. She was—"

"Wait, please," Betty interjected; then she turned again to the *señorita*.

"I have quite a collection of daguerreotype pictures," she said, "and a list of them in my grandmother's handwriting with the dates when they were made. That is a picture of my great-grandmother. It was made on the 17th of June, 1845—seventy-two years ago; and on the day before she was married, which happened on her twentieth birthday. The picture that Katherine refers to was made a year or two afterward; I haven't the date of that one; but the reason why Katherine's family also has a picture of her is because Katherine's great-grandfather and my great-grandmother were brother and sister. So, you see, by collateral descent, Katherine and I are third cousins.

"We have always known that, *señorita*," she went on after the slightest of pauses, during which the others were silent. "My great-grandmother was a Maxwilton, and the great-aunt of Katherine's father—Katherine's great-great-aunt. So, now, what I would like to know is: Where do you come in? It goes without saying that you *belong*. There is Maxwilton blood in your veins—there must be, or—" She stopped for lack of ideas to go on. Then impulsively she cried out as she went forward and peered into the eyes of Señorita Cervantez:

"Are you another third cousin? Are you, somewhere in the past, a Maxwilton, or a Keese? That was my name before I was married to Tom Clancy. Is Cervantez your really-truly name, *señorita*, or is it just a professional name? Yet you speak Spanish, for I heard Mme. Savage talking it to you, and saw that you replied to her with your pencil and tablets. My goodness gracious! How I have been rattling on and never giving anybody else a chance to put in a word."

Roberta had grown pale and paler while Betty talked.

Neither she nor Katherine had noticed it, being more intent upon the problem than with the object of it; but, with Betty's closing remark, Roberta got slowly to her feet from the chair upon which she had dropped when the picture was shown to her.

She still held it in her grasp tightly, as if in dread that it might be taken from her, and she seemed dazed—as indeed she was by the revelations and the mysteries that were a part of them.

Her lips parted as if to speak, but she remembered in time and closed them. She was groping for her tablets with wandering, uncertain fingers when Katherine put her arms around her and drew her into a close and fond embrace.

"It doesn't matter who you are, dear," she said. "Whether you are a Maxwilton or a Keese or if the wonderful resemblance to the old portrait is only an accident, the fact remains that you are here, and that we are both fond of you; that I am certainly. And," she added, with another thought, "I am not going to let you go away, Monday, as planned. I will see to that."

Roberta let go of the tablets which she had found and grasped. She whispered into Katherine's ear:

"I—I don't know anything about it, Mrs. Harvard; nothing at all. It is all a mystery to me. I am dazed, excited, speechless, thoughtless. It is all so wonderful—so overwhelming. May I—may I go to my room now? And may I take the likeness with me, please? I want to study it; I want to think about it. Please let me take it."

Katherine repeated the substance of what she said to Betty.

"Of course you can take the picture," Betty announced; and then they both kissed her good night, and she left the room.

"What does it mean?" Betty demanded of Katherine after she had gone.

Katherine shook her head.

"I don't know," she replied. "I will ask my father about it. He has got the entire Maxwilton genealogy tucked away in his head, ever ready for instant reference. He will be likely to know; or, if not that, he'll be more likely to know how to make guesses about it than we are."

Betty kissed Katherine good night. She started for the door, and stopped half-way to it.

"Katherine?" she began.

"Yes? What now, Betty?"

"Do you think that Mr. Belknap might have known the *señorita* somewhere, sometime, before he met her here?"

"What a question! Why?"

"I have heard that when people walk in their sleep they follow out ideas that were predominant before they went to sleep. And—and, honestly, Kitten, I don't believe he was asleep any more than I am now."

"Why, Betty!"

"You just wait a moment. I saw him before I came into this room. I was on my way to find out if you were still up and to show

91

you that picture. I saw him in the hall and dodged into the room that Bing always reserves for Mr. Chester. I peeked out when he passed the door and saw him plainly, and if ever anybody was wide awake in this world, he was. He was scowling and showing his teeth, and as mad as a bear with a sore paw. Asleep? I reckon not! And he went as straight to the *señorita's* door as a shot out of a gun. He rapped on it, too; and kept on rapping, just as if he had a right to do it; or, if not that, as if he knew that he could *make* her answer him, whether she wanted to or not. And I was scared out of my wits when I sneaked along the hall to this door, afraid that he would see me; but he didn't; and you could have knocked me down with a cobweb when I found the *señorita* here. And, Kitten—"

"Well, dear?"

"While I am on the subject, there is something else that I want to say: Tom doesn't like the man, and I don't either. Tom has put Rodney Rushton onto his track, and—"

"What?" Katherine cried out.

"Well, what of it? He has, anyhow, whether you like it or not. Tom thinks that—"

A wild cry, like the scream of a banshee, instantly followed by three pistol-shots in rapid succession, interrupted her, and both young women stood spellbound and frightened.

"They came from outside—from the gardens—didn't they?" Katherine asked breathlessly.

"I wonder," Betty said, "if Belknap went back to the *señorita's* room to wait for her?"

The wild scream and the pistol-shots that followed it momentarily paralyzed every energy that Katherine and Betty possessed, coming upon them as it did at the moment when they were about to part for the night.

But the effect of them lasted only for a moment. Both of the young women recovered their self-possession instantly, and each of them was courageous, resourceful, and quick to act.

They were close to the door into the hall when the cry and the shots startled them. Katherine reached out and punched the black button of the electric switch, extinguishing the lights in the room; then she darted across it to the window and out upon the balcony— for she was convinced that the sounds proceeded from without the house, and believed that they were not far from her window.

Betty Clancy seized upon the door, opened it, and sprang into the hall—for she was equally convinced that the sounds came from within the house; that is to say, both acted upon the impulse of the moment, without thought.

Each of them was, in part, right.

Katherine, as cool as ever she had been in the old days of her police experiences, was quickly outside on the balcony, and bending over the rail of it, peering eagerly this way and that; and she saw— or thought that she saw, not being entirely certain—the outlines of a human figure as it darted into entire obscurity beneath the shadows of the trees at the edge of the lawn. And that was all.

Betty, as she literally jumped into the hall from Katherine's room, saw nothing at first. But doors were pulled open, timid and shrinking guests appeared as if by magic, frightened figures of women and the startled and questioning visages of the men, materialized from every direction, for the alarm had been one that was not to be ignored. It was not the sort of thing that one hears vaguely in sleep when one wonders even more vaguely about the cause and rolls over into sleep again; it was of the character that compels a person to sit up and take notice.

Bing Harvard came into Katherine's room from his own just as she reappeared from the balcony. He snapped on the lights while she crossed from the window toward him, and she noticed instantly, but without betraying her surprise because of it, that save for the fact that, he was without a coat, he was dressed precisely as he had been at dinner that evening.

His quick questions also surprised her.

"Was any one here with you?" he demanded.

"Betty was here. We were—" she began. He interrupted her.

"Anybody else?"

"No, not just now, when we heard the shots. The *señorita* had been here earlier, but she had gone. Why—there is Betty now!" For Betty had reappeared at the door.

"Come!" Betty called to them from the doorway. "Oh, Bing! I'm so glad that you're here. They say—out there—that it came from Mme. Savage's room."

Bingham and Katherine followed Betty into the hall.

They found that a group had already collected in the corridor near the entrance to the suite occupied by Mme. Savage and her maid, and that a hush had fallen upon those who were gathered there.

The cause of it was at once apparent, for the unmistakable sounds of a woman sobbing could be heard from beyond the door, and mingled with it were the sharp tones of *Madame's* deep voice, almost masculine, in timbre.

Harvard tapped upon the panel, and *Madame's* voice bade him enter.

The old lady was sitting up in bed, and she held in her right hand a small automatic pistol with which she had been gesticulating while she talked to her frightened and sobbing maid who stood facing her across the footboard, grasping it with both hands.

Mme. Savage was a very old lady, it must be remembered; a very young-old lady, with eighty years or thereabouts to her credit, but as youthful as ever she had been, in spirit and thought, and in her outlook upon life. Nor was she one who had resorted to artificial devices to keep herself young; her natural buoyancy, and her ardent love of being in the middle of "something doing" had done that.

"Come in! Come in!" she called out when she discovered the group at her door, headed by Harvard. "I'm not a bit afraid to be seen in bed by all of you. I don't wear a wig, nor do-up my face and neck in an enameling-mask when I retire. My goodness, Bing, did I wake up the whole household?"

"Naturally. Have you been practicing at a target, *Madame*, or were you shooting at your maid? And, if I may inquire, where did you get the pistol?" Harvard was smiling as he put the questions, for he was reassured. It had only been a scare after all, he was thinking.

Madame replied to the last question first.

"Where did I get it?" she retorted. "I've always had it. Not this one, of course, but a pistol of some kind. I'm not used to this new fangled contraption yet, and I shot three times when I only meant to shoot once."

"But, my dear lady, *what* did you shoot *at*?"

"A man. There were two of them, or a man and a woman. I think that I must have winged one of them at that. You see—"

Betty interrupted impulsively.

"But the scream!" she exclaimed. "That came before the pistol-shots."

"Oh! That Nistine is a ninny; she is always scared at her own shadow. It was she who did the screaming. That is what I was scolding her about, and why she is sobbing now, just like a scared child."

"But, *Madame*, how did it happen? What *did* happen?" Bing asked.

"I was reading myself to sleep—I always do that, you know; it's a habit I've had for sixty years; and Nistine was sound asleep in that chair by the window. I heard a noise and looked around and saw

Nistine jump to her feet; and there was a man—I could just see his head and shoulders—climbing in at the window. He had a handkerchief or something tied across the lower part of his face. You see, only this reading-light was turned on, and he must have thought that I was asleep with a night-light burning, or he wouldn't have tried to climb in.

"Well, anyhow, Nistine let out that scream you heard and jumped, and when she jumped she caught her foot in something and fell. But in the mean time I was reaching under my pillow for this. When Nistine fell and was out of the way, I let drive at him, and the thing went off three times instead of once. I guess maybe that night-prowler didn't know that my father and my husband were both cattle-kings in the Southwest, and that I learned how to use a gun at the same time I learned to read a primer. I always sleep with one of them under my pillow, and I always carry one in my hand-bag with my book and lace-needles when I travel. It's the habit of a lifetime; and, besides, this isn't the first effort that burglars and porch-climbers have made to get my diamonds away from me.

"That's the whole story, so—No it isn't, either. I jumped out of bed and went to the window, and I saw two figures disappear among the trees, and one of them either wore a long raincoat—which isn't likely, for it's not raining—or was a woman and wore a dress. That is all. I didn't shoot again because they got out of my sight too soon. But I'll tell you this much: one of them, the one that I'm sure was *not* a woman, acted as if I'd winged him, and I've seen too many men shot not to know pretty well when they're hit. Now, will you do me the favor to send all of these people out of my room? Those burglars had probably heard that I was down here at your place and figured it out that it would be a swell chance for them to get my jewels. They've been hot-foot after my diamond-rope ever since that foolish Sunday newspaper printed a picture of it and told what it is worth. But they won't get it, Bing Harvard! Not while I'm alive, and I expect to be on earth a good many years yet. And, Bingham, come nearer. I want to whisper to you. Now, listen: I think—I don't know, but I *think*—that I could make a good guess about that chap that I did *not* hit. He moved just like—er—somebody I know. But I'll tell you about that in the morning."

CHAPTER XV

A KEY TO THE MYSTERY

The impromptu gathering dispersed; the startled guests departed to their several rooms after Harvard had pooh-poohed any idea of a search of the grounds of Myquest that night.

He followed his wife into her room and closed the door, and was at the point of passing on, through it, to his own, without comment upon the excitement that had just passed, and its cause, when she stopped him.

"Bingham," she said.

"Yes," he replied, and wheeled about and went back to her.

She reached out and rested her hands on his shoulders, then she cuddled her face close against his neck and sighed contentedly; and yet it was a sigh that was much too deeply drawn to express merely content. There was repression in it, too, for she had intended, when she called to him to stop, to tell him everything, but in the barely perceptible moment that intervened had changed her mind.

How she wished, in that instant, that she had told him all about her brother Roderick, long, long ago; for there was not, nor had there been, anything about the circumstances of Roderick's past, or in connection with his supposed death and burial, which Katherine had need to hide from her husband. She had not told him, because it had always seemed so unnecessary to recall the dark and heart-rending chapter in her life, or to harass Bingham by the recital of it.

Her reticence was not the consequence of any reluctance to confide the whole truth about Roderick to Bingham, for if Conrad Belknap had been elsewhere, and temporarily beyond her husband's reach, there would have been none at all; but she knew as well as she had knowledge of anything, what Bing would do to the card-sharper if he was made aware of the things that Belknap had done, and of the threats the man had uttered since his arrival at Myquest.

She knew that the Night Wind would be unleashed again, as it had been during those terrible days of the frame-up when he had been hunted and hounded like a felon, for a crime committed by another.

Above all things else in Katherine's mind was the dread that her father and mother might discover that their son did not lie buried in that grave in Kentucky that was marked with his name; that the dead still lived; that Roderick Maxwilton had not expiated his misdeeds with his life—and any violence on Bingham's part toward Belknap must inevitably lead to such an exposure.

So, in that interval of a second, while Bing returned to her and she clung to him, with her head on his breast, the impulse to tell him everything passed.

Harvard waited for her to speak, but when she remained silent he asked:

"What is it, dear? Is something troubling you?"

"N-no," she replied.

"Are you quite sure about that, Katherine?"

"Of course. I am only—babyish."

"That is not like you."

"N-no. But, then, we are not always immune from nervous shocks, are we, Bingham?"

He did not reply to the question. Instead, he asked one, with a glance as he did so, toward her bed that had not been occupied.

"Why had you not gone to bed, Katherine?"

"I had callers, as I told you," she replied. "The *señorita*, and Betty."

"What errands did they have, at such an hour, to bring them—"

Katherine brightened, and lifted her head as she interrupted him.

"That reminds me," she said, speaking rapidly—for she did not wish to be questioned too closely about the things that had happened after she had said good night to her husband. "The *señorita* must have seen or heard the same burglars that disturbed Mme. Savage. She was badly frightened when she came in. She had seen somebody prowling about outside of the house—a man, or some men, under trees, I think."

"Was that what you wished to tell me about when you called me back just now?" Bing asked her; and when she hesitated for a reply, he added: "There was something that you wanted to tell to me, wasn't there, Katherine?"

"There is something that I want to ask you, dear," she answered, evading his question, and believing that he did not notice that she did so, although he was aware of it, and disturbingly so.

97

"Yes?" he replied, noncommittally.

"Do you think that it would be possible"—(the idea had just occurred to her as a possible solution of her difficulties)—"for us to go away somewhere, very early in the week—just for a short trip—somewhere—anywhere at all?" Being well into the subject, she warmed to it, and went on rapidly: "The guests need not hinder us, you know, if you can get away from the bank. And I don't care to stay long, anywhere. I would *so* much like to go away alone with you for a short trip, *somewhere*, Bingham."

Harvard smiled a bit grimly, although Katherine did not notice that.

"That sounds," he said, "very much as if there is somebody here—a man or a woman, or both—that you would like to be rid of." He hesitated just an instant, and added: "Is there such a person?"

"Why—er—perhaps, dear. I had not thought about it in just that way; but—"

"Have you forgotten, sweetheart, that you have one guest here who cannot very well be gotten rid of for another whole week, without giving offense? Mme. Savage makes her dates for months ahead, and is as exact about them as a railway schedule. Don't you remember that it is only a short time since you told her that we would remain at Myquest all summer, and that you asked her down here for as long a stay as she could make—and she told you the date when she would come—which she kept—and the date, twelve days later, when she would leave us, which she means to keep to the letter? You can't send her away, Katherine. She'd be lost. It would upset her entire system to interfere with her timetable of dates."

Katherine nodded without replying.

"Besides," Harvard went on, "your week-end entertainment that began nine days ago, has developed into a house-party. Demming and Sears, Cora Crane and Di Loring, mean to stay on as long as you will keep them; and—well, there's Belknap, too. He seems to like it so well here that I shouldn't wonder if he decided to stay all summer. No, Katherine, I don't think that we can pitch them all into the highway and go away; but, if you like, you can give notice that we will close the house a week hence."

He was watching her closely while he talked, although his tone was a bantering, rather than a decided one.

He saw that she sighed again, resignedly, and that she was vastly more disappointed than she wished him to know. He was more than ever convinced that she was keeping something from him that she wanted to tell, and which, for some inexplicable reason, she withheld.

"Who is it that you wish to be rid of?" he asked abruptly. "Belknap?"

Instantly she was on guard.

Her husband's question might have been purely accidental, or there might have been a purpose behind it. She did not wait to inquire of her own mind, but replied instantly.

"Did you notice, Bingham," she asked, "that Mr. Belknap was the only one of our entire guest-list who did not appear when Mme. Savage alarmed the whole house?"

"Yes," he replied coolly. "I did notice it; but I knew why he did not."

"You did?" Katherine almost cried out in her sudden alarm. "Why—what—"

Harvard replied to his wife's unfinished question smilingly.

"He, too, like the *señorita*, discovered prowlers in the grounds around Myquest, but with the difference that he actually encountered one of them, and had been very badly handled when he returned to the veranda where I waited him, you'll remember. He had lost his watch, his stick-pin, and some money—and an important message or letter, which he went back to search for at the spot where he was attacked."

Katherine, in her amazement, gasped, and Harvard misunderstood the reason for it.

"Do you mean that he was robbed—actually robbed—in our grounds?" she demanded.

"Yes; perhaps by the same prowler, or prowlers, that the *señorita* saw, and that Mme. Savage shot at. However, you have not replied to my question."

"What was it, Bingham?"

"You would not want to go away, just now, unless there were some persons here whom you prefer to be rid of. I asked you if that person is Mr. Conrad Belknap?"

"Oh. Why, yes, I suppose so, when all is said. He is a stranger to us, isn't he? One can't say that he really belongs, you know. But, dear, the truth is, that I would like to be rid of all of them—every last one of them."

They had remained standing while they talked. Now, Harvard reached out and put his arms around Katherine, and drew her close to him, kissing her brow, and inhaling the fragrance of her hair. Then, holding her so, he asked:

"Has something happened to annoy you, Katherine? Has any person annoyed you, by word or deed? If anything of that kind has occurred I want you to tell me."

"No, no, no, no!" she exclaimed, so vehemently that he suspected she was not entirely truthful. Then she broke away from him and laughed. "How silly we are, just because of a burglar scare," she said. "Do go to bed, Bingham. Do you know what time it is?"

"I wonder," Harvard remarked tentatively, as he turned toward the door to his own part of the suite, and while his back was toward Katherine, "if you, also, saw a prowler under your window, to-night? I wonder if that is what you want to tell me, and are afraid to tell—lest I should go outside and get hurt, or—hurt somebody else?"

Then, before she could reply, he wheeled and faced her—for his own words had provided the key to the mystery that perplexed him so sorely.

"What has Belknap done to you, or what is he trying to do? Tell me!" he demanded.

CHAPTER XVI

AN APPALLING SITUATION

There was a crucial instant for Katherine Harvard when her husband put the abrupt question which was a demand rather than an interrogation.

It was one of those vital instants when one has only a flash of time in which to determine a course which must be adhered to indefinitely—in which a thousand queries and replies pass into and out of one's mind with the rapidity of thought which can span the distance between earth and sun within one ten-millionth of a second.

Katherine realized in that instant—when there was no perceptible pause at all—that she had to choose between a deliberate deception and a complete revelation of all of the facts. Merely a part of the truth, with something withheld, would not suffice for Bingham Harvard, once called the Night Wind by the men who had hunted him.

Katherine lied to him—and hated herself for doing so the instant when it had been done; yet, had she been given an hour or a day to think it over, she must have arrived at the same decision—for the dread of what Bing might do filled her with terror.

"What has Belknap done to you, or what is he trying to do? Tell me!" was the demand that he made upon her; and her reply was ready as soon as the last two words were pronounced.

"Mr. Belknap?" she questioned instantly—and Katherine was a perfect actress in such emergencies.

The pronouncement of Belknap's name interrogatively, was made with such perfect simulation of astounded surprise that it was quite enough without further remark. It was so adroitly done that it disarmed Harvard; and she added: "What has he done, or tried to do—to me? Why, what could he do—what could anybody do—what could any person try to do to Bingham Harvard's wife—or dare to try to do, that might affront her?"

Harvard sighed, unconsciously, and with an inward sense of relief.

"Then, dear, answer your own question—the one that you have just asked," he said. "What has anybody done, or tried to do, that is not to your liking?"

"Nothing," she replied.

Thus Katherine uttered the first lie—why soften it by substituting the word untruth?—that she had ever told to her husband.

Harvard sighed again.

He believed her—because he had never known her to deceive. Yet there remained in the back of his mind a mental reservation of doubt. It was so faint, so obscure, as to be unrecognizable, but it was there.

He kissed her forehead again, curbed and withheld other questions that sought utterance, held her close in his arms for a second, said "Go to bed, now, sweetheart," and left her.

When the door had closed and he was gone, Katherine moved about the room in her final preparations for bed, methodically; automatically is perhaps a better word.

She turned down the bed-clothing, snapped off the lights, returned to her bed, got into it, pulled the covers over her, snuggled into her pillows, and closed her eyes. But—she was another Katherine; she was not the same personality that she had been a little, just a very little while before.

She had told her husband a lie.

Sleepless, although motionless and with closed eyes—for she was trying to sleep—the events of the night since she came to her room from the veranda passed in review before her. She mentally visualized everything chronologically.

Again, in retrospect, she put on her negligée, snapped off her lights, and stepped from her window to the little balcony to enjoy the night air.

Again Belknap made his appearance beneath her window, and dared to address her intimately, by her given name, and by another one which only an extremely favored few were permitted to use; again the *señorita*—Roberta—came to her room, frightened, or pretending to be frightened, by burglars.

Katherine had not believed, then nor did she believe while she thought it over, in the genuineness of that fright. She had thought then, as she still thought, that it had been simulated. But why—for what purpose?

In the light of what had happened afterward—with the appearance of real burglars and the attempted entrance to the room of Mme. Savage; with the absence of Belknap from the scene that followed, and with the *señorita's* too-reluctant reappearance, hovering at the edge of the partly clad group of startled guests—there could be only one answer to those two questions.

Katherine opened her eyes wide, and sat up in bed, startled into sudden revelation when that answer occurred to her; and she whispered it breathlessly, in a hushed whisper.

"That attempt at burglary upon Mme. Savage was real; it was genuine. Belknap knows who those burglars were, and was expecting them. He went from the veranda into the paths among the shrubbery and trees to meet them. They saw him under my window, and they quarreled; perhaps that accounts for his bruises. Roberta is Belknap's accomplice—she knows why he is at Myquest—what he intends to do—and she came to my room to warn me by the only method she dared to use."

Instantly, when she arrived at that solution of the mysteries of the night, Katherine sprang out of bed, seized her discarded negligée, and without switching on the lights, thrust her feet into her bed-slippers and ran—literally ran—to the door.

She opened it softly, passed to the outside, closed it noiselessly, and glided like a ghost in pink, to the *señorita's* door.

She hesitated there for an instant, listening. Then she tapped softly upon it, and waited.

There was no answer, even when she tapped a second time, more loudly, so she grasped the knob, turned it, discovered that the door was not locked, and entered the room.

Señorita Cervantez was not there. The bed had not been disturbed.

Katherine had gone to the *señorita's* room impulsively, without second thought regarding the wisdom of the act, but with the settled determination to "have it out" with the woman accomplice of Conrad Belknap—with the beautiful pianiste who pretended to be voiceless, who was at once so beautiful and so double-faced, so lovable and yet so deceitful.

If Katherine had needed any added conviction of Roberta's connection with Belknap and his aims, she found it in the *señorita's* absence from her room—and it was equally plain that only one reason could have taken her from it at that time; she had gone from it to seek her master—to find Belknap.

"Shall I follow? Shall I seek them?" Katherine asked herself mentally; and shook her head slowly in a negative.

"I will wait," she told herself voicelessly; and she sought a chair in the darkened room, for none of the lights was turned on, and only a dim glow shone into it from the starlight without.

She found one, a big chair upholstered in leather with a high and solid back, and she moved it a trifle so that her presence in its depths could not be seen from the doorway by a person entering the room.

Then she hid herself in it and waited.

During many minutes she sat with her eyes wide open, staring slanting-wise through the open window where the filmy lace draperies swelled and subsided and swelled again in the zephyr-like night breeze.

When they bulged into the room, pressed apart momentarily by the drafts of air, she could see—between the iron spindles of the balcony-rail—the same big balsam-tree out of the shadow of which Belknap had made his sudden appearance when he had startled her so greatly, earlier in the night—and she fell again into going over the details of the evening and night, bit by bit, item by item.

Thus the sleep that would not be wooed when she had gone to bed crept stealthily and silently upon her in the chair beside the opened window, and without realizing it, she drowsed and drifted into obscurity.

The clicking of a latch startled her into wakefulness. A sharper draft of air bulged the draperies into the room.

Katherine was aware that the door opened, and was closed again, although she heard no further sound; but she was certain that the *señorita* had returned and was standing somewhere between her and the closed door, unconscious of her presence, unwise to the fact that she was not alone.

It was Katherine's impulse to speak, but she did not. She sat very still and waited, wishing fervently that she could see; she was, at the moment, sorry that she had so placed the chair that her own vision of the interior of the room was minimized to next to nothing.

She could hear stealthy footfalls, presently, as the person behind her crossed the floor.

Absolute silence followed, and continued so long a time that Katherine found it difficult to restrain her impulse to move ever so little so that she might turn her head enough to discover what was going on; yet she feared to do so, knowing that the slightest of sounds would betray her presence in the chair.

Then she remembered that she was clad only in her night-dress and the filmy negligée that covered it; and therefore there was nothing about her apparel that would rustle if she moved; the soft material of her wrapper would slip noiselessly over the leather covering of the chair.

After another moment a single light was switched on behind her, and by the dim glow of it Katherine knew it to be the green-shaded desk-light in a far corner of the room; but the silence remained unbroken.

Katherine could bear it no longer—and, anyway, since she had gone to that room for the express purpose of having an understanding with the *señorita*, why delay? So she moved ever so little, and turned her head, and fortunately, made not a sound in doing so.

What she discovered terrified her.

For the first time in her life that she could recall she was actually afraid—really scared—panic-stricken.

The person who had entered the room, who had so silently crossed it, who was, in fact, at that very instant moving slowly across the floor toward the very chair upon which she was seated, was not the *señorita*.

It was a man; and the man was Conrad Belknap.

Katherine saw, with that quick capacity for comprehension which one experiences in vital moments, that he held in one hand an opened envelope and an unfolded sheet of note-paper that he had evidently taken from it—a letter, apparently, that he had been reading by the aid of the desk-light; a fact which would account for the enduring silence of his after he had entered the room and crossed it to the desk.

It was, without a doubt, a letter of the *señorita's* that she had left upon her desk. Katherine saw that the envelope had been sealed with wax, and had been ruthlessly broken open.

The green shade over the desk-light was thick and heavy, and there was not sufficient illumination for Katherine to see the man's face plainly, yet she did discern enough to know that he was in a rage—a silent, impotent, helpless rage, about something that was, for the moment, beyond his control.

She had no time in which to determine what to do; there was nothing that she could do.

Belknap had not seen her; she knew that. He was not aware of her presence in the room; but he was approaching her swiftly, silently, implacably; evidently seeking the chair as she had sought it earlier, and she knew that in just another instant she would have to rise in her place and confront him.

CHAPTER XVII

IN THE SEÑORITA'S ROOM

If Conrad Belknap had taken one more step he must have seen her.

He did not take it. There was a sharp click against the knob at the door, and at the sound of it he turned.

Katherine had been on the point of rising to confront him, and she had swayed her body around in the chair, grasping the back of it. She was ready to spring to her feet and to demand of him why he dared to prowl about the house at that hour of the night, when the slight sound at the latch alarmed him and he turned away.

Instead of rising, Katherine huddled herself more closely into the chair, drawing her feet up into it so that she was on her knees, and with only so much of her head above the back of it as would permit her to see what was going on.

Belknap had wheeled around so that his back was toward her, and he stood a little to the right of her line of vision toward the door which fell open quickly after that click at the knob.

The *señorita* entered, turned, closed the door silently, and locked it. Then, with an air that bespoke dejection, she leaned her back against it; and with bowed head, and her gaze evidently upon the floor at her feet, she stood there, relaxed and panting, as if she were badly frightened or had been running.

Thus she did not see Belknap until his voice startled her so that she jumped. Without any sort of doubt she had believed herself to be utterly alone when she came into the room so hastily and locked the door after her.

The move that she did make, then, was bewildering.

It is an axiom that persons thus rudely startled will act instantly and impulsively upon the idea that has been most emphasized in thought immediately preceding the alarm.

"Where have you been?" Belknap demanded without preface. His voice was sharp, cold, and authoritative, and Roberta jumped as you have seen kittens spring into the air when one's foot is scraped sharply upon the floor behind them.

She sprang toward the desk where Belknap had snapped on the light beneath the green shade, which she had not noticed, evidently, till then; possibly she thought she had left it so.

Her body bent forward and her right arm was extended as if she would seize something—without doubt the same letter that Belknap was holding in his hand, and which he had opened and read, and which had angered him, as Katherine had divined.

Also, he seemed perfectly to understand her impulse, for when she turned to face him again, with one hand clasped at her breast, and utterly heedless of his question, Katherine heard him say in that coldly sardonic manner which was so thoroughly his characteristic:

"I found your letter. I have it here. I have opened it and read it."

Bear in mind the fact that there was no light in the room save the very dim glow that escaped from beneath the green shade where Belknap had turned on the desk-light.

It was not sufficient to enable Katherine to observe either of them distinctly. Belknap's back was toward her; Roberta was beyond him, partly facing Katherine. The impressions she got from the scene were the result of intuition combined with so much of observation as the dim light would afford.

She was certain of just one thing, however; neither Belknap nor Roberta suspected her nearness. Fortunately it did not occur to either of them to turn more light upon the scene.

Katherine's terrors of the moment ago had left her.

All of the masterfulness, all of the shrewdness for which she had been noted when she was attached to the detective bureau at headquarters, all of her long latent abilities as one of the keenest and the best of operatives, returned to her in that moment.

She became on the instant once more the Lady Kate of the Police—the quick-witted, far-seeing, inscrutable Lady of the Night Wind—the indomitable personality that had made of her a force and power to be reckoned with during the days of the great frame-up which had made an outlaw of Bingham Harvard, and which, but for her efforts, would have kept him an outlaw for the rest of his days.

She forgot that she was in negligée and bed-slippers, and was the hostess of a house-party who had penetrated surreptitiously to the room of one of her guests—for although Señorita Cervantez was a hired entertainer, she was nevertheless a guest.

Katherine...in the big chair...listening was certain that neither Belknap nor Roberta suspected her nearness.

Roberta—we must call her that, save when requirement renders necessary the name she assumed for use as an entertainer—seemed in the half light of the room to straighten and stiffen where she stood, as if her attitude had become one of defiance.

She did not reply to Belknap's question at all, and there was a perceptible pause before she answered his remark about having opened and read her letter. Even then she uttered only one word. It was:

"Well?" The enunciation of that one word was as clear and distinct as the tone of a bell, and the voice was the same melodious one that had so charmed Katherine upon the wires of the telephone.

"Where were you? Where did you go after you wrote this letter and left it to be found on your desk in case you should not return? Where have you been?"

Roberta did not answer; but Katherine could see that she shrugged her shoulders in a disdainful gesture that was almost as indifferent to consequences as the manner and attitude of Belknap always was.

"Answer me," the man commanded sharply.

Katherine thought that Roberta actually smiled at him then; she could see the flash of her perfect teeth.

Again the pianiste did not reply.

Instead—she was still near to the desk with its shaded light, although her back was toward it—she moved backward and reached out one arm until her hand covered a button that was against the wall beside the desk.

Holding her hand thus she spoke again, and with an element of cool daring in her voice—voice, remember, coming from one who was supposed to be speechless—that was rather amazing under the circumstances; and it seemed to be her turn to make demand.

"Leave the room, C. B.," she said.

Belknap's answer was entirely characteristic—and without words.

He took one step forward and to the right, reached out for one of those small bedroom chairs that are more for ornament than for use, swung it around between his legs so that the back of it was toward Roberta, and sat down astraddle of it.

"Go ahead and ring," he said then, coolly. "It is getting along toward two in the morning. Who would hear the bell? The butler, possibly. Who would respond to it? Again, the butler—or one of the servants. What would he find when he arrived?" Katherine could see the expressive shrug of Belknap's shoulders; then he added: "Ask yourself that question, Berta—and answer it for yourself. You ought to know me well enough by this time to know the answer to it. You won't ring, I don't think! Now, who is outside, in the grounds of Myquest—or, who did you expect to find out there waiting for you? For I very strongly suspect that you were disappointed."

He bent farther forward across the back of the gilt chair and his chin was thrust forward as he added:

"You took a long chance when you wrote this letter and left it on your desk—and you have lost out. Of course you did not suppose that I would dare to come into your room in the middle of the night, as I have done, and find it and read it; but you ought to know by this time that I dare all things when I have a definite purpose in view, and you ought also to know that I shall stay right here where I am until you pull in those little prickly horns of yours which couldn't hurt anybody. You can't do anything but scratch with them, like the feline little animal you are; you couldn't stab with them if you tried; they'd break off before they got deep enough to hurt. I brought you down here to do my bidding, and you've got to do it, and you know it.

"Bring that desk-chair close to me and sit down—and sit facing me," Belknap ordered sharply. "I want to see you while I talk to you. It will be as well to have no more light in the room just now."

"I prefer to stand," Roberta replied. Plainly—to the listening Katherine—she was gaining courage rather than losing it.

"Bring that chair here and do as I tell you or I'll do it for you, and put you on it," Belknap commanded—and although he neither raised his voice nor altered its tone, Roberta obeyed him.

When she had placed it, and seated herself upon it, her position was such that if she should lift her eyes from Belknap's face she would see Katherine; so Katherine permitted her body to settle down in the big chair until she was entirely concealed by it; and she cuddled closely into the depths of it, content to hear, without seeing.

But she did wish to hear everything that might be said between those two; there was strong likelihood that their conversation would enlighten the mistress of Myquest greatly.

Belknap, although Katherine could not see him, seated astride of his chair, was bending slightly forward with his forearms resting lightly across the back of it. His eyes, hard and cold, but piercing, bored into Roberta's gaze as if he would read her very soul while he questioned her.

He still held in one hand the letter he had read, and he tapped lightly upon it with one finger while he said:

"So you have been having another try at stealing my trump card away from me, have you?"

Roberta did not reply. He said:

"Berta, if you don't answer my questions as I ask them I'll make you. Now, answer that one, and answer it straight."

"There isn't any answer," she replied coolly.

"Did you send for him to come down here?"

"Yes, if you want to know, I did."

"To come here to the house?"

"No."

"This letter as good as tells me that you more than half expected to find him in the grounds under the trees waiting for you. Was he there?"

"No."

"This letter was written by you and left on your desk in case you should not return. What did you mean by that?"

"I meant exactly what the letter said—what it says—what you have read—every word of it, C. B."

"So you were going to double-cross me at the same time you made your own getaway, were you?"

"I meant to warn Mrs. Harvard against you—yes—and I will warn her if you insist upon keeping me here. I'll find my voice and speak out. I'll do it in your presence, too; and in the presence of Bingham Harvard, also. Don't forget that he is the Night Wind, C. B. Don't forget that he is the same man that you have so often talked about and wondered about. Don't forget that he loves his wife, and that if his wrath should once be turned against you, you'd be withered and crushed and rent apart in his grasp like a child in the claws of a man-eating tiger."

"There, there, Berta; don't get dramatic. What are you trying to do, threaten me, or are you just trying to scare me?"

"Neither. I am warning you."

"Yes—against yourself."

He chuckled. Then he snapped his fingers. There was something akin to amusement in his voice when he said coolly:

"You couldn't warn Katherine Harvard against me, Berta. You couldn't say anything to her about me that she doesn't already know or guess. I haven't been squeamish in letting her see under my shell of respectability. I don't care if she does know it—all of it. I shall tell her myself, exactly who and what I am, when the proper time comes—when a fitting opportunity shall offer itself. She doesn't know that I'm a crook, but she is fairly well convinced of it already. So, don't you see? You'd better drop that lay."

Roberta did not reply.

"Listen here, you would-be fairy-godmother to the Harvards. I came to Myquest for a definite purpose, and I'm going to accomplish it. I brought you here for a definite purpose, and I'm going to make you perform your part of it. I made you come here because I needed you, and I'm going to make use of you, exactly as I planned to do it—and you can't dodge that fact or avoid it. You might as well put that fact into your little pipe and smoke it, Berta. Are you paying attention to what I am saying?"

"Yes."

"Well, you'd better pay heed to it, too; to all of it."

"Wait a moment," she said coldly. "You know, C. B.—it isn't the first time, either—that I will throw you down the very first time I find the chance. I have told you that before. I mean it. I am tired, worn out—"

"Can that, Berta!" he interrupted her sharply. "Why this sudden spasm of goodness and purity on your part? Eh? What has put the worm into our little apple? Tell me that. What is the reason for this supposed dumbness? This inability to speak a loud word? Who is here, among the guests at Myquest, who might recognize that sweet voice of yours if you should make use of it? Have you and Katherine Har—By God, I've got it! So! That's the idea, is it? I get you, now, you she-cat. You tried to double-cross me even before you came down here, didn't you? And you used a telephone to do it, didn't you? You have talked to Lady Kate on the telephone, haven't you? Answer me!"

"Yes."

"She is the one you were afraid would know your voice, eh?"

"Yes."

"You called her up and—"

"I did not. She listened-in when you called me up. Then, when you hung up, she spoke to me."

"Then why—Oh, I see. You were afraid that if she got onto your curves right off the reel, as soon as you appeared on the scene, she'd fire you on the spot, eh? And you wanted to play us two off, one against the other, while you looked on—for a little while before you made a break. Fine! Fine! Really, Berta, I'll take my hat off to you in some things."

He was thoughtful a moment; then went on, in the same bantering tone, which, nevertheless held a sting:

"I see. I get you. I'm wise. Very clever of you, you panther-girl. You are a sort of panther-girl, when all is said. You're sleek, and beautiful, and graceful, and as smooth as satin, and you can purr as softly as one of their kittens; but you've got teeth and claws, and you can spit—as well as bite and scratch. You were lying back, eh, watching for the psychological moment, so to speak—waiting for the moment when you could bring two certain people together, face to face, while you looked on and patted them on their backs, and played the good fairy. That is what you were up to, is it? That is the way you intended to double-cross me."

He got up from the chair and shoved it aside—Katherine ventured to peek over the back of her chair.

She saw him seize one of Roberta's wrists and jerk her to her feet; she heard him say:

"All right for you. I told you, when you promised to come here, that there was one thing that I would not force you to do; but, just to prove to you that you can't play the cat-and-mouse game with me, I'll make you do it, now."

CHAPTER XVIII

ONE QUALITY OF FEAR

Belknap released Roberta's hand and started toward the door, but he stopped and turned to face her again before he touched it. Katherine dropped out of sight a second time, but was conscious of a touch of sardonic mirth in Belknap's voice when he spoke; she could picture that wolfish smile of his which she had no doubt he was employing.

"I wonder if by any chance you are jealous of the beautiful Katherine," he said.

"I might be jealous for her," was the quick retort from Roberta. "If I thought that you so much as—"

"*Touché!*" he interrupted, and laughed. "Rest easy, my lady-of-the-claws-and-teeth. The charming chatelaine of Myquest does not tempt me. It's her money that I want, not her exquisite self. One or two of her jewels, maybe—one that she wore during the evening, for instance, but not Katherine herself."

Roberta did not reply; he left the door and returned to her.

"On the level, I wouldn't give the nail off of one of your little fingers for a dozen Katherine Harvards," he said, and then Katherine heard the sounds of quick motions and a gasp from Roberta, and a low, chuckling laugh from Belknap.

"Got you, haven't I?" Katherine heard him say, and she ventured to peek once more over the chair back.

He had seized Roberta's wrists and was holding them while he bent forward with his face close to hers.

"I've got you so you can't bite or scratch, so don't struggle. It won't do any good. I am going to hold you till I have said something that I want you to hear. It's—"

"Let go of my wrists," Roberta demanded of him coldly, and without a sign of an attempt to free herself. "If you don't—" She did

115

not complete the sentence, but he seemed to know what she would have said.

"I won't let go until I have finished with what I meant to say when I turned back from the door, just now," he told her. "It's this: you seem to be the only person of my acquaintance who has the power to exasperate me to the limit of endurance. You are the only person alive who can madden me to the point of losing my temper. I who never lose it! And I don't know whether it is because I love you or because I hate you. I—"

She interrupted him.

"It is neither," she said coolly.

"No?" He chuckled again, still holding her hands.

"No," Roberta repeated after him. "It is solely because you know that you are not my master. It is because I defy you—because you cannot make me your slave—because there is an element within me that is so utterly beyond your control that you are mystified. But, after all is said, C. B., those are only side reasons. The real reason why I exasperated and madden you at times is—"

She stopped, gazing frankly into his eyes; and while she did so he slowly released her hands and stepped backward, away from her—and it was noticeable (or would have been so if another could have seen Roberta just then; Katherine did not dare to lift her head above the top of the chair back) that she did not move away from him. She had forced him to become the one who put more distance between them.

When she paused in her speech, he demanded:

"Well, what is the real reason? I would like to know it."

She replied to him slowly, and with quiet emphasis:

"Because, deep down in your heart you are afraid of me. Because I am the only person in the world that you are afraid of; and because the experience is so strange to you—so entirely apart from your regular scheme of things—that although you know it to be true, you will not permit yourself to believe it. You won't admit that it's so."

Belknap laughed softly, showing his teeth wolfishly.

"You are afraid of me," Roberta said again. "You know that I carry around with me the power to kill you as surely and as quickly as the lightning strikes and kills. You know that I carry with me wherever I go the means of ending my own life as suddenly, and you know that I have the will to use that means—against you or against myself. You know, too, that there is only one thing that keeps me from using it—that makes me withhold my hand, and it all

116

resolves itself to the one fact that you are afraid of me. You are in constant and deadly fear lest you go a step too far, and so—" She stopped.

He had withdrawn as far as the door; Katherine realized that when he spoke again. His voice was low, his speech deliberate and filled with menace.

"Sometime," he said, "you will take the step too far. Sometime you will force me to take the step which will compel you to act; but, when I do take it—don't forget this little fact, Berta—you will be the victim, not I. You will take your own life, not mine."

Katherine heard the click of the lock as he turned the key. He pulled the door partly ajar, and closed it again. His cool suavity of manner had returned when he said:

"It is Sunday morning now. To-morrow will be Monday, and I shall see to it that an occasion is made for you to make use of your skill at cards. Do you get that, Berta?"

"Yes."

"I will keep the letter that you wrote for Lady Kate to read in case you did not return. I have found it interesting."

"You can do what you please with it; I can easily write another one, if need be."

"You will not write another one," he retorted carelessly. "There will be no need of one. Our useful friend, for whom you sent to come here, did not make his appearance; and he will not. You will see to that, now. If he does, you will regret it; and so will others whom you have a mind to champion."

He pulled the door open, passed out, and closed it after him.

Katherine kept very still in her hiding-place in the big chair, but she peeped around the side of it and could see Roberta standing with her back toward her, with her face toward the door.

Her attitude, now that Belknap had gone, was one of utter dejection.

Katherine's impulse was to make her own presence known at once; and yet her police training assured her that it was much better that she should not do so. She kept very still, withdrawing into the chair. She knew that it was quite likely that Roberta would presently discover her, and just as likely that she would not. In the one case she intended to appear to be very soundly asleep, and in the other she would wait where she was until Roberta slept, and then steal silently out of the room.

After a time that seemed interminable, so long did Roberta remain in that attitude of thoughtful dejection, Katherine could hear her moving about the room; but she did not turn on any more lights, nor appear to have any thought of preparing herself for bed. All that she seemed to do—for Katherine could only hear, and not see—was to walk slowly up and down the room, and with each turn that she made she sighed deeply, as if the burden she bore was almost too much for her.

Katherine was in a dilemma.

More than once she was at the point of making her presence known; she had, in fact, determined to do so, and had partly lifted her head in the beginning of the act, when, as if Roberta had reached a guiding decision, she passed the chair, went swiftly to the window, and stepped out upon the balcony.

Katherine could see her peering with apparent eagerness this way and that, as if she searched the darkness with her eyes for somebody she hoped to see; and presently she wheeled about, re-entered the room, crossed it swiftly without seeing Katherine, and went out, closing the door softly behind her.

Instantly Katherine slid from the chair to her feet.

At all hazards, and notwithstanding her negligée attire, she felt that it was her duty to follow—for Roberta had said to herself, whisperingly, as she crossed the room:

"I will look again. Possibly he was detained. He may be there, now, waiting for me."

CHAPTER XIX

A MAN IN THE OPEN

Katherine was not to leave the house that night on the track of Roberta in precisely the way she planned, although she did go out into the darkness by another method than the door—by one that was forced upon her, which she would not have attempted, nor, indeed, believed possible of accomplishment had she not been compelled to it, and if she had not been transformed, by the scene she had just witnessed, to the keen and daring Lady Kate of the Police, to the Lady of the Night Wind who had dared so greatly and accomplished so much, long ago, when she had taken upon herself the task of clearing her husband of the framed-up charges against him.

When Roberta went from the room after making those self-addressed whispered remarks about her going, Katherine became suddenly alert and eager.

She was again the shrewd, resourceful, and skilful detective of her "Miss Maxwell" days at headquarters, unafraid, self-confident, and competent. She became, on the instant, the skilled operative of by-gone times.

It did not matter to her then that she was in negligée. Señorita Cervantez, the Roberta of the midnight conversation over a telephone wire, the confederate of Belknap in his schemes, had just gone out into the night a second time to meet somebody she had sent for and was expecting—somebody who was inimical to Belknap and his plans—somebody whose identity Katherine vaguely, very vaguely, suspected—and Katherine was bound to discover who and what that same somebody might be; she was determined to find out if there were any grounds for her faint but insistent suspicions.

She had what Tom Clancy would have called a "hunch."

She guessed that in the conversation she had just overheard, Belknap and Roberta had both referred to her brother Roderick—and yet—and yet—

She darted to the door and pulled it a little way open without a jar or sound.

There was the possibility that Roberta had paused just beyond it; that she might have changed her mind; so Katherine was extremely cautious—and it was well that she was so.

She peered into the hall, which, although dimly lit, was lighter than the room behind her.

Instantly she withdrew her head, reclosed the door, and turned the key in the lock, fastening it. Then, almost holding her breath, she waited.

What she had seen was startling enough.

Roberta had already disappeared—much more quickly than Katherine had believed she could; more than likely she had run to the stairs and down them. But Belknap was returning.

She had caught sight of him at the moment he turned around the post of the balustrade coming from the floor above, where his room was located; she had seen him—and she feared that he had caught a glimpse of her. Not enough to have recognized her; she was quite certain as to that, but his eyes had evidently been on the door when she had thrust her head outward. He had started forward with quickened pace, and—

The knob of the door turned; then when it would not yield, the knob was shaken gently.

Katherine made no response whatever. She stood very still, listening.

Belknap, at the opposite side, tapped lightly against it. Then Katherine heard his voice raised barely above a whisper.

"Let me in, Berta," he said. "There is something I forgot to say, and there is no knowing when there will be another opportunity like this one. You haven't undressed, yet, I'm sure. Open and let me in. I won't stay five minutes. I promise."

Katherine smiled, well pleased to know that he had not recognized her; and, of course, she made no reply whatever.

Belknap did not, immediately, speak again, but Katherine could hear a faint rustling beyond the closed door; and then she became genuinely startled.

She heard the click of metal against metal at the keyhole, and Belknap's muttered remark made at the same time:

"All right. If you won't let me in, I'll go in."

And Katherine understood.

She knew that he was using burglar-forceps to grip the post of the key and turn it, and thus unlock the door from his side, and she knew that it could be done as easily as if he held the key itself. She knew all about such instruments; she had seen many a pair of them in the museum-cabinet at headquarters.

It did not at the instant occur to her to seize the key and hold it—and even if she had done so, Belknap would presently have discovered that it was not Roberta, but another, beyond the door—and he might guess who that other person was. Katherine was very far from wanting him to suspect that she had been a witness to the scene that had just happened inside of the room.

When the forceps clicked against the lock, and she realized what he was doing, she darted away, and by the time he had begun to turn the key in the manner described, she had fled into Roberta's bathroom, and had closed and locked the door after her—and that time she withdrew the key and dropped it to the tiled floor.

But there was no other way out of that room—unless—She glanced toward the high and narrow window and shook her head—but approached it nevertheless—and stepped upon the low chair that stood beneath it while she pushed wide open the hinged screen to peer into the night outside.

"It might be done," she told herself mentally. "It can be done. I must do it. That man shall not know that I—"

Belknap had entered the other room and was rapping softly against the bathroom door.

"Come out here," she heard him say. "What is the matter with you?"

But Katherine was working with feverish haste and paid no heed to him.

There was a pile of bath-towels in the small cupboard where they were kept and they were of generous size.

She seized upon them one by one and knotted them together until she decided that her improvised rope was long enough, for she had made up her mind that she would experience only slight difficulty in forcing her slender body through the window. She had not a doubt that Belknap, when he became convinced that Roberta would not go out to him nor answer him (for of course he could not doubt that it was Roberta inside of the bathroom), she believed that he would do one of two things; he would either try to force the door—an unlikely thing—or he would calmly announce that he would sit down and wait till she came out, if it took her till doomsday to decide—an extremely likely thing for him to do in his present mood.

Well, he could wait; but Katherine did not propose to remain where she was to be waited for. Roberta might have done so; she would not.

She tied one end of her rope around the pipe of the hot-water-heating apparatus that passed from floor to ceiling in the corner beside the window; then she got upon the low chair again and began her strange exit from the bathroom.

She could hear Belknap talking, but she paid no heed to what he was saying.

She had to force her way head first through the window—there was no other way—but she kept a firm grip upon her towel-rope.

Head and shoulders first while she clung with one hand to the rope of towels, she forced her way through the narrow space.

Katherine was slender and willowy. There was but little impediment of clothing to overcome, as we know.

It was a tight squeeze, nevertheless; but she made it inch by inch, by squirming and edging her body forward a little at a time, first at one side and then at the other, emerging finally at the opposite side in the position of one who dives into the water.

When at last she was free from the window casings, she did dive, but she clung desperately to her rope as it caught her weight and whirled her body over.

The impetus of her fall and the sharp jerk upon the improvised rope proved too much for the knot she had tied around the water pipe; it was not equal to the sharp and sudden strain upon it.

It came loose, and she fell, a few feet only, and upon the soft sod, so that in her quite natural excitement of the moment, and her glee over the escape she had made, she was barely conscious of the shock of it—and the knotted towels fell with her, and she gathered them up as she got upon her feet and sprang into the deeper gloom of the night among the shrubbery.

So Katherine was free from the house, leaving Belknap none the wiser.

She smiled at the thought of his amazement, if, while he waited beside the locked bathroom door, Roberta should return—and remembrance of Roberta brought to mind her original purpose.

But a moment of thought convinced Katherine that it would be worse than useless to seek her under the circumstances.

Roberta had gone out with a definite purpose, and doubtless to a definite place; there was no such thing as guessing where that place might be located.

Moreover, now that she was in the open air, she needed, and very much wanted, clothing.

There was no means of re-entering the house at once; she knew that she would have to wait until morning to do that—if she hoped to accomplish it without betraying the unusual circumstances of her being outside, and she had no notion of letting anybody into that secret. It was wholly her own, thus far, and she meant to keep it so.

She did not know where she could go.

There was always the Nest, her one place of secure refuge from any and every sort of storm or stress. There was everything that she might need there; and never yet had there been a time when she was so thankful for its existence—so grateful for that whim of hers that she had coddled and encouraged since childhood, which had induced Bingham to let her build it—never had she appreciated the fact of it so much as at that moment.

It was her "mystery place," her very own sanctum, and with a smile of content she made her way swiftly along the winding paths among the bushes and shrubs toward the artificial lake beside and above which it was located.

She glided along like a spirit—and with scarcely more noise than one might make—and so she came at last to the shore of the little lake, to a pathway that followed the indentures of it and would lead, presently, to another one that ended at the Nest.

Katherine was too impatient to keep to the path; the way across was shorter, and she knew every inch of it even if the darkness was deeper among the towering trees from beneath which every scrap of lesser growth had been cleared away.

Gliding noiselessly onward, flitting like a sprite from tree to tree, she came to a sudden stop, and sniffed the air like a hunting-dog that has caught the scent of game.

It was the unmistakable odor of a cigar that Katherine had sensed, and as she came to a halt and listened, peering eagerly this way and that, she detected the low murmur of voices in conversation—just the low hum of them, with nothing distinct about it.

"Roberta!" she thought quickly. "Roberta, and the man she came out to meet. And he is smoking. Foolish man! But he could not guess that a regular old-timer detective would be out here on his trail."

She smiled broadly at her own facetiousness while she stood very still and listened intently in order to catch the exact location of the sounds she heard. Then her face took on a serious expression; and as she moved slowly forward toward the sound, she murmured to herself:

"Can it be? Oh, can it be possible that—that he—No, no; I can't believe it. But, if it is not that, it must be another part of this hideous plot; and, whatever it is, I mean to know about it."

CHAPTER XX

THE FACE IN THE FLAME

A broad-spreading box-elder tree grew on the bank of the lake just where Katherine approached it from the wood. Its long, thickly leaved, horizontal branches extended above the water in one direction, and as far back from the shore in the other, creating a perfect and extensive shade in the daytime, and enveloping all things beneath it in black darkness at night. There was a rustic bench under it, where Roberta and her companion were seated, facing the lake, and therefore with their backs toward Katherine as she stealthily approached them from among the trees.

Under the tree, against the surface of the water that shone in the starlight beyond, Katherine could discern the outlines of both figures with just enough distinctness to determine one from the other—to know which was the man, and which was the woman.

They were seated very close together; the man's left arm was stretched along the back of the bench behind Roberta; they seemed to be conversing earnestly, but their voices were tuned to a pitch so low that even when Katherine had approached them as near as she dared, she could hear no word distinctly that was uttered between them.

It became very quickly evident to her that whatever might have been the reason for the clandestine interview, its purpose had been already accomplished, for even as Katherine attained a position from which she might have overheard them had they continued, they got up from the bench and stood facing one another.

Katherine stood behind the trunk of a giant, old-growth hemlock, with her lithe and slender body pressed closely against it, and with her head bent forward so that she could look past it; but the drooping branches of the box-elder hid their heads and shoulders from her sight. But she was able to see that the man held both of

Roberta's hands tightly clasped in his—and she was aware that he bent nearer as if to touch his lips lightly against Roberta's forehead.

They parted then—and Katherine had heard not a word that had passed between them.

Roberta glided away swiftly and noiselessly, and was lost to sight around a winding of the path along the shore, which, by the way, would have brought Katherine directly upon them had she pursued that course instead of cutting across through the trees on her way to the Nest.

The man remained.

He stood quite still until Roberta had disappeared; then he sat down on the bench again, struck a match, and applied the flame of it to his cigar with the burning match cupped in his hands, but with his back toward Katherine, for all the world as if it were done purposely to tantalize her.

She had the mad notion that the man was her brother Roderick, and she could not rid herself of the conviction, and yet, strange paradox, she felt, she almost knew, that it could not be so.

He was tall, broad of shoulder, well built, and carried himself like a soldier; she had been able to discern that much. Every item of that description, so far as it went, would apply to Roderick Maxwilton; but so would it apply as precisely to thousands of others.

She had not heard, with any distinctness, the sound of his voice, and she was by no means sure that she would remember Roderick's if she could hear him speak. She believed that she would, but she was doubtful, too, so many years had come and gone since she had listened to it and loved it.

She had been only a girl, then, with her hair in braids down her back. Precocious and wise beyond her years, perhaps, but a girl, nevertheless. And Roderick was already a young man with a drooping though somewhat scanty mustache, with coal-black hair that he had permitted to grow quite long, after the fashion of the Southern youth, at that time, and he had been addicted to frock coats and wide-brimmed hats, string ties, and a touch of "swagger"—like other young Kentuckians of his class.

Besides, during the three years that had immediately preceded his "going away from home," Katherine Maxwilton had seen very little of her brother—less and less with each succeeding day and week and month.

He had been wild, untamed, and untamable; she, only the kid-sister at home. He had raced his horses, drank his toddies and juleps and smashes, played cards, made love, and sowed his wild oats

126

broadcast with generous indulgence; she had been the kid sister at home who saw him scarcely at all, save when—as quite often happened—in the dead of night, or at dawn, she stole down the stairs to help him into the house and to his room, without waking their parents.

She had idolized him and worshiped him, nevertheless—her only brother; for he had been the eldest and Katherine the youngest among five, and of the three who had died, she had no recollection whatever.

So she panted with expectancy and dread while she stood behind the trunk of the hemlock watching the man on the bench who smoked on as unconcernedly as if he had not a care in the world beyond the immediate consumption of the cigar.

She wished that he would throw that one away and light another, and turn so that he would face toward her when he did it. She was certain that she would know him if he were Roderick. She was not sure about the voice, but she knew that she could never forget the handsome, somewhat dissipated, but wholly patrician face of her brother.

After a time he stood up again, tall and stalwart, with his head and shoulders veiled within the black gloom above him, and Katherine crouched low behind her tree.

Then he did precisely what she had been hoping that he would do; having turned his body slowly around, gazing first out across the lake, then toward the buildings of Myquest, he presently faced directly toward herself as if he looked at the trunk of the very tree behind which she was crouched.

He struck a match; he held the flame of it before his face while he applied it to the cigar so that every line of his features showed plainly—and Katherine was conscious of a sharp pang of disappointment.

She saw no resemblance to her brother Roderick in that flame-illuminated face.

Katherine's disappointment was so keen that she closed her eyes in the spasm of regret that followed it; she had not realized how earnestly she had hoped, nor how confidently she had expected, that the flaring light of the match would reveal the face of her brother.

When she opened them, and lifted her gaze again, he had gone.

It amazed her that he could disappear so swiftly and silently; but the fact of it reminded her of Bingham when he had been the Night Wind, and a hunted man.

127

She kept very still for a time after that, for she did not know that the strange man might not be close at hand where he would discover her if she started away; but ere long she became convinced that he had really gone, and so she continued on her way toward the Nest.

The artificial lake was the gem of Myquest.

It was somewhat more than two acres in extent, and had been made by erecting a dam across a narrow ravine to hold back the waters of a brook of sweet cold water that had no doubt once been a torrent. It was fed by numerous springs as well as by the brook, and was clear, and cold, and deep, and was well stocked with several varieties of trout which the guests at Myquest always found delight and entertainment in feeding.

There was a boat-house and two bath-houses at the shore-side nearest to the Myquest home, while upon the higher of the two bluffs that bordered the ravine, Katherine had had built, under her personal supervision and direction, and after her own self-made plans, a Swiss chalet; and the building of it had been a whim of hers which Bing had indulged to the limit—and then some.

It was Katherine's very own—more individually and exclusively hers than in her wildest imaginings she had ever dreamed of—for her husband had gone her one better in every suggestion she had made about it until it had become a veritable Castle of Seclusion for the indulgence of her own pet hobbies, theories, tastes, and talents, and into which no other human being than herself had penetrated since the moment when the last of the imported workers upon it had completed his task and gone away.

She would have admitted Bingham to it, gladly, of course; but she was none the less secretly pleased when, at its completion, and in reply to her suggestion that he should go inside with her to inspect it, he had said, laughingly, yet with seriousness:

"No, sweetheart. That little chalet of stone and cement and tiling is, and shall continue to be, your very 'onliest' own. No foot but your own shall step across its threshold; not even mine. You planned it yourself, you built it, you selected every field-stone for its construction—every hollow tile and ounce of cement, almost. It is the perfection of your own vision of such a place, that you have so often told to me; it is your childhood's dream come true. Another presence than your own, inside of it, would be desecration—even your husband's. You are the hermit thrush, and the chalet is your nest."

The Nest she had named it forthwith.

Katherine had no reason for desiring such exclusiveness save the whimsical one of absolute personal possession entirely free from

128

interruption and the fear of interruption; a retreat that was all her own where she could seek and find seclusion and solitude whenever she wished, and where both would be perfect and inviolate.

Her favorite etchings and drawings, her choicest books, her sentimental *penates* that she had selected and preserved since childhood, her tenderest keepsakes, were there.

So was her easel, before which she passed many hours with palette and knife and brushes, or with pencil and crayon as the whim might take her.

So was her desk there, over in one corner between two windows that overlooked the lake at different angles—windows which permitted of no vision of the interior from without; as, indeed, was the rule without exception for every other window, too.

She passed many silent and happy hours at her desk, writing, as also at her easel, painting; but these were little secrets of her own, shared by none as yet.

Katherine required no key with which to enter the Nest.

The lock which guarded its one door of entrance had been made and adjusted for her by the so-called best lock makers in the world. It had neither dial nor keyhole; it was invisible, and its presence unsuspected—and was as great a mystery from the inside as from without.

Simple enough, all of it, to Katherine; yet a stranger outside of that chalet could not get in, and, by the same token, a person inside of it and unwise to its secret, could not get out; for the windows were guarded as thoroughly and as skillfully, and by the same sort of mechanism as the door. When she was inside, the steel blinds that covered them were shoved aside by the mere pressure of one of her fingers upon the secret springs; and even then their arrangement was such that prying or curious eyes could not see past them to the daintiness and homeyness inside.

The ventilation was ample and complete, and could be rendered greater, or less, by the pressure of a finger. Indeed, very many mysterious things could be accomplished there by the touch of Katherine's fingers.

The Nest was really a wonderful place.

It contained every comfort and convenience of a tiny home; and it stood high perched upon the bluff at one end of the dam that was as solid and substantial in its way as that one of Ashokan.

The little house was made of uncut, hillside stones. The roof was of terra-cotta tile. The door and the windows were framed with oak encased in steel. It was built at the pinnacle of the taller of the

two bluffs, which stood at either side of the narrow ravine like senti-
nels on guard above the dam, and there was but one pathway to it
with a flight of stairs at the top which could be transformed into no
stairs at all by another touch of one of Katherine's fingers inside of
the house, or below the stairs outside of it.

There were many other secrets, also, than those already described, connected with Katherine's whimsical hobby—but they
need not be gone into just now; we will learn more about them later
on.

She had day-dreamed of some time possessing just such a place
ever since, as a child, she had fallen under the fascinations of Sir
Walter Scott's masterpiece; and when Bingham's foster-father, Mr.
Chester, made her a belated wedding present of Myquest, she at
once chose the tall bluff over the ravine as the proper location for
the fulfillment of her lifelong dream.

So she mounted the steep path to the bottom of the stairs, touching, as she drew near, the small spring that made them practicable,
and pressing upon another one after she entered the house, which
restored them to their former condition of steep and smooth inacces-
sibility; and it is worthy of note that if one had stood at her elbow
looking on while she performed either act, one could not have seen
her do it, nor have told how it had been done.

Then—

Sleep—blessed sleep—contented sleep. The sleep of perfect se-
curity, of utter safety, of complete seclusion. Even her own bedroom
in the great house beyond the lake had never been so much her home
as the Nest. There she could be found, and routed out; at the Nest
there was no such possibility.

Bing would know, when he missed her in the morning, where
she had gone; he would not know why, but he would not be impatient to know even that—and if he should particularly want her,
there did exist a secret means of communication between the two
places, known only to themselves, by which he could call to her.

Katherine slept.

Within the great house Conrad Belknap also slept—in the
depths of a big chair that he had pulled across the floor until it confronted the bathroom door beyond which he believed that Roberta
had locked herself away from him.

And thus, upon entering softly, Roberta discovered him.

130

CHAPTER XXI

FLINT AND STEEL

Roberta's entrance, even though it was accomplished silently, roused Belknap, and he was wide awake on the instant.

He yawned, stretched his arms, and showed his teeth in his wolfish smile. He wheeled the chair slowly around to face her, without leaving it. He opened his mouth to speak, but he started to his feet instead, stared an instant at her, and then sprang to the bathroom door and seized the knob of it. It would not open at his touch, of course.

He had known that even before he made the effort.

His quick and observing eyes had noticed the moisture of dew on Roberta's shoes. He knew, in that instant, that it was not Roberta who was locked inside of the bathroom—who had been locked in it—who might be—who doubtless was—still there.

Again he started to speak and withheld the words he would have uttered.

He had seen the amazement in her eyes when he sprang to the door and attempted to open it.

His first thought was that the man whom she had gone out earlier to meet was there; his second one was the same, although he added to it the belief that Roberta was unaware of the fact. Being puzzled, and also intensely curious, he was silent.

It was Roberta who spoke first.

"What are you doing here?" she demanded.

"I might reply by asking what the devil you've been doing outside of the house a second time to-night," he answered.

"Who is locked in the bathroom?" she asked in utter amazement.

"I thought you were—until this moment."

Roberta shrugged. She did not believe him.

"Who is in there?" she repeated.

"I don't know—unless it is the man you expected here to-night," he answered, leaving his chair and standing facing her.

"Then why don't you open the door and find out?"

"There are several very good reasons for that," he drawled. "I could not use the forceps because the chap inside withdrew the key. I could not pick the lock or force the door because I haven't my tools with me—and I didn't think it wise to leave the room long enough to get them. You fooled me, you see. I really supposed that you were the person in the bathroom."

Roberta was plainly puzzled—a fact which Belknap was not slow to see.

"Don't you know who is in there?" he demanded, bending nearer to her.

"No; and I don't believe that anybody is there. It is a trick of some sort that you are attempting, C. B. One of your Machiavellian schemes, doubtless." Her voice and manner were so sincere that he was suddenly convinced that she told the truth.

"Was somebody besides ourselves in this room when I came here the first time?" he asked sharply.

"No. Or, if there was, you should know it. You were here when I returned."

"How long a time had I been gone when you went out again?"

"I don't remember. Five—ten minutes. Perhaps more than that."

"And I was gone no longer than that when I returned. Somebody was here, then. Somebody partly opened the door into the hall to go out; I saw the door move, but I did not see the person, although I knew that one was at the door. That person locked it and—It all resolves itself into the fact that we were spied upon. Somebody knew that I was in this room with you to-night, and probably overheard our conversation. Do you insist that you do not know who that person was?"

"I not only do not know, C. B., but I don't believe there was such a person. I don't in the least know what you are up to, but whatever it is I wish you'd unlock that door and have done with it. I am very tired, and I want to undress and go to bed—but I'd like you to unlock that door before you go. Besides, it is very late, and if you were found here—"

"You would be compromised, eh?"

"Compromised! As if you could compromise me. I care less than that"—she snapped her thumb and finger together contemptuously—"about such complications. In fact, I would welcome such an

interruption. I'd be glad, overjoyed, right now, to see Bingham Harvard himself walk into this room followed by the entire household.
It would not result in my undoing, but in yours. I would betray you,
wholly, on the spot—root, trunk, bark, and branch."

Belknap reached out and seized her by one wrist and held it.

"Listen to me," he said, speaking with cold precision.

"Well?" she demanded, meeting his eyes unflinchingly.

"I can't unlock that door—unless I leave you long enough to get
my tools to do it with, and I won't bother to do that. Whoever went
into that bathroom to avoid me has probably gone out of it by way
of the window. It is big enough to get out of, and it isn't much of a
drop to the ground under it. That incident is closed so far as I am
concerned. But I want answers to a few questions. When you have
made them, I will go. I will know if you lie to me."

"Ask them."

"Did the man you sent for come—and did you see him when
you went out the last time?"

"Yes."

"It was—" he went on, but Roberta interrupted him.

"Yes," she said again.

"Where is he now?"

"I sent him away."

"Why?"

"Because the fact that you had discovered that I had sent for
him spoiled my plan. It is evident enough, isn't it? Wait, C. B. You
need not ask questions; I will tell you all that I will say in almost one
sentence. I sent for Roderick Maxwilton to come here. It was my
wish that he should make himself known to his sister. I believed that
I could persuade him to do it. In case he should insist upon not doing
it, I had made up my mind to go away with him. Is that plain
enough, C. B.?"

He nodded.

"If he consented to my plan, I meant to bring him directly into
the house, to Mrs. Harvard's room—and to-morrow morning you
would have seen the end of your career, no matter what the consequences might have been to me, or to him, or to anybody. You
spoiled both or either of those plans by finding and reading that letter. It told you that I had sent for him, and you guessed the rest. You
guessed who I had sent for, and why I had summoned him. He did
not come at the appointed hour. I decided that he declined both of
my pleas: the one to make himself known to his parents—because
he dreads the effect of it upon them as much as his sister does; and

the other one (in case he refused the first), my offer to go away with him to the other side of the world—away from you and your schemes, forever and ever. If he had taken me at my word in that I would have gone with him—and that is why I wrote and left that letter for Mrs. Harvard, that you found and read. When I returned and found you here, and knew that you had read my letter, both of my plans, or either of them, were spoiled—particularly that one upon which I had hoped the most: to go away with Roderick Max-wilton, and to escape from you forever."

While Roberta talked, Belknap regarded her with a careless, although inscrutable smile. There was a commingling of amusement, interest, and concern in his expression. He had succeeded in removing nearly all of the outward evidences of his encounter with Bing Harvard under the tree, and he was really handsome—even if a trifle diabolical—in the green tint of the shade over the desk-light. He shrugged when she finished.

"Sometime," he said, "I wonder why you don't take yourself off with your Roddy-Max. You have succeeded so well in keeping him out of my sight that it is a little bit strange that you don't get out of it, too—only, I guess you know mighty well that you couldn't keep out of it. Also I sometimes wonder why—since I wouldn't know him by sight—he doesn't slip a knife between my ribs, or put a bullet into me; one more crime to his record would not make him so much worse off than he is now. But I guess that—"

He stopped, for Roberta's eyes were suddenly glowing. His words had given her an idea. Roderick had said nothing about it in their interview, but then, that would be like him—to keep silent.

She spoke quickly, impulsively. She said:

"There are marks of recent scratches on your face, C. B. You have tried to hide them, but they are there. I saw you fighting, under the trees, to-night. Oh, yes, I saw enough to understand what was happening; and I know now, by your manner and your words, that you have not read the message I dropped to you from my balcony, and so, it follows that the man you were struggling with took it from you. Has it occurred to you that the man might have been 'Roddy-Max,' as you like to call him, in the belief that it angers me?"

Belknap was, however, above being disturbed by that suggestion. He only shrugged again, and smiled the more; and another idea, Roberta's original one about the affair, recurred to her.

"Or," she added, "perhaps it was Harvard himself; the Night Wind."

"More likely than the other, but equally absurd," he agreed, still smiling. "Either of them might have taken your message, having seen you drop it, but neither of them would have stolen my money, and watch, and stick-pin. Oh, no; that man was an accident—a wandering yegg—the subsequent porch-climber of Mme. Savage's room, doubtless. But, really, Berta, I don't care so much as the flip of a coin who it might have been. However, since you have reminded me of the message, what was it?"

"It was—" she began, and stopped; then she added: "—of no importance. The reason for it has ceased to exist."

Then, before he could stop her, she stepped quickly past him to the door into the hall and opened it.

"Go," she said. "If you stay here another minute I will go to Mrs. Harvard's door and call her."

Belknap smiled more broadly than ever; he bestowed a mocking bow.

"Monday I shall ask you to be my partner at bridge," he said coolly, and went from the room.

Roberta closed the door after him, locked it, withdrew the key, and stuffed a corner of her handkerchief into the hole.

CHAPTER XXII

THE FORBIDDEN NAME

Katherine had not forgotten her father's lifelong habit of early rising, so, notwithstanding the fact that it was after three o'clock that Sunday morning when she lost herself in sleep at the Nest, she was wide awake again soon after five.

It was a bright and beautiful morning in June, as near to perfection as one might wish.

Having selected a dainty morning costume from the abundant wardrobe that she kept at the Nest, she stood at one of the windows that overlooked the lake, beyond which a three-pronged vista through the trees and shrubbery beyond it had purposely been trimmed out so as to command three distinct views of the house.

After a little time, as she had anticipated, she saw the tall, dignified figure of her father as he descended the front steps from the veranda and paused at the bottom of them while with uplifted head he seemed to be drinking in the beauty and peace of that perfect morning. So she went to him, touching the proper mechanical buttons as she left the Nest to restore it to its wonted condition of somnolence and isolation.

Truly it was a wonderful place, the Nest, with its hidden secrets and mysterious mechanical contrivances—more wonderful and marvelous, indeed, than Katherine had intended it to be in the beginning, or than she had dared to hope that it could be made; but, as has been said, Bingham had given her a free hand in the construction of it, and there had been no counting of its cost.

Imported labor from far and near, the best mechanical geniuses that could be found in the length and breadth of the land, and the highest skilled artisans in every branch of the work required, had alike given the best that was in them to the working out of Katherine's desires and plans, and her plans had broadened, and length-

136

ened, and deepened as they were fulfilled one by one; others had been added to them until the Nest became, under the skilled touches of those workmen, a veritable network of hidden secrets and mysteries that were almost unbelievable until one actually witnessed the workings out of them.

The Nest was created in the second decade of the twentieth century, when every perfected device and power of our own wonderful and marvelous age was available.

Where hydraulic power was needed, the lake supplied it. Whatever of electricity was required, the lake supplied that, too, through the hydraulics—for the Nest had its own small dynamo, its own storage batteries, and was not dependent upon outside sources for the working of its mysteries. Whatever of compressed-air resourcefulness was employed in the operation of heavy steel blinds and doors, and the like, was produced from that same placid source, the lake. Nature has not blessed us with another power so manifestly stupendous as the pressure of water.

Ah, yes, the Nest was a wonderful place, indeed—as we will discover.

Katherine passed outside in that early Sunday morning in June, and went swiftly to her father, former Senator Maxwilton, "the Senator from Kentucky."

"It is such a comfort to have you here with me," she said softly as she slipped a hand under his arm, and they strolled along one of the paths which would lead, ultimately, to the stables—for well Katherine knew that they would have been his goal that early morning had he been left to his own devices. The Senator was all Kentuckian in his love for horses, and Katherine's inheritance of that love had not been marred or lessened by the high-powered cars in her husband's garage.

"I want you to see Daniel Boone, 3rd," she said, while her father gently patted the hand that clung to him. "I call him just Dan, and he knows his name so well—all of it, I mean—that it would make you smile to see his appreciation of the different uses of it that I make. You see, he is very playful, and awfully mischievous. When he is just a little bit naughty, I say, in a surprised and dignified way, 'Daniel!' and he looks as conscious as can be. When he is very mischievous, I say, 'Why, Daniel Boone!' and he drops his ears and his tail and looks as sorry out of his eyes as a chided puppy-dog. Then, when I think he is thoroughly repentant, I say, 'All right, Dan!' and instantly he arches his neck, lifts his crupper, and dances like a happy child, nuzzling with all his might to express his affection. Really, father, he almost talks."

The Senator nodded. It was his favorite topic.

"He's a thoroughbred, Kitten; he almost ought to talk," he replied. "Let's see, he's almost five—five next month. He was just three when I sent him to you. He ought to be a beauty by now."

"A beauty! Well, I should say so. He walked off with the blue ribbon in his class at the horse show without a competitor that approached him. The judges pronounced him an absolutely perfect animal."

"Of course," the Senator replied complacently. "That is what he is. I could have told the judges that without their bothering about it. That is the only kind we raise on the old place, Kitten. I hope nobody rides him but yourself."

"Certainly not. That is to say, of course Smokie. He is almost as fond of that boy as he is of me. Sometimes I'm almost jealous."

The Senator laughed.

"Kitten," he said, "that horse knows how to keep Smokie in his place just as well as you do. He knows, just as well as we do, that Smokie is a little black boy that's his servant, made to wait on him, and he loves him in just the same way that we love our colored people who serve us faithfully and long. Here we are. Has Bingham added any new stock to his stable since last year?"

"Just an Irish hunter that was a present. I'll have him brought out so you can see him."

Thus father and daughter inspected the stables, talking horse, laughing together over the Senator's criticisms and suggestions— father and daughter chums, as they had been in the past, before Katherine went to New York—for this morning, beside her father, with the mysteries and perplexities of the past night temporarily forgotten, Katherine was a girl again.

When they came away from the stables and started to return to the house, Katherine was laughing merrily over one of her father's inimitable stories of the doings of his black retainers on the stock farm—and so they rounded the end of the piazza where they met Bingham.

"Now, that's too bad!" Bing exclaimed with mock regret. "I guessed that you two were at the stables together, and I was going to approach stealthily so as to hear what the Senator had to say about Erin, the Irish hunter."

The three breakfasted together on a side piazza, and were greatly surprised, and not a little pleased, when, before it was half finished, Katherine's mother joined them—for early rising was not a habit with Lady Kate's delicate, flowerlike mother.

"You see," she explained to Bingham, "I knew that Katherine and her father would inspect the stables together as soon as the sun was up, and I reckoned that you wouldn't be very far off, Bingham, so I thought it would be nice if 'papa and mama and the children' could have their breakfast together." Her smile was good to see, then.

Bing put his arms around the fragile but stately lady of the old South, and kissed her.

"God bless you, mother," he said, holding her and speaking very low. "You make me very happy—more happy than I can tell you—because you are the only mother I ever knew."

"And Bingham," she replied, "you are just as near and dear to me as you could be if I were indeed your own mother, in fact—as if you were my own son, my very own." Then, with just a suggestion of hesitation, she added: "Katherine had a brother Roderick, my first born, my hope, my pride, my idolatry. We lost him. He is buried in Kentucky. I—I have given you a place in my heart close beside his memory, Bingham, my son."

The Senator sat very still and erect.

Katherine lifted her eyes to her mother in amazement and repressed joy.

It was the first time in many years that Roderick had been mentioned openly between the daughter and her parents.

That Sunday passed uneventfully, save for a few minor incidents which seemed, on the surface, to be of no importance, but each of which was destined to be recalled later by those most interested. In the order of their happening they were:

1. Former Detective-lieutenant Rodney Rushton, now at the head of an agency of his own, stopped for an hour at Myquest in the middle of the forenoon ("ong-passong," as he expressed it), to pay his respects, as, indeed, he was in the habit of doing whenever opportunity offered.

His real purpose was, of course, in response to Tom Clancy's suggestion, and to give Mr. Conrad Belknap what Rushton called "the once-over," which is to say, to have an opportunity to observe the man carefully, to recall, if possible, any memory of him of the past, or, failing that, to provide a memory of him for future occasion; for Rushton possessed to a large extent what in police parlance is known as the "camera eye."

2. A stranger came to Myquest in the early evening—a tall, soldier-like figure of a man, who might have been handsome of feature but for a terrible disfigurement of his face caused by a livid scar that extended from the top of his forehead above the left eye, down and over the left eyelid, across the bridge of his nose, past the right corner of his mouth to which it appeared to impart a sardonic twist, and thence on, under the right cheek bone until it disappeared beneath his collar.

His hair was abundant, and of the whiteness of fresh milk, although his brows were coal black. If you observed him when his back was toward you, and were asked to guess his age, you would have placed him as anywhere from thirty to forty-five, and prematurely white; but if in the next breath he turned to face you, and you had noticed the scar, and the lines between his eyes and radiating from their corners, you would have amplified your own statement with, "anywhere from forty-five to sixty, but with an extraordinary physique and bearing."

He arrived, also, so it would appear, *en passant*—like Rushton; which is to say that one of Harvard's friends who was also a banker, with whom he was motoring, stopped for a short call in passing.

Naturally the stranger was duly presented to the guests who were present at the time, and was made welcome, and notwithstanding the hideous scar on his face, he seemed to cast some sort of a charm or spell upon those with whom he chatted, while Harvard and his banker friend strolled up and down, almost—but not quite—within ordinary conversational distance from the veranda.

The *señorita* was not present. She left the group and entered the house through one of the French windows just at the moment when Mr. Morton Saulsbury's car was driven under the porte-cochère—and during all of the time that the callers remained, she sat at the piano, playing softly, modulating from key to key, and from major to minor and back again. To Betty Clancy, who was very still and silent in her chair near the rail, listening to and observing the stranger with the scar, it seemed almost as if the *señorita* were indeed talking to all of them at once with her magic fingers.

Belknap was present—and was strangely silent—for him. When the stranger appeared he pushed his chair into a deeper shadow.

The call did not extend beyond twenty minutes, but nevertheless it seemed to have left a marked impression—particularly in regard to Mr. Carruthers. A different one, too, it appeared, with each of the Myquest guests to whom he was presented.

When it came to an end—when Bingham and his banker friend having concluded their conference, returned to the veranda, and the latter announced to Carruthers that they had better be on their way, and the two had got into the car to depart—Bing called out, suddenly, and with every outward appearance that a happy thought had just occurred to him:

"Wait a moment, Saulsbury, I have got an idea," and he half turned his head and shot a smiling glance at his wife before he added:

"When we came down to Myquest it was our intention to have a series of week-ends throughout the summer, but this one has developed into a house-party, instead." Bing had again turned his back toward the group on the veranda and was addressing only his banker friend, but he spoke with a distinctness that rendered every word he uttered plain to all.

"I am a bit seedy, myself, and although I shall probably drive into the city now and then just to look things over, I have decided to stay down here this week—and possibly next week, also—for a little vacation and rest, and I'm going to ask Clancy to do the same. He'll do it, too. Tom nearly always does what I suggest. But the thing that I'm getting at is this: why can't you and Mrs. Saulsbury join us, for this week anyhow, and bring Mr. Carruthers along? Eh? Just say that you will, and come along down as early as possible to-morrow."

Katherine, who, after greeting Saulsbury and his companion, had withdrawn from the group, and was hovering in the background, listened to her husband's totally unanticipated announcement in unconcealed amazement—a fact which Belknap was quick to notice as he shot a glance at her beneath half-drooped eyelids.

He left his chair and strolled carelessly toward her with his ears keyed to catch Saulsbury's reply, and he knew that Katherine was waiting for it as eagerly as he was; although he could not guess what her interest in it might be.

But Katherine acted quickly, accepting Bing's cue, and acting upon it as he threw another quick glance over his shoulder in her direction.

Before Belknap could get to her—before Morton Saulsbury had opportunity to respond to the invitation so cordially given, she stepped quickly forward and down the steps to her husband's side.

"Do, Mr. Saulsbury," she said. "I shall be delighted to have Miriam with us; and"—she permitted her gaze for a moment to rest upon the scarred visage of Daniel Carruthers—"I am sure that Mr. Carruthers will find it possible to come with you, for I heard him say

141

only a moment ago, to Miss Loring, that he is idling his time with you because he had found that he has a month's time on his hands with nothing to do."

"I fear that I am too busy just now to accept for myself, Mrs. Harvard," Saulsbury replied smilingly, "but there is no reason why Miriam can't come, nor why Dan Carruthers cannot come with her. Eh, Dan? You can do that, can't you? And I'll come down Friday afternoon for the week-end."

So it was arranged that Carruthers would arrive with Mrs. Saulsbury the following day, and the banker departed with his scarred-face companion.

Then happened the third incident which several of the group on the veranda were to recall to mind later.

The butler came out to them, crossed directly to Belknap, and announced:

"You are wanted at the telephone, Mr. Belknap—a long-distance call—from the city of Washington, the operator said."

Belknap thanked the butler, and with a nod of apology toward the others in general, entered the house.

Instantly there was a chorus of exclamations and interrogations all around Bing and Katherine concerning the stranger whom Saulsbury had brought to Myquest in his car, and who was, thenceforth, to be of their party.

They all agreed that he was interesting, and would have been strikingly handsome but for the disfiguring scar across his face. Diana Loring thought that the scar was the most fascinating thing about him. Betty announced that, "Scar or no scar, I think he is splendid," and Tom, grinning while he lighted a cigar, asked:

"Who the devil is he, anyway, Bing? Banker or baker or candle-stick maker? And, for the sake of a few of the ladies present, is he benedict, widower, or bachelor? That is the main idea. Is he married or single?" to which Bing replied:

"Search me, Tom. He is Morton Saulsbury's friend, and that's enough for me!"

CHAPTER XXIII

THE GENTLEMAN FROM KENTUCKY

In mid-June the sun gets up early.

So do babies, and small children, and old people—and such others as love the air and the sunlight and the freshness of the early morning hours, while the dew is on the grass and leaves, and the air is as if it has been washed and polished, and hung out to dry.

Senator Maxwilton was one of such; and that morning was like the preceding one, although Katherine was not waiting to greet him as she had been yesterday.

The earliest of the servants invariably encountered him in one of the paths, or saw him seated upon one of the veranda chairs, or found him in the stables among the hunters and cobs, petting them, and feeding them sugar. The Senator was a typical Kentuckian, and loved horses.

He came out that Monday morning with the first rays of sunlight—came out, as had been his habit in his own Southern home, and continued in his daughter's, by one of the windows.

His movements, without intention, happened to be noiseless, and as he stepped outside he saw Belknap—and was on the point of going forward and speaking to the man who "had beat him to it," when some indefinable thing about Belknap's attitude made him hesitate, and then step backward, within the window, where he stood still, and observing.

He had not seen Belknap about at that hour before, and, although in riding togs, the man appeared to be without intention of seeking the stables.

More than that, he was passing up and down a short stretch of pathway in the vicinity of Katherine's favorite rose bower, and glancing this way and that, from side to side, in front of, and behind him, furtively, and with rapid motions, exactly as if he were on the watch for something or for somebody.

Belknap had been there—and elsewhere among the paths—two hours and more, if the Senator had but known it, and was both exultant and disappointed, both pleased and angry, both annoyed and delighted; likewise, and without the paradox, he was tired of his vigil.

The long-distance-telephone conversation to which the butler had summoned him the preceding evening, had in a measure upset many of his calculations, although he was inclined to doubt the logic as well as the fact of the warning that had been transmitted to him from Washington.

Nevertheless he had passed a more or less sleepless night, and with daybreak, before the sun was up, he had donned riding togs—as being the most appropriate and palpable explanation for being about so early—and had gone outside.

There was a threefold purpose in that: he wanted the air and the exercise; he wanted to secure a saddle horse from the stables at rather an early hour, to ride alone to meet a messenger at an appointed place as announced in the telephone talk the preceding evening; and, quite an important and imperative in case there were logic and fact (and therefore danger to him) in what he had been told and what the expected messenger was yet to impart, he greatly desired a short but uninterrupted conversation with Katherine Harvard.

He knew that it was her habit to rise early, and to ride Daniel Boone, 3rd, cross-country, and alone, at sunrise or soon thereafter, over the extensive acres of her own estate of Myquest. Belknap had no notion of accompanying her—he had other fish to fry that morning—but he had determined that he would see her and talk with her before she started, and so, he was watching out for her when the Senator stepped from the window and saw him.

He did not discover the nearness of the Senator—when the latter, grown tired of watching him from the window, approached—until, close at hand, he heard the quiet deep-toned voice of the statesman greeting him.

"Good morning, Mr. Belknap," the Senator said. "Have you been riding so early?"

"Ah. Good morning, Senator," Belknap replied in his imperturbable manner. "No; I haven't been riding—yet. It was earlier than I supposed when I came out. Nobody was about when I went to the stables."

"You were"—the Senator smiled—"searching for something? I have been observing you from the window. Have you dropped something, or lost something, or"—again that inscrutable Senatorial smile—"perhaps there is another early riser whom you are expecting?"

"You have guessed it, Senator," Belknap responded, returning the smile in kind if inscrutability be the criterion. "Mrs. Harvard, your daughter, is in the habit of indulging in early morning rides, cross-country. I thought I'd beg permission to ride with her, but—the men must be about by now so I think I'll go ahead."

"Why not wait a little longer? I don't know if she intends to ride this morning or not, but she is sure to come out soon. She always gets up with the sun, no matter at what hour she retires. And, by the way, since we have met so auspiciously this delightful morning, I am reminded of a question that I have wanted to ask you."

"Yes?"

"Are you, by any chance, related—kin, we would call it—to the Beldings, of Kentucky?"

Belknap who had not lessened his watchfulness over the approaches to the house, and who was still casting furtive glances along the path that led to it, narrowed his eyes a trifle, and an almost imperceptible crease showed between his brows when the question was put to him. It was as if he were startled by it, although he replied instantly, and smiled as he did so:

"Not by any chance in the world, Senator." He laughed aloud, then. "Have you discovered a fancied resemblance?"

"No. Not a resemblance—not a facial one, certainly."

Belknap made no comment. The Senator continued:

"I should call the resemblance, if there is one—a reminder, would be a more appropriate word—temperamental; a trait, rather than a likeness. I am—er—pleased to know that you are not a kin to the Beldings of my acquaintance sir."

"Thank you. I assume that you are not favorably disposed toward them."

"Was not. The branch of the family that I refer to has died out. I—er—assisted at the last—er—function, so to speak. He was named Cranshaw Belding. He—er—was hung."

"Were you the hangman?"

The senator ignored the insolence of the question; possibly he did not notice it. He answered quietly:

"No. I sentenced him. I was on the bench, then. He murdered the mother of his child—a woman who was not his wife, although she believed that she was—but who nevertheless, had been his good angel, or had tried to be. He—er—escaped with the boy, after he had killed the mother, and was not caught till two years later. After his trial, after sentence was passed upon him, he announced that he had killed the boy also. I have always—er—hoped that he did so, although I didn't believe him at the time. That boy would be—let me see—thirty-five or so, by now, if he is living." The Senator seemed to be reminiscing rather than addressing Belknap. Thinking aloud, rather than talking.

Belknap was plainly frowning. He had ceased to watch the approaches to the house or its entrances. He was standing very still, staring straight ahead of him without motion, apparently without the flicker of an eyelash.

His lips were drawn tightly together over his teeth, in a straight line; a physiognomist would have said that he was straining every effort in his power for self-control—as, indeed, he was.

He spoke, after a moment, in a low, monotonous tone, devoid of anger, but nevertheless coldly ominous.

"Your remarks, Senator Maxwilton, are capable of unpleasant inference. Am I to assume that you so intended them, sir?"

"God bless my soul, no! Forgive me, Mr. Belknap. I was dreaming—remembering—harking back into the past. I hated—I disliked that man greatly."

"I see. The girl, also, doubtless; the mother of the boy."

"No. I honored and esteemed her. She did not know that she was not a wife. It was because she discovered the truth that Cranshaw Belding killed her. She was a—she belonged to one of our oldest and best families."

Very slowly Belknap withdrew his gaze from the distance—distance is the precise word of it in this case, for the Senator's remarks had expelled from his thoughts all immediate recollection of the expected messenger, and of Katherine. Although he seemed to continue to stare at the house, he was visualizing other things.

"Senator," he said, and his voice seemed to carry a chill with it, "if the idea were not preposterous I might easily infer that you are seeking to connect me, in some remote way, with your retrospective remarks. Such a thing would be absurd, naturally—particularly so, since it is not even a fancied resemblance that brought back the memories. You called it a trait—I suppose you meant a mannerism, didn't you? What was it, pray, that brought to mind the memory of your friend, the wife-killer? For, if the woman honestly believed herself to be a wife, she was one. No lack of priests or proper ritual,

146

no absence of prescribed sacrament, could deny that sanctity to her. What was the mannerism, Senator?"

The Senator, like many Kentuckians, was tall and straight. Age had not bent his soldierly figure, nor wasted it. He carried his years without a suggestion of them, and one found it only in his wealth of snow-white hair.

He met Belknap's gaze calmly, looking down upon the man from his greater height, and said, with slow emphasis and quiet dignity:

"I have offered my apology, Mr. Belknap."

"Quite so, sir; and I have accepted it as offered. Also, I have ventured to ask you a question—a natural one under the circumstances. If I am addicted to a mannerism which suggests memory of a man who was hung for murder, I would like to know what it is, so I may avoid it in the future."

The Senator shrugged. Then he smiled.

"Do you recall," he asked, "that you gave me the impression that you had lost something, or that you were impatiently awaiting the coming of another person? I had been observing you from the window. The mannerism—if you insist upon that word, although it is a much stronger one than I would apply to it—was in the way you moved your head and eyes as you glanced along the paths, and toward the house; it was your impatience of restraint; your repression of eagerness; your attitude of commingled expectancy and apprehension. I was reminded—without a reason in the world, of course—of the man whose name I have spoken—of his demeanor throughout his trial. Pray forget it."

What reply Belknap might have made may not be known, for at that instant Bingham Harvard came out of the house, sprang lightly over the rail of the veranda, and approached them swiftly along the path, moving, as Belknap could not help but notice, with that feline, leopard-like grace of alertness and power that had so frequently been described in the newspapers in the days of "Alias the Night Wind."

Belknap was startled in spite of his outward calm.

CHAPTER XXIV

BLACK JULIUS RIDES

Just why Belknap was startled by the sudden appearance of Bingham Harvard he could not have told himself.

Possibly it was because it interrupted his train of thought engendered by the Senator's remarks—perhaps they had stirred latent memories in the back of Belknap's mind. Possibly it was because Harvard's sudden appearance brought to mind Roberta's suggestion that it might have been the Night Wind himself who attacked him under the tree after he had caught the old letter which Katherine had unknowingly dropped into his grasp from her balcony, and after he had received the note which Roberta had dropped to him—neither of which he had had a chance to examine.

Whatever reason there might have been for it, he was entirely his cool and smilingly inscrutable self by the time that Harvard joined them—and if he had harbored any real fear, it was instantly dispelled by Harvard's cheery greeting.

"Monday morning, and all's well," Harvard said after he greeted them. "I feel like a schoolboy on the first day of his summer vacation: I don't know what to do with myself. I see that you"—addressing Belknap directly—"are togged for the saddle. If I had known it I'd have gone with you."

"Mr. Belknap is waiting for Katherine," the Senator remarked.

"Ah? That's odd. She was dressed and ready to come down when I left her just now, but not in her riding togs. Perhaps she forgot—"

Belknap laughed pleasantly.

"Mrs. Harvard doesn't know that I'm waiting for her," he said. "I was only hoping that she would let me go with her if she was riding this morning. You see, I didn't read my watch correctly when I got up. I thought it was two hours later than it was. I think that I'll

148

go ahead, alone, if you don't mind. Will you suggest a horse for me, Harvard?"

"Yes—if you want a real one—one that will make you pay more attention to him than to the scenery. Ask for Comet."

When Belknap had gone the Senator linked his arm in Bing's, and as they started along one of the paths, he asked, in his deep-toned, leisurely manner—a manner which any one of his old colleagues of the Senate chamber would instantly have recognized as indicating extreme interest, although not a suggestion of it appeared:

"Is Mr. Belknap an acquaintance of long standing, Bingham? Do you know him well?"

"Oh, he is new to all of us," Bing replied carelessly, "even to the Archers, who are responsible for his presence. But, he seems a likeable chap, don't you think? Then, without waiting for a reply, he changed the subject. "Jove! but I'm glad that I took the figurative bull by the horns and decided to give myself a vacation this week—particularly because you and mother are here with us."

"I am glad, too," the Senator rejoined earnestly. Then: "I quite took a liking to your friend Saulsbury last night, Bingham, although I saw next to nothing of him. He is an old friend, isn't he?"

"Yes, indeed. He is considerably older than I am; graduated at Harvard two years before I matriculated. His father and Mr. Chester are great cronies. I have known him since I can remember."

"Fine chap. I like him," the Senator remarked with emphasis, and they strolled on in silence for a time. Then: "what about his friend—that Mr. Carruthers?" The Senator chuckled, and went on before Bing could reply: "I reckon that when one gets to know him well enough not to see that scar, he'd be a fascinating sort of a chap, eh?"

"Yes," Bing replied. "I liked him at once—and you may be sure that anybody whom Mort Saulsbury vouches for is all white, clear through."

Followed another silence until they were within sight of the stables and saw Belknap riding down the driveway on Comet, who was dancing and cavorting with tripping feet and arched neck and tail. But Belknap sat him like a Centaur, with perfect poise and loose rein, thoroughly at home in the saddle.

"The chap rides like a Kentuckian," the Senator remarked.

"Or a cow-puncher," Bing suggested.

"Both," the Senator rejoined. Then he stopped in the path, thus forcing his son-in-law to pause also, and, in a tone that was at once serious and emphatic, and which carried a little note of pleading in it, he said:

"Bingham, yesterday morning when we were breakfasting, your mother mentioned the name of our son, Roderick. I gathered from the expression of your face at the moment that you had not known, till then, that Katherine ever had a brother. Is that true?"

"Why, yes; but—"

"Pardon me, Bingham. Perhaps Kitten should have told you about him; possibly she thought best not to do so. But, now that his name has been mentioned, I feel that it is my duty to—"

"Please, Senator—please, father, wait a moment. Forgive me for interrupting you. I know by your manner and your words that it is a subject that you would prefer not to discuss. Will you, to please me, let it rest where it is? If there is anything that needs to be told to me, Katherine will tell it in her own good time, and I prefer that it should be left that way. I have never had occasion yet to see unwisdom in our Katherine's judgment."

The Senator sighed, plainly relieved; and as they started on again, remarked:

"I think, Bingham, after breakfast, I'll try that Erin-hawss of yours—that Irish hunter."

"Do, father. He's a wonder, really. You'll like him—only, he isn't gaited like one of your Kentucky horses. He is—Hello! Now what do you suppose is taking Julius off for a cross-country ride at this time of day, and all by himself? Some errand for Katherine, doubtless."

He had seen Julius in the act of taking a fence beyond the pasture behind the paddock—saw him for an instant only before he disappeared from view, and thought no more about it.

Black Julius was not, however, on an errand for his mistress, although he was, most certainly, bound upon one which he thoroughly believed to be definitely in her interest.

Julius did not like Conrad Belknap—had not liked him from the moment of his arrival at Myquest—had taken one of those instinctive dislikes to the man which are characteristic of the loyal and faithful colored folk of the South whenever a person who is inimical to those they serve appears.

He had kept a furtive eye upon Belknap from the first. He had seen and taken mental note of as many trivial incidents as had Betty Clancy, or Tom, or Bing himself; not the same ones, perhaps, but as many, or more; and his devotion to his mistress had made him, even more surely and more quickly than others, determine, intuitively, that the man was a fly in the ointment of that house party, and that Katherine disliked him—and for some inexplicable reason, feared him—or dreaded him—or at least would be glad to be rid of his presence at Myquest.

It had so happened that Julius was talking with the butler at the moment when the telephone call from Washington came over the wire, and while the butler was gone to summon Belknap, Julius had not hesitated to plug the switchboard in such a manner that by making haste to his own cottage he would be enabled to "listen-in" to a part of the conversation that was to follow, at least.

If Julius had been thoroughly versed in contemporary slang he would have said that he did it because he considered it an opportunity to "get a line on Belknap's curves."

Anyhow, he made the most of it, and although he did not hear the beginning of the talk, he did hear much of it, and although he did not get the line on the curves that he might have wished for, he did discover that a friend or an associate of Belknap's in Washington was warning him against the appearance at Myquest of a man whom they both had good reason to fear, and that Belknap was requested to meet a messenger at a stated time and place the following morning, who would impart such further information on the subject as was not wise to discuss by telephone. Julius had heard enough to make him want to hear more. Also he believed that the appointed place was such as to afford him every opportunity to do that very thing if only he could get to it before Belknap arrived.

There are still in existence in various places on Long Island the picturesque ruins of two-century-old (and more) saw and grist-mills, some of them tide-water mills, some of them otherwise, which the owners of the estates upon which they are situated have preserved for their picturesqueness. The telephone-made rendezvous was at one such, and was on the Myquest estate.

To get to it by following the highways (as Belknap had been directed over the wire), was a roundabout route that covered three miles or more; by the route that Julius selected, over fences, through by-lanes, and across fields, the distance was barely a mile.

Thus, he did get there first, so that he had ample time to tether his mount where it would not be discovered, and to creep into the ancient edifice and conceal himself before either of the parties to that arranged interview arrived.

He was well hidden, where he could hear without fear of discovery, when Belknap, who was the first of the two to arrive, appeared.

After that there was a wait of fully half an hour before the other man came, during which Belknap strode up and down with every evidence of exasperated impatience.

CHAPTER XXV

THE MAN FROM WASHINGTON

Black Julius, after all, had his labor for his pains.

He could hear every sentence that passed between Belknap and the other man at that meeting in the old tide-water grist-mill, but he could not understand a word of any of it.

The two talked in a language that Black Julius did not know, although he rightly assumed that it was Spanish.

Nevertheless, he was no wiser when he went away—a full half-hour after the two had gone—than when he arrived; no wiser save for so far as his intuitive perceptions, and his steady regard of their faces while they talked, rendered him. But he was more than ever convinced of his opinion of Belknap.

Nearly all of the guests were assembled at the breakfast table when Belknap joined them. Asked, casually, where he had been, he replied, addressing all of them generally:

"I don't know, exactly, only that I found the shore, and an interesting old mill that must be two or three hundred years old if it's a day."

"Two hundred and forty-two," Tom Clancy announced solemnly. "It was built in 1676. I wasn't present, but I've been told about it."

"I ran into a chap while I was there, and we got to talking, which explains why I am late," Belknap added, and thus accounted logically for the incident in case he had been seen in the company of that other man.

When they left the table he managed to place himself beside Katherine, to whom he said, in a sharp undertone:

"I must have a talk with you, Mrs. Harvard, as soon as possible, and where there will be no fear of interruption."

"We will walk down the—" she began, but he interrupted.

"No," he said decidedly, and in that tone of command which he had assumed toward her of late which he seemed so greatly to enjoy for the sole reason that he knew that she so bitterly resented it. "We will ride, if you please—or whether you please or not—in your roadster; and without a passenger in the rumble. You will invite me, presently, to drive with you to some point of your selection."

Katherine turned to face him, to resent, hotly, his assumption of giving orders, but already his back was toward her and he was moving leisurely away.

She flushed angrily, bit her lips, then smiled, and accepted the situation—for Katherine had decided that morning to meet Belknap on his own ground, henceforth, and to puzzle him, even to deceive him, by an outward appearance of entire acceptance of the inconceivable situation.

"Oh, Mr. Belknap," she called to him, and he paused and turned. "It has just occurred to me," she went on, "that since you seem to be interested in old mills, there is another one about twenty miles from here that is even more interesting than ours. If you will go to the garage, I'll join you there, presently, and take you to see it."

"Why can't we all go?" Betty Clancy demanded.

"You can," Katherine replied. "Suppose we do! We will picnic there; it is a beautiful spot. I will give directions about the hampers, now, and the rest of you can trail along as soon as you are ready. Mr. Belknap and I will go on ahead in my roadster."

* * * * * * *

"You arranged that very deftly, Lady Kate—to be accompanied without having company," Belknap remarked as they drove out past the lodge gates.

Katherine shrugged.

"I suppose I must endure it," she said resignedly, and shrugged a second time.

"Endure what? The 'Lady Kate'?" he asked, with his wolfish smile, which, however, she did not see, because her eyes were upon the road ahead of them.

"Your utterly contemptible and discourteous assumption of familiarity whenever we happen to be alone together," she said coldly. "Of course I can't stop you, if you insist upon keeping it up, but"— she shot a glance at him—"you will find me much more tractable to your whims and fancies, Mr. Belknap, if you cut it out."

He laughed aloud.

"You ought to be glad that I do not seek other familiarities than the mere use of names," he said coolly; and, after a moment of pause, added: "when I look at you, Katherine, I sometimes find myself wondering why I do not demand that prerogative also. You are a very beautiful woman, my lady, with all of the witchery—"

"And you are a despicable scoundrel!" she interrupted.

"Granted," he replied, and laughed outright a second time. "I think I like you best when you are angry—that is why I tease you. Almost, when your eyes flash and flame, and you lift your pretty chin in that defiant gesture of yours—almost, I say, but not quite—I could fall at your feet and worship you, and give up the worldly world for love of you, and promise to be good and proper for the rest of my life for your caresses, which I know perfectly well you would never bestow. Really, it is rather an interesting as well as a pleasant psychological study, when I am alone, and thinking about you, to try to discover why I have not capitulated—why I know that I will not succumb to your undeniable charm, Lady Kate."

Katherine slowed the car and turned to face him, but the derision and mockery that she saw in his eyes reassured her.

"Did you force me to take you to ride in my car to tell me that?" she asked coolly.

"No, dear lady, I did not." He laughed again. He seemed to be greatly amused, and it appeared to be real. "But, you see, you tempt me. I rarely find an opportunity to talk, on equal terms, with real ladies—thoroughbreds; and, besides, you amuse me. Come; that is a compliment with a sting in it."

"Why did you demand this opportunity for an uninterrupted talk?" she asked unmoved.

"Because I have a request to make."

"A request, did you say?"

"Call it what you like. For the moment I am a monarch whose requests are commands. I hoped that the softer word might please you."

"What is it?" she asked him, pressing the accelerator and returning her attention to the roadway before them.

"Before I state it, there is a question—possibly two or three of them."

"Well?"

"Have you any idea as to the identity of that chap who came here last evening, and who is due to return to-day?"

155

"None, save that he is Mr. Daniel Carruthers, and a friend of Mr. Saulsbury."

"Dear lady, he is neither the one nor the other. He is a certain Mr. Bruce Brainard, an operative in the secret service of the United States government. Carruthers is not his name, and for that matter, Brainard my not be either. Nor is he a friend, in the sense you mean, of Saulsbury's. He may be an acquaintance, although, even so, he is doubtless a recent one. And, now—yes, there is another question. Do you guess why he comes to Myquest?"

"Not unless he is after one Conrad Belknap—in case that happens to be your name."

"Splendid! You're a corker, Lady Kate. You score a bull's eye first shot."

"How do you know this—if it is true?" (Katherine was inclined to doubt, attributing his statement to one of his odd methods of annoying her. His reply convinced her.)

"My call to the telephone last night was to warn me of his coming, although neither the name nor the description confirms it. When I rode out to the old mill this morning I went to meet a messenger who was sent to me with more particulars than could be rehearsed over the phone. Even the description did not tally with the man; but, I have no doubts about it, just the same."

"You say that he is after you? To arrest you?"

"He seeks several persons, of whom I happen to be one. So far as arresting me is concerned, he will do that in his own good time— if he can—and at his own pleasure and convenience—if he is permitted to have his way about it."

"Why?"

"Would it interest you to know?"

"I would not have asked, otherwise."

"It is too long a tale for now, dear lady. Later—when you have hidden me away securely, if the necessity arises—I will tell you."

"Why do you tell me this? Don't you realize that—"

"That it gives you a power over me, you would say, to betray me to him? Not at all. That it offers an opportunity for you to rid yourself of my presence? Again, not at all, sweet Katherine of the immaculate heart. It does neither. You could not betray me because you have nothing to betray; and you cannot be rid of me, because I will not be gotten rid of—until I have accomplished what I came to Myquest to do."

"You intend to stay on, then, and defy him?"

156

"I intend to stay on—yes; and to defy him, also, up to a certain point. And this, Lady Kate, brings me to the crux of this interview. I shall not leave Myquest before it is my pleasure to do so, no matter what happens—not even if I have to commit a murder in order to stay on. Oh, don't be shocked, pray. I wouldn't do it myself; I would have it done for me. I said just now that I would defy him up to a certain point. I will. But, when that point is reached, if it is reached"—he bent forward and touched her shoulder with his fingers while he went on with slow emphasis—"you must have made ready for me, at Myquest, a place of concealment where that man cannot find me, but where I may, nevertheless, see you daily. There is such a place, doubtless, and if there is not one now, you must make one."

CHAPTER XXVI

THE RETURN OF CARRUTHERS

They drove on in silence for a time.

Katherine was thoughtful, and so was Belknap. Presently, when she stole a covert glance at him, she saw that he was staring at the roadway ahead, and that his somewhat thin lips were set in a straight line. Katherine was psychologist enough to know that he was thinking upon the subject that he had just mentioned to her—the true identity of Carruthers, and the reason for his appearance at Myquest.

She could read, also, that he was counting the risks he would take in remaining and daring—for a time at least—to brave the presence of a secret service operative; that he was figuring up the chances he would take; his chances of success in whatever it could be that he had determined to do, and getting away with it. And she realized, likewise, that there was not a shade of fear or hesitancy in his expression.

He would not be foiled in his purpose, or permit himself to deviate from the direct course to its accomplishment—and while she hated and despised the man, she could not deny to him a modicum of admiration for his courage and daring, his cool and calculating cock-sureness, and his apparently utter indifference to consequences for his acts.

Almost unconsciously—certainly before she thought how it would sound—she gave voice to the thought that was uppermost in her mind at the moment.

"What a pity it is that you are not a good man," she said, speaking her thought.

"Why do you say that?" he demanded, turning his head quickly toward her.

"Because you have it in you to accomplish great things if only your aim was right, and your target happened to be good instead of evil."

"Yes," he replied in the same tone that she had used, "you are right, Mrs. Harvard. I have it in me—I have always had it in me."

He was looking straight at her, but seemingly through and beyond her into the distances of the past, and for the moment during that retrospect his face was transformed. She could scarcely realize that he was Conrad Belknap, the cheat, the blackmailer, the self-confessed crook. He went on:

"I was born under a cloud. My life was begotten in felony. I was bathed in the blood of an awful crime when I was less than a year old. My boyhood and youth were years of close association with criminals. My young manhood was still worse." He lifted his head and laughed aloud, harshly, and the Belknap that she knew, and hated, and despised was predominant again. "So," he went on, "I grew up to be just a human tiger, of the man-eating variety. I dominated all of my associates because the blood of many gentle generations on both sides flowed in my veins—because I had inherited brains, and knew how to use them—because I have never known physical fear." He laughed again, softly, and added:

"So, you see, what you said was true: if my aim happened to be right, and my target happened to be good, there is nothing that I could not accomplish."

"Is it too late to try, even now?" Katherine asked softly.

"Too late? Dear lady, it was too late for that before I was born. I have said that I am a sort of human tiger. Would you bring a tiger from the jungle, half starve it until it attained maturity, and then turn it loose among a lot of children and expect it to fawn upon them and lick their hands? Too late? It was always too late. I will confess one thing to you, Katherine. This: I have never, by my own choice, committed but one honorable act since I have been a man. I mean by that that never but once have I chosen the honorable course in preference to the dishonorable one—and I have regretted it ten million times. It was my one and only attempt to aim at good, as you expressed it, and I missed, and I got what was coming to me.

"That's all, sweet lady. We will change the subject. We'll get down to cases again. I have said that a moment is likely to arise within the next few days, or hours, when I will ask you to put me in hiding at Myquest, or so near to it that I can reach out and touch it. When I make that demand upon you, it must be met. It must be. Is

159

there such a place? And if there is not, will you see that one is prepared so that it will be ready when I have need of it?"

Katherine had been thinking swiftly, too, during that silence, just before these last remarks, and she had determined upon a course which, an hour earlier, she would not have dreamed of considering. She replied instantly:

"Yes. There is such a place."

"Very good. And you will have it ready for me."

"It is ready now—at any moment you need it."

"Where I will be close to Myquest, and can have frequent interviews with you—in case it is necessary?"

"Yes—to both questions. Now, I will ask you one."

"As many as you like."

"Where do you find the courage to ask this of me when you must know that having hidden you away, I could so easily direct your enemies where to find you? When you must know that my every impulse under such circumstances will be to betray you, and so to be rid of you? Surely you must know that I could, under such conditions, anticipate your betrayal of my secret, and render your knowledge of it impotent."

"Lady Kate," he said slowly, "my favorite pastime is the study of character. I know that it is as impossible for you to do wrong as it is for me to do right. You would no more betray me in that manner than you would betray your husband in another one. Likewise, you are what men call a good sport."

"Then why aren't you one?"

"I will be, Lady Kate."

"You mean—what?"

"I mean that while I shall compel you to assist me in the fulfillment of my plans down here, I will not, hereafter, needlessly offend you—other than by the use of your given names."

"Thank you—for that much. Will you tell me why you came to Myquest? What your plans are? Just what it is that you seek? And let us get it over and have done with it—if it must be done?" she asked with a touch of wistfulness in her tone.

"Not now. Another time. When you have hidden me away—if that has to be done."

"Is it money that you want, Mr. Bel—"

"I have answered that question before. No; it is not. Don't question me now."

They arrived at the mill shortly thereafter, and had been there only a little time when the remainder of the house party joined them—and in the last car, which Bing drove himself, came also Mr. Daniel Carruthers.

Katherine stepped forward at once to welcome him.

Notwithstanding the hideous scar on his face, there was something about the man that fascinated her attention. When he grasped her hand in greeting, the touch of it thrilled her strangely. She studied the expression of his eyes during that brief interval, and wondered vaguely what it was that she saw there that seemed to convey unintelligible words and phrases that did not enter into his speech, and when she turned away, it was with the feeling that she had known him and liked him in the past, although she knew that she had not; but, as if he were somehow mixed with an incomplete and forgotten dream.

In turning away she encountered Belknap, who drew her aside and away from the others with a pre-text.

"I was right," he told her in a low tone. "It's Brainard, of the secret service. I know, because of one sure point that the messenger gave me. I shall seek him, now, and talk with him. Keep an eye on me, Lady Kate, and if this wild aster"—he plucked one and fastened it in the lapel of his coat—"should disappear, it will mean that you must hide me away at once, upon our return to Myquest."

Belknap sought, rather than avoided, the society of the man with the scar—and the feathery, purple-hued aster did not disappear from the button-hole in the lapel of his coat.

It was still there when the party returned to Myquest. Belknap had found opportunity to say to Katherine just before the return start was made, that inasmuch as the aster was destined to fade, he would replace it with some other flower when necessary, and that whenever she chanced to discover him without the decoration of a boutonnière, that fact would be the signal for immediate action.

Harvard rode back with Katherine. Belknap went in the car with Tom and Betty Clancy, Mrs. Saulsbury, Diana Loring, and Carruthers.

"Truly," Katherine thought as she saw them depart, "Conrad Belknap is not of the breed that runs away." Nor did she believe that his insistence that she should hide him when he gave the signal, was because of fear of the secret service officer. Rather, she was of the opinion that he had selected that course because he believed that it would serve his own interests better in carrying out his secret plans.

Over and over again she puzzled her brains in the effort to determine the ultimate object of Belknap's visit to Myquest; but search as she might, she found herself at fault with every turn of thought.

He had not come with intention to rob the house of its plate, or her guests of their jewels; of that much she felt assured. His winnings at the card table, although she knew they must be considerable, she regarded as a by-product, merely, of his real purpose. To win at cards by cheating others was a characteristic of the man which he as thoroughly enjoyed as a marksman finds delight in making bull's-eyes.

Katherine had intended that day, during their ride together, to ask him for particulars about what he knew concerning her brother Roderick, but when he made the strange request that she should hide him away, if need be, she determined on the spot to defer such questionings till later—for the Lady of the Night Wind had then, very quickly, formed a little plan of her own concerning that hiding stunt; a plan which would prove to be considerable of a surprise to Mr. Belknap; a plan that—she smiled when she considered it calmly, and thought of what the outcome of it might be.

"Here is a letter of yours that I found under your balcony," Bingham said to her while they were on their way back, giving it into her hand. "It is the one your mother sent, announcing the time of her arrival."

"Oh, yes," Katherine replied without surprise. "I was using it as a bookmark—Saturday, I think. It must have dropped out; thank you."

Bing regarded her partly averted face in silence, vaguely disturbed.

He had hoped that with the production and return of the letter that had dropped from her balcony when Belknap had so startled her Saturday night, she would have something to say, something to tell him, about the circumstance, but she said nothing.

He had read the incident correctly, although he did not know that. He had assumed that Belknap had come upon her unexpectedly, and startled her, when he had found that what he had first supposed to be some sort of a written message had turned out to be a two-weeks-old letter from her mother.

The other paper that he had taken from Belknap on that occasion had been no more enlightening.

True he had seen it dropped purposely into Belknap's hand, and he now knew that the *señorita* had dropped it, but the contents of it told him nothing whatever. Indeed, it had appeared to be merely carelessly scribbled balderdash—unless, indeed, it might be some sort of cipher.

162

Bing had puzzled over it so much since it so strangely came into his possession, that he had learned it by heart, and while he covertly watched his wife, he repeated it in thought. It was:

> When every arm resists entirely, we are then concerned how effort, done before endeavor, will award rebellion's end.

Such had been the *señorita's* message to Belknap that she had deliberately—so it had seemed—dropped into his outstretched hand from her balcony, Saturday midnight. It had the appearance of a meaningless quotation, and the more Bing thought it over, the more inclined he became to consider it in much the same light as the old letter that had dropped from Katherine's balcony—an accident.

Yet, deep down inside of him he knew that that was not so, and the thing that puzzled him most while he rode on in silence beside Katherine, was the fact that she did not tell him about the unlooked-for appearance of Belknap beneath her window that night.

"How does Mr. Carruthers impress you, Katherine?" he asked her presently.

"He impresses me very strongly," she replied, "but just what that impression is I don't know. I am very much inclined to like him, if that is what you mean, Bingham."

"Yes; that is what I mean," he returned.

"Is he a business man, or does he belong to one of the professions?" she asked, with a quick glance toward her husband out of the corners of her eyes, for she had in mind the things that Belknap had said about him.

"I don't think that he is in business," Harvard replied evasively, "so we may assume that he belongs to one of the professions."

Abruptly Katherine changed the subject.

"Why didn't you bring Señorita Cervantez with you to-day?" she asked. "I was surprised not to see her at our picnic. Did you forget to ask her?"

"No. I asked her. She whispered into my ear, in that breathless way of hers, that she hoped I would make her excuses to you, and I clean forgot to do it."

"Was she present when Mr. Carruthers arrived? Did she meet him?"

"She was on the veranda when he drove in with Miriam, but she went inside while they were getting out of the car."

Therein, Katherine thought, was partial confirmation of what Belknap had told her; for Katherine remembered that Roberta had gone inside to play dreamily upon the piano the preceding evening when Carruthers came to call, with Mr. Saulsbury—and again she seemed to have purposely avoided meeting him.

Did Roberta know—as Belknap confidently believed that he knew—that Carruthers was in reality a certain Bruce Brainard, an operative of the secret service? She decided then and there that she would lose no time in bringing the two face to face, and that she would watch them closely when she did so.

As matters stood, the key to her entire problem was concealed within the real object of Belknap's presence at Myquest. If only she could discover what that was!

Bing drove home rather slowly. They had been the last to leave the old mill where they had picnicked. They were nearly half an hour behind the others in returning. When Katherine ascended the steps to the veranda, almost the first thing that she noticed was the fact that Roberta was seated on a chair at one corner of it while Carruthers was leaning against the rail directly in front of her. Evidently he had just made some remark, for Roberta was writing on her ivory tablets at the moment, and she passed them to her companion even while Katherine approached.

Belknap came out through one of the windows at that moment, and the fact of his appearance at just that instant convinced Katherine that he had been watching the two from inside of the room.

"Will you be my partner at bridge, *señorita*?" he asked at once, fulfilling, as Katherine knew, his threat to Roberta made Saturday night. But Roberta had evidently expected it, and was equal to it. She wrote rapidly on one of the tablets and passed it to Belknap:

"Thank you," she wrote, "but I do not play bridge. I have never learned the game."

CHAPTER XXVII

THE SIGNAL

The cool effrontery of Conrad Belknap and his utter indifference to consequences were never better exemplified than by a (to Katherine) startling episode that occurred in the evening of that day.

The weather was unusually warm, even for late June. Nobody cared to remain indoors, even for the attractions of bridge or music.

Roberta improvised some dreamy airs on the piano for a time, but presently came out through one of the windows where Katherine was seated with Carruthers and Belknap.

"Come with me and I will show it to you," she heard Katherine say to Carruthers; and as they got upon their feet and started slowly away, Belknap remarked coolly:

"Ah; here is Señorita Cervantez. We will go with you, if the *señorita* will do me that much honor." And he added, by way of explanation: "They are going down to the lake. Will you go?"

Roberta knew that the polite question was intended for a command, but she would not have hesitated to deny him as she had done in the matter of the game of bridge, before dinner, if it had not been her whim at the moment to go.

So the four walked down the path toward the lake together, with Katherine and Carruthers in the lead, but not far enough ahead to render their conversation unintelligible to the pair who followed.

Roberta, whose understanding of Belknap's moods and methods was the consequence of long and varied experiences, knew perfectly well that he had a definite purpose in following the others, and she had her own reasons for desiring to be present to witness whatever might occur.

She was glad that Belknap kept so close to the leaders that there was no opportunity for confidences—as she also knew, because of that same fact, that he was meditating some sort of preconceived coup at the first opportunity that offered; and that he was actually making that opportunity.

They came to the lake at the boat-house and bathing pavilion, and went out upon the wide and spacious platform in front of the former, which extended above the water.

"It is much cooler here," Carruthers remarked as he brought some chairs forward for the ladies, and proceeded to light a cigar. Then his eyes rested for a long moment upon the Swiss chalet perched at the top of the bluff opposite, where the glory of the moon but added to its picturesqueness.

"What is that building over there?" he asked Katherine.

"Oh; the chalet?" she replied indifferently. "Everybody who comes here asks that question, Mr. Carruthers. It is really, I suppose, a sort of storehouse for the accommodation of articles that I don't care to keep in the house. It is closed and shuttered, and tightly sealed—unused, practically. Mr. Harvard and I have some plans regarding it, but, you know that procrastination is the thief of time."

"By the way, Carruthers," Belknap spoke up before a reply could be made, "I have been puzzling my head about you ever since you came here yesterday, to call."

"Yes? Have you, indeed?" the man with the scar replied, uninterestedly; but Roberta bent slightly forward in her chair, convinced that the moment had arrived when Belknap would make the play that had brought him out there with the others.

Katherine, because Belknap's remark, and the manner of it, had startled her, half turned toward them to listen; and Belknap—well, whatever it was that he intended to say, he knew himself to be master of the situation, for he knew what the other man could not know (as he figured it)—that both of the women present were more or less in his confidence; at least he was not afraid of anything that might be said in the presence of either of them.

"I have," he rejoined, without hesitation. "I thought, last evening when you came, and I am quite certain, now, that we have met before; only—"

"I have no recollection of such a meeting, Mr. Belknap."

"Possibly not. It happened some years ago. You have met with a serious accident since then. You did not wear that scar at the time"—he hesitated while Katherine caught her breath and bit her lip in amazement at his insolence, and while Roberta sat bolt upright on her chair as if petrified; and Belknap deliberately plucked the boutonnière from his coat and tossed it into the lake—"and," he went on, "your name was not Carruthers, then. It was Brainard—

Bruce Brainard. You were, so I was informed, an operative in the secret service."

It was all said very deliberately, concisely, and in a tone of finality that left no room for argument or denial.

A pistol shot exploded immediately behind them could not have been more astounding, although it might have produced a different effect.

As it was, all three of his listeners sat very still and silent. Belknap alone of the group was on his feet.

There was a space of perhaps a full second, but which seemed, to at least two of the four, to be many seconds, during which nobody spoke; then, as deliberately as Belknap had spoken, Carruthers replied:

"Your memory is remarkable, but—misleading, Mr. Belknap. It is remarkable because I happen to be acquainted with the Mr. Brainard to whom you refer, who is, I believe, a member of the secret service, and who, quite unaccountably, resembles me, save for the facial disfigurement to which you have so delicately referred. Shall we stroll on, Mrs. Harvard, along the lake shore?" he added, before Belknap could reply.

Katherine left her chair instantly, glad to be relieved of the strain.

Belknap, apparently, had no desire to pursue the subject. He knew that Katherine had seen him pluck the boutonnière from his coat, and that she had understood the signal. Also, he had accomplished his purpose, which had been to inform Carruthers that he was "on to" him—and to defy him.

It was plainly up to Roberta to follow Carruthers and Katherine, if she so desired, but she kept her seat and let them go—and watched them in silence until they were out of hearing. Then, in a tone so low as to be barely audible, she said to Belknap:

"Why did you do that, C. B.?"

He shrugged, and indulged in his sardonic smile.

"Because it pleased me. I was warned of his coming by telephone last night. I got the particulars early this morning. The man is Brainard, of the secret service. There is no doubt about it."

"And he is here"—she hesitated, and Belknap noticed for the first time that she was pale and tense—"why is he here, if you are right about him?"

Belknap smiled even more pronouncedly as he replied:

"There is only one reason why any of his kind would be after me. You know that. It is old, to be sure; but, you know that legend,

167

don't you, that Uncle Sam never lets go? A thousand years are as a day, and all of that rot. He hasn't got the gall to try to put irons on me, even if he is sure that I am I—which I doubt; and if he did it he could not prove his case, Berta. Bah!" he snapped his fingers, "I don't fear him that much."

Then he turned sharply upon her.

"What did you guess at, about him?" he demanded.

"Nothing," she replied, calmly returning his gaze.

"I was watching you this afternoon when you talked together on the veranda. I could not hear what he said, and of course I couldn't read your written replies; but, your manner and his were not as between total strangers. I saw something that smelt of an understanding between you, I thought. Are you trying in another way to double-cross me? Did you supply the information that brought him here? Somebody did, and if it was you—"

He did not finish, but he managed to convey a world of menace in what he left unsaid.

Roberta did not reply, for at that moment several more of the guests joined them on the platform.

Belknap excused himself and returned to the house as soon as the other guests came upon the scene.

Miss Loring and Demming were seated together on the veranda, and saw him enter the house. Black Julius, passing through the main hall, saw him ascend the stairs as if he were going to his own room, and a maid on the third floor saw him enter it. Nobody, on the following day, remembered having seen him after that; at least, nobody admitted it, if he was seen.

Katherine saw and understood the signal of the boutonnière when he plucked it from his coat and threw it into the lake at the boat-house, and so, instead of wandering along the shore with Carruthers—although for reasons of her own she did wish very much to do so—she guided him away from it, and, by a roundabout way, led him back to the house, where she left him on the veranda and went inside.

She wrote a single line upon a sheet of paper—"The rustic seat under the box-elder, after midnight," was what she wrote—folded it, carried it to the next floor, and slipped it beneath Belknap's door unseen. After that she went outside and joined the others on the veranda.

"The others" were scattered along the length of it, save for the *señorita*, who was inside at the piano, playing for them; and presently, while she was rendering Chopin's "Polonaise Militaire," Carruthers tossed aside his cigar and entered at the window beyond which the piano stood.

At first he began idly to turn over some sheets of music on the top of the piano, as if seeking a choice selection, and soon, having found it, apparently, he carried it around the end of the piano to her.

"Will you play this one for me, please?" he asked, fixing it against the rack; and while he bent forward to adjust it, Roberta murmured:

"He knows you. What will you do?"

"Nothing at present. I'll wait—and watch."

She began to play, but Carruthers, in withdrawing his hand, dislodged a sheet of the music so that it fell to the floor. When he stooped to regain it, she murmured swiftly:

"I must talk with you. How can you manage it?"

"Go where you met me Saturday night," he replied softly. "The bench under the tree by the lake."

"What time?" she asked, while he readjusted the music on the rack.

"After midnight, Bobbie. Who arrives first will wait."

She nodded as if to assure him that the music was well placed at last, and he passed again around the end of the piano and dropped upon a chair to listen to her playing.

Thus it will be seen that the coming of Carruthers to Myquest, the first time, to call, and then to remain as a guest, was not unexpected by at least one of its guests—that the stranger with the scar was the same man who Roberta had gone outside to meet in the wee small hours of Sunday morning—that he was the same man whom Belknap had thought for a time was locked in Roberta's bathroom—and that he was the identical individual whose face Katherine had observed in the glow of a lighted match beneath the box-elder when she fled to the Nest, which she had hoped she would recognize, but did not; and, wholly as strange and inexplicable as any part of the preceding, she had not remembered it at all when that same person appeared at Myquest Sunday evening with Morton Saulsbury. And thus it appears, also, that there existed between him and Roberta a degree of intimacy which nobody but themselves knew about.

The man whom Katherine saw under the tree had worn no scar. She would have seen it in the glow of the lighted match had there been one. He had been bearded and shock-headed—but wigs and false beards are not readily discernible at night, under trees; and he had been enveloped in a raincoat that reached nearly to his heels.

No; Katherine had not suspected that Daniel Carruthers, so called, was the same man who had talked with Roberta under the tree that night. Such an idea had not occurred to her at all.

But we know something more which none of them guessed at.

Two appointments had been made, to take place at the same spot, at approximately the same time, for the night that had just begun; Carruthers and Roberta were to meet there for a private conference which she had insisted upon making; and Katherine was to meet Belknap there to conduct him to the hiding place which he had insisted that she should provide.

And there were two more incidents connected with the same matters which none of the parties most interested knew about:

Betty Clancy had gone into the house by the doorway at the same time that Carruthers entered it at the window; and she had turned into the music-room through another doorway, but had stepped backward again when she discovered, or thought she did, two significant gestures that passed between Carruthers and Roberta while he searched among the music sheets.

Betty kept her place, too, and looked on, with more or less understanding, at what followed.

The other incident had bearing, also, upon what was to follow.

Harvard, a trifle earlier, entered Katherine's room from his own, in search of such a trivial article as a pin. He saw one that had been dropped on the blotter-pad of her writing desk, and as he bent forward to secure it, he saw something besides.

There was a half sheet of note-paper there, with the tracing of a pencil upon it that had been impressed through another half sheet from which that one had been torn; and the impression was as easily legible as the literal pencil-marks would have been.

"The rustic seat under the box-elder after midnight," was what he saw and read.

When he went from the room he forgot to take the pin with him.

CHAPTER XXVIII

A NIGHT OF MANY DANGERS

"The rustic seat under the box-elder, after midnight," Bing repeated to himself as he went out of Katherine's room totally forgetful of the pin he had gone after; and he added, perplexedly: "In Katherine's writing—written upon another half sheet and impressed through it upon the one I saw. She had torn that half sheet from this one and carried it out with her, so it was intended for somebody—for whom, I wonder?"

He joined the others on the veranda, and although he responded to such conversation as was addressed directly to him, and occasionally made a remark himself, his mentality continued to dwell upon the mysterious message he had seen and read in Katherine's room.

"The rustic bench—after midnight," he kept on repeating to himself. "After midnight might be any time between twelve o'clock and daylight. Can it be possible that Katherine has made an appointment to meet somebody there at such a time?"

He could not understand it, and least of all could he bring himself to believe it; but there was the evidence of his own visual sense, the certainty of her handwriting, and the seeming fact that the half sheet upon which the actual message had been written had been torn away to save bulk, probably, and carried in the hand to deliver—yes, to deliver unseen—into the hand of the person for whom it was intended.

He noticed, then, for the first time, that Belknap was not present on the veranda.

"Where is Belknap?" he asked generally.

Nobody answered; nobody knew; then Miss Loring remarked:

"He has probably gone to his room, Mr. Harvard. I saw him go into the house about nine o'clock." Bing looked at his watch and found that the time was a few moments past ten.

He left his chair and strolled down the steps and along one of the paths to think.

There was no definite objective in his mind, but after a time, and somewhat to his surprise at that, he found himself before the rustic bench under the box-elder, by the shore of the lake—so he sat down.

Betty Clancy had been likewise disturbed by what she had seen in the music-room, for she had seen enough for her quick wits and lively intuition to read with more or less correctness.

She was convinced, for example, that Carruthers and the *señorita* were by no means strangers to one another, although they maintained the attitude of appearing to be; also, she had convinced herself that there had been a passage of words between the two at the piano while Carruthers was arranging the music on the rack, and picking up the fallen sheet which she believed to have been purposely dislodged.

Now, Betty was mischievous rather than suspicious.

She read nothing more in the episode at the piano than a hidden and unsuspected romance; but romances interested her, always, whether between book covers, or in the open, between persons of her acquaintance.

So, Betty was watchful; she scented an approaching love-scene between the man with the scar and the pianiste; she knew that since Carruthers's arrival there had not been opportunity for the exchange of confidences between him and the *señorita*, save that brief interchange at the piano, and, therefore—well, it was plain to Betty that they had agreed to seek a better opportunity before the night was done, and while any idea of spying upon them was farthest from her thoughts, she did want to satisfy herself that she had guessed correctly. She made her own plans accordingly.

Black Julius was also vaguely disturbed and uneasy that night.

The scene that he had witnessed at the old mill in the early morning had thoroughly convinced him of Belknap's duplicity—and that it was the sort of duplicity that seemed to him to threaten his beloved mistress, or her husband, or their property: the latter more likely, since Julius had convinced himself that Belknap was a thief in disguise.

So, Julius, hovering about among the paths, but keeping himself unseen, watched the lighted windows of Belknap's room until, somewhat after eleven o'clock, they became suddenly black—and Julius had already been so mindfully suspicious of Belknap's character and habits that he knew it to be unprecedented for that person to retire so early.

Julius waited, thinking that the man might appear on the veranda; but when, after a reasonable time, he did not do that, Julius entered the house at the rear, ascended to the third floor, and deliberately tapped at Belknap's door, with an excuse ready if the man were there to answer.

There was no response, so Julius turned the knob and entered the room.

Belknap was not there; the bed had not been disturbed; and Belknap's evening clothes had been flung carelessly across the back of a chair, showing that he had changed before he went out.

Julius searched farther, then, by the aid of a small flash-light that he always carried for emergency use around an automobile; and because he had been the one to direct the stowing of Belknap's effects when they came down from the city, he soon found that a black leather handbag which should have been there was missing.

Julius was gravely puzzled, and he hurried down the stairs to inform his master of his discovery. "Mis' Kittie," he decided, "mustn't be bothered with such trifles."

But Harvard was not to be found anywhere, and the black, after waiting around for a time, figured it out that Belknap's interview with the stranger at the old mill that morning had been for the purpose of perfecting plans for the robbery of Myquest that night, and he decided that he would remain in the grounds and watch—till daylight, if need be.

There is just one more thing of which cognizance must be taken if we are thoroughly to understand the events that followed.

Ex-lieutenant Rodney Rushton, whose services Tom Clancy had retained for reasons already known to us, possessed one gift that had taken him over many a difficulty that might have put a shrewder man at fault: tenacity of purpose.

Having been directed to "Find out who Belknap is," he had never had an idea of stopping investigation until he did find out. Having been balked in Arizona, and in New Orleans, he had sent a boy with a camera to the neighborhood of Myquest, and he had secured a snapshot of Mr. Conrad Belknap (among others, to be sure) without arousing suspicion.

He had had that one head of the group enlarged, and hundreds of the enlargements had been printed for him. He had sent them broadcast over the country, accompanied by the simple request: "Please identify, if possible."

173

It was by the last mail that Monday evening that he received the first definite reply—that the first information on the subject came to him that was worth consideration as a possible clue.

He realized the importance of discussing the matter with Clancy without delay, but a telephone call to Tom's home informed him that Mr. Clancy was staying at Myquest for the entire week, so he called him up at Harvard's home, and announced that he had something important to discuss, and would drive down late in the evening.

Unexpected duties detained him, so that it was late when he started, but he called Tom up again in the meantime, and asked that he should meet him at the lodge gate at twelve, which was the earliest that he could get there, possibly.

Truly that forthcoming midnight promised to be replete with incidents, as it already was with appointments and surveillances.

Katherine was to seek Belknap beneath the box-elder by the lake, after midnight. Roberta and Carruthers had made the same appointment, and the Night Wind was already at the spot, waiting. Black Julius was hot on the trail of Belknap. Betty had planned to watch the *señorita*, and Rushton and Clancy were also to be abroad that night.

CHAPTER XXIX

THE HOUSE OF ALADDIN

When Harvard seated himself upon the rustic bench under the tree, the time was approximately half past ten, and he had been there a full hour when he roused himself to a realization of what he was doing.

"Good Heavens!" he exclaimed audibly, but softly. "What am I doing! Spying upon Katherine." But instantly he denied the charge that he had made against himself.

He had not gone there to spy; he had not thought of such a thing; he had been puzzled, and he had wandered to that spot merely because the location of it had been uppermost in his mind.

"My goodness!" he murmured, smiling. "What a thing for me to do—to come here and sit down and wait, simply because—" He got to his feet and strode swiftly away, taking a course that led him to the lodge gate and out upon the highway, for he felt the necessity of the exercise that a long and rapid walk would give him. "Katherine may meet whomsoever she pleases, at any time and place that best suits her, if she wishes to, and she can inform me about it at her own good pleasure. She always has reasons for doing things, and her reasons are always good ones," he announced to himself as he passed the gate.

The saving grace which assisted Belknap's plans—and Katherine's—that night was that both were a trifle ahead of time in arriving at the appointed place.

Belknap left his room soon after eleven. He had stowed some necessary articles in the black bag which he lowered to the ground from one of his windows by a cord—after the watchful Julius had transferred his espionage from the windows to the veranda.

He then descended the stairs nonchalantly to the first floor, and encountered nobody, as it happened, although he was prepared for such an event; but everybody was outside.

He went out at the side entrance, darted into the shadows, made his way cautiously to the point under his room windows, secured his bag, and went swiftly toward the lake, having determined that he would conceal himself in the woods behind the rustic bench, but at a point where he could keep an eye upon it, until Katherine should appear.

A strong point with Belknap was that he never neglected caution: therefore, without having made a sound in his approach to the place, he made the discovery that the bench was already occupied— and by a man.

He watched and waited, not without misgivings, a time that seemed interminable; but at last Harvard left the bench, and Belknap recognized him—and attributed the circumstance of his being there to accident.

Fifteen minutes later Katherine came—fully ten minutes before midnight.

She also approached the spot through the woods, and so silently that even the watchful Belknap did not hear her; but when she crossed the open space to the elder, he saw and recognized her.

Instead of following after her, his caution being predominant, he uttered a low whistle, which brought her to a standstill, listening. When he repeated it, she went to him among the trees.

Neither of them suspected that other ears than their own had heard that warning whistle; but there was one who did—who heard it and crept toward the sound of it—who caught a recognizing glimpse of Katherine as she returned from the tree to the wood—and who very nearly forgot to watch on, because of the utterly amazing fact.

Katherine went close to Belknap.

"Do not speak," she said in a whisper. "Make no sound whatever, if you can avoid it. Follow me."

She led the way among the huge trees where the darkness was so deep that Belknap felt as if he was pursuing only a shadow that was more dense than those around it. Meanwhile, the owner of those other ears that had heard the whistled signal, came to a full stop, stood irresolute for a moment, and then deliberately turned away in the opposite direction.

Katherine led her companion to a point where she halted a moment as if to rest. In reality she did it in order to press a finger upon a certain spot in the bark of the tree against which she leaned. After a second or two she went on.

They came, presently, to a long flight of hard wood steps which she proceeded to mount. When they were nearly at the top, Belknap murmured:

"Can I venture to make a remark, Mrs. Harvard?"

"If you speak softly, yes," she answered without turning her head. "What is it?"

"I thought that I had thoroughly looked over the place, but I never saw these steps before. I didn't know they were here."

"They weren't," she replied laconically. "Come on, please."

A steep and winding path succeeded the steps. It twisted so amazingly about between boulders that it was not discernible as a path even in daylight.

Again Katherine paused, half-way along the winding path. She pressed upon two more secret places without Belknap's suspecting that she did so. The first pressure converted the stairs they had just climbed into a smooth and steep and inaccessible surface; the second one converted the same sort of inclined surface above them to steps.

Thus, presently, they arrived at the door to the Nest, which was wide open—for Katherine had negotiated that secret mechanism while she climbed the last flight of steps.

She passed inside, into black darkness. Belknap followed her, wonderingly; and as he was on the point of asking a question, he heard the click of a closing door. There was no other sound or jar to it.

Then, so suddenly that it startled him, the room in which they stood was flooded with light, and Belknap discovered that he was facing Katherine across a huge, square-cornered table of solid oak, in a great room that might have been "the dream come true" of any artist, musician, writer, or pronounced sybarite.

Long accustomed as he was to manifest no surprise at anything, Belknap could not conceal his amazement.

"Aladdin's lamp!" he exclaimed. "Where do you keep it concealed, dear lady? And where is the jinee?"

"The jinee," she replied, smiling a little, "is here. Would you like proof of it? Look behind you."

He turned slowly.

As he did so the lights went out—all save one which glowed faintly by comparison with the recent illumination in the ceiling over their heads.

Even Belknap's stoic self could barely repress a startled exclamation and an involuntary shudder when he discovered that he had been standing within a few inches of a floorless space into the black depths of which a spiral staircase descended; and as he turned again to question Katherine, the last light was shut off.

"Oh, I say!" he exclaimed with a half laugh, and yet with a touch of petulance; but before he could add to that remark all the lights were turned on again, and he saw that Katherine stood near the center of the other half of the room beyond the table. The trap in the floor behind him had closed itself without a sound.

"Be seated, Mr. Belknap," she said to him formally. "That is not a trap in which to catch the unwary, that I showed you. It is my cellar—my storehouse, carved out of the solid rock. It is one—only one—of a thousand secrets of this place."

"Why did you show me that much?" he asked, shrugging his shoulders. "Was it to warn me, perhaps?"

"I did it as a reply to your former question—to prove to you that the jinee of my conjuring is constantly at my hand, in this house, prepared for instant obedience."

"I understand," Belknap replied soberly. "That is at once a warning and a threat. Have no fear of me, Mrs. Harvard. While I am here I will be a 'slave of the lamp.'"

Katherine, in the coldly formal tone in which she had last spoken, instructed Belknap concerning his surroundings.

"Over against the wall behind you, there is a wide and soft couch where you may rest, and sleep," she said. "Such conveniences as you require, you will readily discover, if you seek them. Before I go I will switch off the major part of the lights, leaving the others burning, which you may turn on and off at will. Such doors as you find fastened against you, may not be opened by any skill of burglary. I mention that fact merely to spare you useless effort in case you have brought your tools of the craft with you in your bag."

"I assure you—" he began.

"Don't. It is unnecessary."

"We are inside of the Swiss chalet, on the bluff, are we not?" Belknap asked.

"Yes."

"What about this brilliant illumination—in case somebody outside should look in this direction?"

"Not a ray of light within the house can be discovered from outside," she answered. "You will find reading matter here, if you want it," she went on. "There are cards for solitaire in the table drawer;

also chess, for working out problems, if that pastime entertains you. If you can cook, there are electrical conveniences, and material for anything which I have thought you might require; only, while you remain, you will have to forego fresh meats and vegetables. You will find sufficient canned goods, however. The water which constantly flows in and out of the porcelain tank in the electric kitchenette, is from a never-failing spring, and is nearly as cold as ice-water. That, with tea, coffee, and perhaps chocolate, must suffice you as beverages.

"When occasion makes it necessary that I should come here to see you, you will hear the humming of an electric buzzer, and I will invariably announce my approach at least twenty minutes before I will appear."

She stopped a moment, and an enigmatical smile softened her expression. Then:

"I will suggest that you had best not stand too near to the door when you are expecting me to arrive. The jinee is always there on guard."

"Will you tell me what you mean by that remark, Mrs. Harvard?" Belknap inquired, impressed by her manner.

"I mean that in case you should be too eager to receive me, when you have been signaled that I am coming, it would not be safe for you to stand too near to the door. There is another entrance to my cellar in the rock, just in front of it, which I shall probably open as I approach. You might get a nasty fall, you know, for there is no spiral staircase there."

"By Jove!" Belknap could not refrain from exclaiming in his admiration.

"You are the only person," she went on, unmoved, "save myself, who has set foot within this building since it was completed. Nobody comes here—"

"Not your husband?"

"Nobody—and none will come."

"What if I should want you to come to me—in case you should remain too long absent? Is there some method by which I can signal to you—from a window—or—"

"Mr. Belknap, while you remain here, you will not see daylight once. There are windows, but they may not be opened—if you would be entirely secure. You will have plenty of air, however—the ventilation system is perfect, but electricity must take the place of sunlight. But, if you should want me"—she crossed the room swiftly and lifted a small Japanese idol that stood upon one end of the granite shelf above the fireplace—"you will find a button here. By pressing it five times in succession—remember, *five* times—it will convey a silent signal to me which I will presently discover. That is all for the present, I think."

She turned abruptly and moved swiftly toward the door, which, to his profound amazement, swung open as she advanced.

He darted forward to detain her—not by force, but by expostulation and argument—for there was much that he wished yet to say to her, and to hear her say; but she had passed the threshold before he could take the second step in her direction; the massive door closed itself swiftly and silently—without a sound save a delicate click of its mechanism; and Belknap could see, when he stared at the place beyond which she had disappeared, only a smooth surface, unrelieved by knob or bolt or visible hinge.

CHAPTER XXX

BLACK JULIUS SPEAKS

Katherine, making her way back to the house, touching hidden secrets here and there as she progressed—to facilitate her progress, and, metaphorically, to "shut her gates behind her"—selected the same route by which she had led Belknap to the Nest.

Naturally she passed again quite close to the rustic bench under the box-elder—and as naturally she glanced toward it in passing.

She halted.

Outlined against the opalescent surface of the lake beyond, she plainly saw two persons seated there, side by side, and quite close together; moreover, they were so perfectly silhouetted against the faintly shining background that she recognized both, on the instant.

"Strange," she thought, and moved silently backward, away from them, before she continued on her way. "Roberta and Mr. Carruthers seated there together at this hour, and in an intimate position that suggests former acquaintance. I wonder—"

She did not complete the conjectural thought, for just ahead of her, in one of the paths that led to the house, she saw Betty Clancy hurrying away.

"That is strange, too," Katherine commented silently. Then she smiled, and added to her thought: "Why, of course! Betty walked down to the lake with them, and, little matchmaker that she is, scented a possible romance, and so sought the first excuse she could think of to leave them together."

She permitted Betty to enter the house before her; then, as she ascended the steps to the veranda, she encountered Black Julius.

"Why, Julius!" she exclaimed. "You ought to be in bed."

"Yes, Mis' Kitten, I know it. But I thought I'd wait fo' Mr. Harvard. He hasn't come in yet; and Mr. Clancy is out, too."

"Where did they go?" she asked, assuming that they were together.

"Mr. Harvard went down toward the lake about half past ten, so Mr. Archer told me. And Mr. Clancy went out 'bout half an hour ago, Mis' Kitten."

"Oh, well, you need not wait for them, Julius. They are doubtless taking a walk together. They are just 'boys again' whenever they can get by themselves"; and with a smiling good-night to her faithful servitor, she entered the house and sought her own room.

Julius stared after her, slowly shaking his head. He was deeply puzzled, and profoundly troubled.

"No," the black muttered to himself "She wouldn't take that man to the Nest. She has just sent him off about his business; but—but—but—"

Down at the lodge gate, Harvard, returning from his long and rapid walk, came upon Tom Clancy and Rushton engaged in earnest conversation.

"What the dickens—" he began; but Tom interrupted.

"Gee, Bing. I'm glad you happened along. Rushton has made a most extraordinary discovery about that guy Belknap—if only it turns out to be true. And, say, we'll have to take the old Senator into our confidence in order to determine that point."

"What in blazes are you talking about, Tom?" Bing inquired impatiently.

"I'm talking about Belknap. Rushton has got a line on him. Come on into the house, Rushton. We'll go to Bing's den and talk it over."

When Harvard, accompanied by Clancy and Rushton, approached the veranda, Black Julius stepped out from a shadow among the shrubbery just in front of them, and his appearance was so unexpected that Rushton's right hand flew to the pocket were he carried a weapon; but he grinned in the darkness, and drew forth a handkerchief instead as he heard Julius say:

"Mr. Harvard, sir."

"Yes, Julius. What is it?" Harvard returned.

"May I speak with you a moment, sir?"

Clancy and Rushton moved onward, and Julius, in a low tone, made the report to his master that he had determined upon.

"I ask your pardon, sir, for doing things that are outside of my duties," he began (Julius, remember, was an educated negro, and his language, save for an occasional slurring of the vowels, was nearly always correct). "But I have seen certain things that have made me watchful, and—I have discovered other things which I think I ought to tell to you."

"Won't they keep till morning, Julius?"

"No, sir; begging your pardon."

"Things about what? Things about whom, Julius?"

"About Mr. Belknap, sir."

"Are they matters which you believe I should know about to-night?"

"Yes, sir."

"Very good. We are going to my lounging-room now to discuss that same person. You may come with us, Julius."

In Harvard's den, behind closed doors, he announced:

"Julius has something to tell us about Belknap. I think it will be well to hear what he has to say before we listen to your report, Rushton. It begins to look, to me, as if everybody save myself has dug up some definite criticism of Belknap. I am thoroughly opposed to discussing the character of one of my guests in this manner, but, because only my best friend, my confidential employee, and Julius, who is always trustworthy, are here, I will consent to it. Now, Julius, what have you to tell us?"

"Mr. Harvard," Julius replied soberly, "in the beginning, I just didn't like Mr. Belknap; that was the onliest thing I had against him; but, sir, I set myself to watching him. At first I didn't see anything that I could put my finger on, that was against him, only"—he turned toward the others—"you must remember that I have been Mis' Harvard's special servant ever since she was bo'n, and there ain't no expression of her face that Black Julius don't know the meanin' of. I was going to say that at first I didn't see anything, only that Mis' Kittie—excuse me; Mis' Harvard—that she certainly did seem to me to despise him, an' to be just a little wee scrimpsy bit afraid of him. That set me to watchin' closer."

"Get down to the facts, Julius," Harvard commanded.

"Yes, sir. There wasn't any facts till Mr. Belknap was called to the telephone last night. I knew it wasn't right, sir, but I fixed the switchboard so that I could hear, too, and—"

"Julius!" Harvard exclaimed, aghast.

"I know, sir, it wasn't right; but I did it just the same, and I'm glad of it—seeing what has happened since. I didn't hear all that was said. A man in Washington was talking, and he didn't say much, 'cept to tell Mr. Belknap to go to the old mill on our place the next mawnin' to meet a man who would tell him the rest. Well, sir, I went to the old mill, too. And I got there first. They didn't talk English, so I couldn't understand what was said—'ceptin' when they used names."

"What names did you hear them use?" Rushton demanded, intensely interested.

"I wrote them down, sir, so I wouldn't forget them—those that were not familiar. One was Bruce Brainard; an—"

"What?" exclaimed Harvard. Then: "Go on, Julius; I understand."

"Another name was Saulsbury, and a third one was a name that I used to know, years ago, down in Kentucky. It was Belding."

It was Rushton's turn to manifest surprise.

"Belding, did you say, Julius? What was the first name that went with it?"

"It wasn't mentioned, sir; but the first name of the Belding that I knew about, years ago, was Cranshaw. Yes, sir; Cranshaw Belding."

"Gee-whillikins! You don't say!" Rushton exclaimed. "Now, what do you know about that! How old was he when you knew him, Julius, and what became of him? How long ago was it when you knew about him?"

"It is a good many years ago, sir—when Senator Maxwilton was a judge. More than thirty years ago. Cranshaw Belding was a little under forty years old, then. He was hung for murder, and it was Judge Maxwilton who sentenced him."

Rushton, manifesting considerable repressed excitement, turned to Harvard and Clancy.

"That seems to clinch matters so far as my report is concerned," he said; "and the Senator will know more, likely enough. The Cranshaw Belding that Julius knew must have been the father of—what am I talking about? You haven't heard my report yet. Say, Julius, is that all you can tell us?"

"No, sir; not quite."

"Well, then, give us the rest of it."

"You see, sir, I was afraid that those two who met at the old mill were planning to rob us, so I kept an eye on Mr. Belknap all day. But I reckon I was mistaken, because he has gone away!"

"Gone away? Left Myquest? Gone, without saying a word about it to anybody? Is that what you mean to say, Julius?" Clancy demanded.

"Yes, sir—with a satchel—soon after eleven, to-night. He went through the woods at the south side of the lake—skulking-like. I saw him myself."

"Did you follow him, Julius?"

184

"No, sir."

"Was he alone when you saw him? Did that other chap—the one at the mill—meet him? Did you see anybody with him?"

"Yes, sir, I saw somebody meet him, but it was very dark under the trees, and—well, sir, one couldn't see more than the outlines of a person." (Julius would have lost his right arm rather than tell anybody that the outlined figure of the person who had met Belknap in the woods was as familiar to him as his own face in a mirror.)

The three white men of the group were silent for a space; then Harvard spoke.

"What Julius has told us compels me to say something that I had intended to keep to myself," he said. "You noticed my surprise when Julius mentioned the names of Brainard and Saulsbury. Bruce Brainard is here. Carruthers is Brainard. Saulsbury brought him first, yesterday, to ask me if I would receive him as a guest, under the assumed name. The man is a secret service operative. He is on the trail of a man whom he believes to be identical with Conrad Belknap. I refused to receive him, at first, but Saulsbury overrode my objections. Carruthers's scar, by the way, Tom is not a real one, although it is as perfect as if it were. It is stained on. Saulsbury told me that he is wonderfully adept at disguising himself, and is considered one of the best operatives in Washington. I—"

"Say, Mr. Harvard," Rushton interrupted, bending forward.

"Well, Rushton?"

"I think that it's about time that you listened to my report; and, likewise, I think that you'd better wake up Mr. Brainard and bring him here before I make it. Maybe it will help him in his work, and more'n likely he can help me in mine."

"Very well, Rushton. Since we have gone to such lengths already, no doubt you are right. No, Julius, I will go myself."

CHAPTER XXXI

BRAINARD, OF THE SECRET SERVICE

When Harvard stepped into the corridor on his way to Carruthers's room he discovered that gentleman in the act of ascending the stairs toward it. He turned about when he heard Harvard's low-toned call.

"You have been outside?" Harvard asked abruptly.

"Yes."

"On the trail of your man?"

"No."

"Belknap has gone. I thought, possibly, you might know it."

"Gone? Gone, when—and where, Mr. Harvard?"

"Come with me, please," Bing said, instead of answering the question. "We are holding an impromptu conference in my den. Mr. Clancy, and a detective in whom I have every confidence, are there; also Black Julius, who is a privileged person in this family. Julius has told us some surprising things about Belknap, and Rushton still has something more to say about him. He would also like to hear what you may be willing to tell. Will you come, please?"

"Yes, thank you. I will be glad to. Have you told them who and what I am?"

"Yes; and also that you are Brainard, instead of Carruthers."

Introductions were quickly made. At the last, Harvard added: "And this is Julius, Mr. Carruthers. (We will stick to that name, and not use Brainard, I think.) He has served in Mrs. Harvard's family all his life."

It was the first time that Julius had seen Carruthers close up. As he turned to face him, the others saw the negro give a violent start, heard him catch his breath in a short, quick gasp—saw him lift one hand and brush it across his eyes. They supposed it was the livid scar that startled him so, notwithstanding that he had been told that it was not a real one—or, possibly it was astonishment because the stranger grasped him by the hand, as he would have done to a white man.

"I foresee that Julius and I will be friends," Carruthers said while he held the negro's gaze for a short moment. Then he turned to the others, and Julius crossed the room on a pretense of bringing up another chair, although one had already been shoved forward.

"You may be seated, Julius; there is no necessity for you to stand," Harvard remarked. "Tom, will you, as concisely as possible, tell Mr. Carruthers of what has already been said?"

Clancy did so, rapidly; and although Carruthers listened intently, he made no comment.

"Now, Rushton, we will listen to you," Clancy finished.

"Mine'll be short, but to the point," Rushton answered—and it was noticeable that he addressed himself directly to Carruthers, as if in him he had already recognized a master mind for criminal investigation. "Mr. Clancy didn't cotton to Belknap from the first. He asked me to find out who he was—and is. I couldn't get no satisfaction from any lines that we already had on him, so I sent a kid down here with what looked like a toy-camera. He's a little guy, but older than he looks; and he's smart. I figured that nobody'd pay any attention to a kid takin' snap-shots with a toy. See?"

Nobody replied. Rushton continued:

"He got two. One of 'em was a corker. I had it enlarged, and a thousand of 'em printed. I sent one to the police of every city, big an' little, an' to almost every town I could think of, with the request, 'Please identify, if possible.' When I'd finished sendin' 'em, I had a dozen of 'em left. Then I got a hunch. Says I to myself, 'That guy went to Archer's just to get himself took to Myquest. He ain't there on no common stunt, either, and he ain't no common crook, or I'd have had a line on him before now. What's his lay?' says I. 'Card-sharpin', mebby, or blackmail.' Blackmail sort of fitted my sconce; and, if that was his lay, it followed that he thought he knew something about the Maxwilton family, or about Mr. Harvard, that would draw coin. Well, I sent the dozen pictures I had left to every place on the map around about the locality where Lady Kate was born, in Kentucky—sent 'em to constables, and all that. Then I had another hundred printed and sent more to other places down there; and I looked up a list of Mr. Harvard's classmates in college and sent them some—and so on.

"Well, Mr. Carruthers, I got this letter this afternoon. You read it out loud. It's the finish of what I've got to say."

Carruthers received the letter, glanced through it, and then did as requested. It was dated from a town in Kentucky that was located less than a score of miles from the homestead of Senator Maxwilton. The letter was as follows:

DEAR SIR:

Your letter with picture received. First off I didn't think I knew any such person, but when I looked at it some more I got to reckoning that I'd seen him somewhere; and finally I remembered a man who'd been to our place two or three years ago asking for old Judge Marbury, who's dead and gone ten years. He had asked me about the judge, and I'd sent him to the judge's son, who's practicing law now in his dad's place. I was certain it was the same man, so I ups and takes the picture over to young Boyd Marbury—he's only twenty-five now. Soon's I showed it to him he says: "Yes, sir; I knew him." And that's all I could get out of him for a while. But Boyd likes me, and bimeby he tells me this—seeing as how a regular detective wants the information, only he made me swear that I wouldn't tell nobody else. The man came here to ask about some property, says he, that he understood that Cranshaw Belding (who was hung for murder thirty years ago) had left behind him. Said he was distant kin to Belding. He got mad when he found that it had all been sold for taxes years ago, and done some cussing. Then he went away without paying young Boyd a cent. Well, sir, Boyd and me we put our heads together, and we (that is, I did) remembered that Cran Belding had a son that was three or four years old when he was hung, that he *said* he'd murdered at the same time he killed the mother. And then I remembered a kind of a jerky way that the stranger had had about him that was a whole lot like what I'd seen Cran Belding do lots of times. So, I says to myself, I'll bet a cooky that Cran didn't kill his boy, and that the chap that came here was that boy growed up.

That's all I know, Mr. Rushton, and it ain't much. You can take it for what it's worth, if it's worth anything at all. He don't look like Cran did, but he acts like him, and he's got a way of jerking his head that's like him—and I wouldn't wonder a mite if it was him—that is, if the man whose picture you sent to me ain't Cran Belding's boy growed up.

Yours truly,

Jasper D. Seelover,
Town Constable

Although Carruthers read the letter through almost without expression, his remarkable eyes were all aglow when he lifted them to encounter Bing Harvard's gaze. When he spoke it was in the same quiet tone that he had used before, indicative of nothing.

"Mr. Rushton has done me a great service," he said; "he has done the department that I serve a greater one. Cranshaw Belding, addressed as 'C. B.' by his intimates, is the name of the man I want, and without doubt Conrad Belknap—the initials are the same, you observe—is the man."

"I have heard him called C. B.," Bing said, "on one occasion."

"That gives us added assurance. Julius overheard the name Belding at the old mill. Belknap's information in regard to my coming here was accurate; he proved that to me to-night at the boat-house, when he claimed to have met me before, without the scar, and under the name of Brainard. His cheek and assurance are phenomenal. He is a cool and capable scoundrel. I am not at liberty at the moment to tell exactly why Uncle Sam wants him, and has wanted him for some time. But, with the information now at hand, I shall not hesitate to arrest him as soon as he can be found."

"Can you tell me why, in the devil's name, he came to Myquest?" Harvard asked.

"I can only guess as to that, Mr. Harvard, and this is too serious a matter to guess about. I will tell you all this: if he did not leave Myquest till after eleven o'clock, he did not go far. I am not alone on this case."

When the conference and exchange of opinions came to an end, Carruthers signified his intention of accompanying Rushton to his car. Harvard and Clancy at once sought their respective beds.

"I was wonderin'," Rushton said to his companion as soon as they were in the open, "if you was figurin' on tellin' me anything more about that guy. I could see that you wasn't ready to give it all up to Bing Harvard and Tom Clancy—but me! That's different, ain't it?"

"Yes, Rushton. That is why I came outside with you. This Cranshaw Belding (I have personally known that Belknap is Belding, for a long time; and an acquaintance of mine has also known it, although neither of us were in a position to prove it) has a long criminal record, and a bad one. It began when he was a mere boy, and he is now, according to my best information, thirty-four years old. He was born with brains; he is superlatively intelligent, and he has courage. I don't think that he knows what physical fear is; nor mental fear, either, for that matter. He has good blood in him, too—the best that Kentucky boasts, on both sides of his ancestry. But he is unmoral; a man who apparently was born without morals. The combination creates a dangerous character to be at large. He is utterly unscrupulous, save in one particular, and that one to which I refer is remarkable because it is the one scruple that one would never expect in a man of his characteristics."

"Say, what is it—that thing that you're talkin' about?" Rushton asked.

"He respects, and is known to be fastidious in his regard, for women. It is an anomaly in his general character, inherited, probably, from his mother's family. At all events, he has it, as has been proved by his acts, many times, to my personal information and belief."

Rushton grunted. It was plain that he received that statement with a large grain of salt; but the only response he made was to put another question.

"Do you mind tellin' me what he's wanted for? Why your department is after him?" he asked.

"Not at all. I have told you that his criminal record began when he was a boy. It is, in fact, nearly as old as he is. He was brought up, and trained, almost from babyhood, in the family of a man who was probably the greatest, shrewdest, keenest, and ablest criminal who ever defied the government authorities—the most expert bond-forger, bill-forger, and all-around counterfeiter of bond-plates, bill-plates, and of all sorts of negotiable securities, that the world has ever known."

"Say, Brainard, you don't happen to mean old Brock—"

"Yes. He is the man I refer to. He has been dead some years, now; but—"

"Eight or ten," Rushton interpolated. "Well, what do you know about that!"

190

"The old man," Carruthers continued, "found in the young one, an apt pupil, a venturesome one, and a competent successor. After the death of the old man the government believed that all of the counterfeit plates with which he had carried on his business had been rounded up and accounted for; but ever since then, at intervals—and in widely separated localities—a counterfeited bond, or stock certificate, or a bill, or something of that character, has made its appearance. So, we have known, without being able to prove it, that young Belding has been carrying on the work of his teacher.

"I am giving you only a bare outline of things, Rushton, and there are two more matters connected with them which I want you to take into consideration. The first one is (I am speaking officially now, not personally, please understand that) that the name of Cranshaw Belding has always been regarded by the department as a sort of a myth. It was known that there was said to be such a person, or actually was one, but no definite description of him could be obtained. There were a dozen descriptions of him, but each one was totally different from any of the others, and not one of them could be relied upon as authentic. The other matter to which I referred just now, the second one, is this. Nearly two years ago an operative of the department sent in a report to the chief in which he stated with emphasis that he had succeeded in trailing Belding; that he knew him, and was prepared to prove identity; that he was going after his man as soon as he finished the report he was writing; that he was positive that he would 'get' him, and also many of the plates that were wanted; and that he would have proof sufficient the following day to send Belding away—well, for keeps. That night, Rushton, two men were killed. One of them was the operative in question (whose name does not concern us just now). The other one was a youngish man whose pockets contained what appeared to be unmistakable proofs that he was Cranshaw Belding. The two had killed one another when the operative went to arrest his man.

"It so happened that I, personally, was in a position to know that the dead man was not Belding; but I could not prove it. Also, it was a long and a difficult task to convince the department that I was right. My source of information was such that I could not use it—nor could I reveal all of the facts about it that I did know, because my informant was a person whose name must not be mentioned, and whose testimony, even if the name should be revealed, would not be regarded by one of our judges as sufficient proof. The things that I did know—which I thoroughly believed that I knew—were that the real Belding had, for several years, cloaked his identity behind that

191

of the dead man who had posed for him as Belding, and that the real Belding had deliberately supplied the operative who was killed with the information that had taken him to his death. It probably was not within his plans that his own impersonator should lose his life, too; but it is reasonably certain that he coldly planned the killing of the operative. So, you see, he is actually responsible, and therefore guilty, of both of those killings.

"That, Mr. Rushton, is all that I need to tell to you now."

"Uh-uh," Rushton rejoined. Then he added: "You remarked while we were all chinning together in Harvard's room, that if Belknap didn't make his getaway before 'leven o'clock, he wouldn't get very far, because you are not alone on this case. I'd kinda like to know just what you meant by that."

"When I came to Myquest, on Belknap's trail—being convinced that he is the real Belding—I was sure in my own mind that he had reasons for being here which were not connected with his past record; and I had my own reasons for determining that he must not, and should not escape me this time. So I asked that certain of our men, whom I named, be assigned to assist me. There are several of them in this neighborhood. You can accept it as a fact that Belknap will not be able to get past them, day or night, by train, by automobile, on foot, or by any other means. He would be seen and recognized, and would be stopped before he could go very much farther."

"Suppose he does get through, just the same?"

"He won't. He can't."

"All the same, suppose that when to-morrow comes, he's still missin', and that none of your outfit has pinched him. What will you think about that?"

"I won't think about it; I will know."

"What'll you know?"

"I'll know that while he has been here he has arranged a temporary getaway and hiding place within the boundaries of Myquest— say at the old mill that Julius told about, or in an outbuilding, or in the ravine below the lake, or something of the sort—to which he has fled, and where he will stay in hiding as long as he pleases, or until he is rooted out. And, Mr. Rushton, believe me, no matter where that hiding place is, or how skillfully he has arranged it, he will be rooted out before long."

"Say, has it occurred to you that maybe somebody might help him to hide, eh? He might have a confederate among the help, in the house, or outside of it. Guys like him don't usually work alone."

"He will be found, Rushton, never fear," was the confident re-ply.

CHAPTER XXXII

BELKNAP'S DILEMMA

In the meantime the object of so much interest had been undergoing—rather than enjoying, be it said—quite a variety of mental gymnastics.

Belknap, for once in his venturesome life, had had "one put over on him."

He was loath to admit the fact, even to himself, at first; but before he had passed an hour in examining his surroundings in the Nest, and in some rather forceful thinking, he was compelled to recognize the bald fact of it.

Katherine's manner of leaving him—the suddenness of her going—the swinging open of the door without visible act on her part as she approached it—the quick and noiseless closing of it after she passed the threshold—and the very apparent fact that he would not be able to open it in her absence, brought plainly home to his understanding the fact that he was virtually a prisoner.

He had walked deliberately, and with wide-open eyes, into a trap that she had prepared for him—a trap that had closed around him as solidly as ever a wire cage has snapped shut upon an unsuspecting rodent.

A very slight examination convinced Belknap that he could not get outside of the Swiss chalet until the chatelaine of it elected to let him out.

Who ever heard of a house that one could not get out of? Not he, certainly.

Even prisons, with their locks and bars and guards and surrounding walls, were negotiable oft times, by the wiser ones among the desperate men who were confined in them.

He very quickly discovered that there was no way out, unless, in the event of his applying his brains to the problem, he had the intelligence to find some of those secret buttons and appliances which supplied the open-sesame for doors and windows, and other things.

And Belknap had no notion of passively submitting to imprisonment.

"I will have it out with her the first time she comes to see me," he told himself with one of his wolfish smiles; but even as he made the remark aloud, the smile changed into a half-sheepish grin, for he remembered how perfectly self-assured she had been; how secure she had seemed from any possible attack; how totally without fear her attitude had been.

But this—the condition of his surroundings—was not at all what he had anticipated when he had demanded that she should hide him.

He had expected to be located so that he could give his orders to Katherine as he pleased—and what he pleased—and expect her to fulfill them; instead, he was as thoroughly a helpless prisoner as if he were already a convict in solitary confinement.

She could visit him when she pleased, or not at all if she preferred.

He could not wait for her at the door and seize upon her when she entered; indeed, she had deftly warned him against undertaking that very thing—and there was not the slightest doubt left in Belknap's mind that there existed many other mechanical protectors around and about him, over his head and under his feet, to which she would have recourse if he "got fresh."

He had seen one opening in the floor into which he might have been tumbled headlong, easily, had she so willed; he had been told, and did not doubt, that there was another one at the entrance door; and he began to think that they might be anywhere, and that the beautiful owner of the Swiss chalet could, with the lifting of an eyelash, drop him through the floor at almost any spot, or herself disappear before his eyes at will.

"What a woman! By Jove, what a woman!" he exclaimed aloud, and with undoubted admiration and respect. "She has got me dead to rights—literally where I can't help myself, unless—unless I've got the brains to study out and uncover some of the secrets of this house of mysteries; and, by Jove, I think I have the wit to do that very thing. Yes, I believe I have the brains to do that. Anyhow"—and he again smiled his undoubted admiration of the woman who had bested him—"she's got me where I am utterly helpless to carry into execution any of the threats I have made. I can't tell her father or mother about Roderick, for the simple reason that I can't get to them to tell them; I can't cop any more coin at cards; but, more than all, I can't get hold of the thing that I came here after, unless I can induce her to let me loose some night long enough to get it. I wonder if she could be prevailed upon to do that? I wonder. I wonder!

"Lady Kate would be surprised if it occurred to her that my chief reason in asking her to hide me was to provide the opportunity, while I am supposed to be miles away, to get my fingers onto that priceless gem; and now, by jingo, she has got me fixed so that I can't do it.

"She would be still more surprised if she knew that I don't even know that precious brother of hers by sight, and that I could no more send him to prison than I could send her to one. I could let the authorities know that he is alive, and I could give a hint that would lead to his trail; but—Oh, well, there is one thing that I could do in that line, if I chose; and sometimes I have thought that I would do it: I could direct them to Roberta. She knows, confound her! She knows who Roderick Maxwilton is, where he lives, what name he uses, and how he earns his bread and salt. But I could never make her tell me, and I doubt if all the authorities in existence could force her to tell them. Roberta is—Roberta."

Katherine, it will be remembered, had left a few of the electric lights switched on so that he could make use of them; there was a reading light near one of the easy chairs, and there were others quite sufficient for his needs; but all of them combined were far from providing what one might define as illumination.

Having, in a sense, thought himself out in conjecturing, Belknap devoted nearly two hours to careful search for concealed buttons and springs, for that one beneath the little Japanese idol on the shelf had given him an idea.

He searched with great care and method, but after the two hours of utterly fruitless effort, he desisted.

"I'll sleep on it," he thought at last. "When I wake up I'll begin where I leave off now."

Katherine, when she got to her room that night, was quite content. She was smiling while she undressed and went to bed.

She knew—none better—that she had "put one over" on Belknap; and she had already decided that she would give him a continuous forty-eight hours for solitary meditation before she would visit him.

More than that, she had determined to keep him exactly where he was until he was ready and willing to reveal to her the whole plot that he had in mind when he came to Myquest—exactly what his

196

real reasons were for visiting Myquest at all—and until he told her all that he knew about Roderick.

She dropped asleep, still smiling.

The following morning, at mid-forenoon, Harvard, who had been seeking Señorita Cervantez, came upon her unexpectedly where she was seated with some embroidery, in the rose bower—for Harvard had one little incident up his sleeve which he had not talked about at last night's conference.

"*Señorita*," he said, "I have here something that I want to ask you to explain; a matter of eighteen written words which I believe you can explain. I saw you drop this message to Mr. Belknap from your balcony the other night. It reads: 'When every arm resists entirely, we are then concerned how effort, done before endeavor, will award rebellion's end.' It read like a poor quotation, or like utter nonsense, until it occurred to me that it might be an acrostic. When I thought of that, I read the first letter of each word, and put them together. I found: 'We are watched. Beware.' Will you, *señorita*, be good enough to explain?"

The *señorita* started to her feet when Harvard began to speak to her.

It was plain in his manner of address that he was gravely serious—and then she saw and recognized the slip of paper that he held in his hand.

Instantly she realized two things; that it had been the Night Wind who had attacked Belknap under the tree; and that he had succeeded in deciphering the message that she had dropped which he had taken from the man for whom it had been intended.

But Roberta was, nevertheless, not at all afraid.

She had prepared herself for just such an emergency, because she had more than half believed that it would happen; and if the truth be known, she was, deep down inside of her, glad that it had happened.

Before she could reply to him—if, indeed, she intended to make reply, for she hesitated while she asked herself if she should resort to her tablet, or should admit by word of mouth that she was not without a voice—he added:

"I should say, perhaps, that I doubt your inability to use your voice. I heard you, before you dropped this message, call out to the person for whom it was intended—although you did make use of a sibilant whisper. But it was sufficiently penetrating. I heard you call two letters. I will pronounce them; and when I have done that, and while you are explaining things, I wish you also to inform me what other name the two letters stand for besides Conrad Belknap. They are 'S-e-e B-e-e!'"

"Yes, Mr. Harvard," she answered at once, but in a tone so low that it was almost a whisper, "I have a voice, and I can use it. I have deceived everybody. I want to explain. I had brought myself nearly to the point of doing so before you spoke just now."

"What wild and vicious plot is being concocted here in my house under my nose?" he demanded sharply.

"Wait, please," she answered, still in that nearly inaudible tone.

"Why wait, *señorita*?"

"Because the things that I have to tell you cannot be told in a moment. Because there is much that I should say in order to make you thoroughly understand; and I do not think that this is just the right place to say it."

"Perhaps not," he admitted.

"Can we not seek a place where we will be undisturbed—where we can talk without the fear of interruption?"

"Yes," he replied, "there is the lake. Come with me. I will row you out to the middle of it. You can talk there."

"No," she said, and shook her shapely head. "We would be seen, and an observer would know that I was talking. I ride well, and I have not been in the saddle since I came here. Can we not ride? We would be alone in that way."

Harvard made still another suggestion, however.

"If you will walk slowly to the gate at the lodge," he said, "I will pass there soon in one of the roadsters. I will invite you to go with me. Then we can talk."

She nodded, murmured a "Very good, Mr. Harvard," and started away.

Ten minutes later he picked her up at the lodge gate, and they drove away side by side.

Two small incidents happened as they did so: one was that Roberta, believing that nobody was near, spoke to Harvard in her natural voice as she climbed into the seat beside him; the other one was that Katherine, who had entered the unused lodge for some reason a few moments earlier, heard the car and her husband's voice, and went quickly toward the door to inquire where he was bound. She stepped into the open doorway just as Roberta was in the act of getting into the car, and at the very instant when she used her sweetly melodious voice in addressing Bing.

Katherine stepped swiftly back again out of sight.

Utter amazement is the only adequate manner in which to describe her sensations; not because Roberta happened to be at the lodge gate when Harvard was driving out, and that he should ask her to ride with him, but that Roberta should speak to him in a perfectly natural manner, inducing no surprise on his part that she used her voice (she who was supposed to be without voice) but precisely as if he had known from the beginning of things that she could talk.

Katherine walked very slowly on her return to the house. She had much to think about.

CHAPTER XXXIII

WHAT ROBERTA HAD TO TELL

Harvard did not speak again for some time after Roberta was seated beside him. He drove the car in silence, guiding it, at the first opportunity, out of the main highway into less frequented thorough-fares. After a time he slowed down until they made less than ten miles an hour.

"Mr. Harvard," Roberta began, "there is so much that I must tell to you, and so much also that I should leave unsaid for others to inform you about, that I shall ask you to hear me through to the end of what I have to say, with as little interruption as is possible."

"I will interrupt you, *señorita*," he replied, "only when a question that I regard as important seems necessary."

"In that case," she said, "I will begin by making a statement that will amaze you, perhaps, more than anything else I will have to say."

"The entire situation is sufficiently amazing," he replied. "But what is the statement you refer to?"

"This: the man whom you know as Conrad Belknap is my husband. I have been his wife ten years. I was married to him when I was seventeen. When I was nineteen—somewhat less than two years after our marriage—I left him, and hid myself away where I hoped he would never find me. It was not until nearly five years after that when he did find me. I was in the far West—in Idaho—teaching school; and I had secured a divorce from him three years before he discovered me."

"Then you are not his wife—unless you remarried. Did you?"

"No. I used the present tense in referring to the subject for the sake of directness and to be explicit. I have never been his wife since I left him more than eight years ago, but I have been more or less closely associated with him and his evil ways ever since he discovered me in Idaho between three and four years ago. He has compelled that—has forced me to do what I have done; to seem to condone his criminalities; to associate with crooks and criminals; to sometimes go the length of actual participation in his crookedness (or of seeming to do so)—he has compelled that much of complacence on my part by holding over me a threat which, until now, I have not had the courage to defy."

"One moment, please. Why 'until now'?"

"I will reply to that question ambiguously, and explain more fully when I get to it. Something happened Saturday night which was established to my satisfaction on Sunday, and which I became positively assured of only last night, that has made it both possible and logical for me to defy the man you know as Conrad Belknap."

"I see. You will explain that point later, you say. But you have twice used the expression, 'the man I know as Belknap.' Am I to understand that the person's right name is not Conrad Belknap?"

"Yes. His name is—"

"Wait! Is it Cranshaw Belding?"

"What? You know?" Roberta exclaimed.

"Yes. I know," Harvard returned quietly.

"While I was in Idaho," Roberta continued slowly, after a moment's contemplation of Harvard's face, "I met, and learned to love, and was loved, by another man. I had already secured my divorce, so there was no obstacle of that character to our marriage. But, there were two obstacles—serious ones, both—nevertheless. One of them was occasioned by his point of view; the other one was by my own. He was living under a cloud, in disguise, and was known by a name that was not his own; and there were many reasons beside the actual cloud to which I have referred why he should not resume his own name and seek to prove—as he believed he could do—his innocence of the act which had been charged to him. He would not ask me to be his wife until he could stand clear before the world, clothed in his right name. But, Mr. Harvard, even so, I would have prevailed upon him, and we would have fought out our battles side by side but for the one great and insurmountable objection that *I* had.

"It was this: I knew that if Cranshaw Belding should find me, and know that I had married another man, he would kill that other man, or have him murdered without compunction. I knew Cranshaw Belding better than he knew himself. I knew that my marriage to another would be the death-warrant of that other. And now, Mr. Harvard, I have another surprise for you. The man who I would have married in Idaho bore the name (not his family name, remember) of Bruce Brainard."

"Bruce Brainard? Carruthers? The Se—" He stopped.

"Yes," Roberta calmly replied. "The secret service operative who is called Bruce Brainard, whom you have received in your home at the solicitation of your friend, Morton Saulsbury, under the name of Daniel Carruthers, and whose real identity I know as well as I know yours, is the man I love, and who loves me; is the man who has been wrongly charged, in the past, with a crime with which he had nothing to do; is the man whose battles I have helped to fight, and who has helped me to fight mine; is the man of all others whom I have ever known who is the soul of honor and upright manhood."

Harvard drove on in silence for a time. Presently:

"Have I permission to mention you to him?" Bing asked.

"Yes. I want you to do so, please."

"Did you know that he was coming to Myquest before he actually appeared?"

"He told me Saturday night that Mr. Saulsbury would bring him to call Sunday to ask you to receive him the following day, under another name, as a guest. He also told me that his chief was to arrive at Mr. Saulsbury's home Sunday night at twelve o'clock, and that he had decided to tell the entire story of his life to his chief, in the presence of Mr. Saulsbury. Last night I met him again by appointment after midnight. He told me then that his chief had merely chuckled when he heard Mr. Brainard's story, and had replied: 'Why, Brainy'—that is what he is called by his intimates in the service—'I have known the truth about those matters two years; ever since six months after you became one of us, in fact. It is part of my duty to know, thoroughly, the men who work for me. The man who was guilty of the things you were accused of has been in the federal prison at Atlanta more than a year. You are like some doctors that I have heard about—entirely efficient when another is ill, but absolutely inefficient when they get sick themselves. You aren't worth your salt when it comes to doctoring yourself.' Then he added: 'I have not mentioned this to you because I preferred to let you tell me about it yourself in your own good time after you had screwed up the necessary moral courage to do it.'"

"*Señorita*—I will continue to address you so—are you willing to tell me who Bruce Brainard really is?"

"No, please. That is one of the subjects that I referred to in the beginning when I told you that there are things which I must leave unsaid, for others to inform you about."

"Brainard himself, or others?"

"Brainard himself and others."

"Why did you pretend to be voiceless when you came to My-quest?"

"Because I had spoken with Mrs. Harvard over the telephone, and did not know until she greeted me that day that she was the person with whom I had talked."

"Wait. Was your talk with her that you refer to in the middle of the night?"

"Yes. Before I was summoned to come to you as a pianiste."

"Well, well," Harvard said, under his breath, recalling the disturbance he had felt because of his knowledge that Katherine had used the telephone one midnight and another night. "You talked with her more than once, didn't you?"

"Twice; both times after twelve at night."

"Correct. I'm glad you told me that."

"C. B. planned my coming to Myquest," she said. "I did not want to come—I had my own reasons for not wanting to do so—but he made me do it."

"He has made a catspaw of you."

"Literally that, Mr. Harvard."

"Tell me—for you must know—why Belknap elected to visit Myquest at all."

"I can't tell you that because I do not know."

"Is that statement literally true, *señorita*?"

"It is literally true, Mr. Harvard. I thought I knew, at the beginning, but I was mistaken. I have conjectured about it since, only to find myself again mistaken. His ways are past finding out. He is an accomplished scoundrel who compels others to do his bidding. Beyond cheating at cards, he considers himself above actual outlawry; he forces others to commit his crimes for him. If he should determine to rob your bank in New York, he would, himself, be a thousand miles away when it was done. If he should attempt to blackmail you, his own hand would not be visible in the consummation of it. If he sought Mme. Savage's jewels, he might locate them, but he would take no part in securing them. If he desired the death of Bruce Brainard, the murder would be committed, but there would be nothing to connect him with the crime. I can conjecture a score of reasons why he is at Myquest, and yet not hit upon the right one."

"That reminds me," Harvard said quickly. "Did you know that he is no longer at Myquest?"

"No," she replied calmly; "but I suspected that he was making ready to disappear, because of his defiance of Mr. Brainard, at the boat-house, last evening. Doubtless you have been told about that."

"Yes; Carruthers—that is, Brainard—told me."

"I ought to warn you, Mr. Harvard, that C. B. is more dangerous when absent than when present. If he has gone, as you say, he has not gone far. Rest assured that he is making preparations for the final coup that brought him here."

"H-m! Perhaps there is something in what you say. It is in line with Brainard's assertions. Will you tell me now why you dropped that acrostic warning to him from your balcony?"

"Certainly. I did it wholly on my own account, to put an obstacle in the way of his seeking conversations with me. I neither knew that we were watched nor cared if we were, but I did wish to startle him into leaving me alone."

"I see. Can you tell me anything about that attempted burglary the other night?"

"I can only guess as to that, but I think it will be a good guess."

"Let me hear what it is, then."

"I have told you that he has underlings who do his dirty work for him. My guess is this: that he has promised them some pickings from the plate and jewels and other valuables to be obtained in your home, and that one of their number, who is also a leader, and jealous of C. B., has worked upon their impatience of restraint, and prevailed upon them not to await his pleasure. It is unimportant. Nothing happened. What did happen could have had no connection with the actual reason for C. B.'s presence."

"Here is another point," Harvard said, after a moment of thought. "Cranshaw Belding is the name of the man whom Brainard is actually seeking. The department he serves has been held at bay because there was no proof of connection between Belknap and Belding. Yet for more than ten years you have known that the two were identical; and for half that time, at least, Brainard has known it. Why, then—"

"Please wait. I know what you would ask. Mr. Brainard's unsupported testimony would not be proof of the fact; my additional testimony would be regarded as biased and insufficient. C. B. would have slipped out of the law's grasp. More; Mr. Brainard has not been willing that my association with C. B. should be disclosed. He has insisted that other means could and would be found to establish the identities."

There was silence after that which endured for many minutes. Then Harvard, with a measure of restraint in his voice, said:

"I must ask you something more in regard to Belknap's possible motive, or motives, for coming to Myquest."

"Please don't, Mr. Harvard. Ask Mr. Brainard, if you will. His opinion—and it would be merely an opinion—is vastly better than mine."

"Very well, then. But I shall ask one certain thing of you, nevertheless."

"Yes?"

"It is that when we return, or as soon thereafter as possible, you will relate to Mrs. Harvard precisely what you have told to me; and that you will tell her that you have told me. Will you promise me to do that?"

"Yes."

"Thank you. I wish to discuss the subject with her, but I prefer that you should tell your story to her first."

CHAPTER XXXIV

THE DEVOTION OF JULIUS

When Bing and Roberta got back, luncheon had just been announced, and the guests were already assembling for the midday meal. Belknap's absence had not been generally noticed until then.

After it there was some discussion of the subject, and Harvard—considerably to Katherine's astonishment—allayed the curiosity of all by saying casually:

"Mr. Belknap was called away suddenly in the night. He took only a bag with him, so it is not unlikely that he will return at almost any time."

Katherine, watching her opportunity, withdrew from the group on the veranda silently and unnoticed.

She had determined that she would not visit Belknap at the Nest before the day to follow, which would have given him from twenty-four to thirty-six hours to accustom himself to the fact that he was a prisoner; but there was one subject which filled her with impatience of restraint of any sort, and she was eager to question the man. The subject was her brother Roderick.

"Why wait?" she asked herself as she stepped backward through an open window and glided swiftly away. "No matter how angry he may be at finding himself helpless, I need have no fear of him there. I will be amply protected by a hundred devices that he is ignorant of."

So she did not seek her room.

She passed through the house and left it at the rear, and she followed the longest route that she could have taken to bring her to the Nest.

Nevertheless, as she approached it at last, through the wood, and when she was nearly to the point where she manipulated the mechanism of the first stairs, she came, quite unexpectedly, upon

Black Julius, who had been leaning his back against a tree, but who started forward eagerly as she drew near.

"Why, what are you doing here, Julius?" she asked him quickly.

"I was waitin' fo' you, Mis' Kitten," was the astonishing reply, given with the freedom of his class when devotion to their "home-folks" is the incentive.

"Waiting for me? Here?" his mistress demanded with a show of impatience.

"Yes, Mis' Kitten; waitin' just the same as I uster wait, when you was a little wee mite of a girl, only so high, every time that I thought you had somethin' on youah mind that you'd like to tell Julius about. I knew that you'd come along past heah sooner 'r later, an'—an' you mustn't be mad at me, Mis' Kitten, please—I reckoned that mebby you'd let me help."

Poor Julius was terribly disturbed. He had passed the last half of the preceding night, and all of that day thus far, in a state of mental torture. Particularly had he suffered since the revelations at the conference in Harvard's den, and at the risk of mortally offending his beloved mistress, he had made up his mind to speak.

"You must tell me, quite plainly, what you are talking about, Julius," Katherine said.

"Mis' Kitten, I suspect mebby you'll never fo'give me, but I was watchin' that Belknap white trash last night. I'd been watchin' him all day, too. I had seen enough to know that he was crooked. I suspected that he was a thief. But it don't make any difference what he was or is, I was watchin', and I knew when he left the house. Then I lost sight of him fo' a while, but I found him again, hidin' out heah behind a tree, an' waitin' fo' somebody. I suspected that the somebody was another white trash like himself, an' that mebby they was goin' to rob the house; but I saw you meet him—please, please fo'give Black Julius, Mis' Kitten—an' I saw you lead him away, goin' toward the Nest. But I couldn't believe that you would take him there, where nobody but youah own self has ever been—an' I didn't believe it till last night, when I found that—that—Oh, Mis' Kitten, there is something else that I found out last night, too, that I jes' must tell you about as soon as I get through with this."

Katherine, with her eyes steadily upon the black, listened without motion or expression, too greatly astonished and too profoundly moved to speak before she had heard all that Julius had to tell.

"I didn't believe that you had taken that man to the Nest last night until I found out that there is a lot of men hangin' around Myquest to gobble him up if he tries to get away; and then I knew that you must have done it. And I knew that you would be going there sometime to-day to see him again; so I waited right heah."

"Why? To tell me that you had been spying upon your mistress?" Katherine asked coldly.

"Mis' Kitten, I ain't been spyin' on you; I've been spyin' on him, and I just happened to see you. And I waited because I wanted to ask you if you please, please, would let ole Black Julius help you in whatever it is that you're doin'."

There was suspicious moisture in Katherine's eyes as she took a step forward and rested one hand on Julius's arm.

She understood the depth of his devotion. She knew, without asking, that he had told nobody of what he had seen.

"Yes, Julius," she said softly, "I will let you help me. I am glad that you saw, and that you found the courage to speak. You shall help me—but not just now. Go to your cottage and wait there for me. Sometime this afternoon, or evening, I will seek you, and then I will tell you what you can do. Wait, Julius!" as he started away obediently. "What was the 'something else' that you found out about last night which you 'just must tell me about'?"

"Mis' Kitten, it is something that's mighty important; but—but—will you please wait till you come to the cabin to see me, an' let me tell you then? Please?"

Katherine nodded, and smiled, and passed on. Julius stood quite still, watching after her; and as he watched he murmured to himself softly:

"Bless her sweet heart! I wonder what she'll say when I tell her that Mister Roddie is right heah at Myquest, without her knowin' a word about it?"

When Katherine stepped upon the threshold of the door that had mechanically opened to admit her to the Nest, she saw Belknap standing beside the big oak table, with one hand resting lightly upon it, regarding her with a half-quizzical smile which, for once, was without its wonted wolfishness of expression.

Between them, close to the open door, yawned an oblong hole in the floor—as she had warned him might happen—which was silently filled while she waited, although he could not discover any act of hers that operated the mechanism of closing it.

When she passed inside, the door closed automatically behind her. As soon as that happened, Belknap spoke.

"Please wait a moment where you are, Mrs. Harvard," he said. "I want to ask you a question."

"Yes?" she replied, pausing.

208

"What is there to prevent me from leaping forward, now, upon you, and seizing you, if I were so disposed?"

"Tell me first why you ask the question; then—perhaps—I will reply to it," she answered him.

"I ask it because I have discovered that I am a prisoner here; that I cannot get out of this house save at your own good pleasure—unless I seize you and compel you to let me out. What is there to prevent me from doing that very thing? For if I should seize you, I could make you do it. You know that."

"Are you very curious about the answer to your first question?" she asked, and gave him an inscrutable smile.

"Yes."

"There is nothing to prevent you from attempting it, Mr. Belknap. There is something to keep you from accomplishing it. If you doubt me, try it. I am here; you are there—at a distance of about three yards. Spring, if you like; seize me, if you can. If you succeed—if you can get close enough to me to touch me with the ends of your fingers, I will promise to let you out of this house whenever you have the desire to go, day or night. Try it," she repeated, mockingly.

"By Jove!" he exclaimed, "I have the will to try it."

"Do so; only, be warned. You will sincerely regret the act."

For a moment he regarded her steadily, and she realized that he was actually on the point of making the attempt. But he hesitated; and hesitating, surrendered.

"You win," he said, and grinned, as if it was an actual pleasure to him to be bested. "I don't know whether you are bluffing or not. If you are, you're the champion bluffer of the continent. Anyhow, I won't call you this time."

"Thank you," she replied. "Now, will you be so good as to seat yourself in the armchair behind you? When you have done that I will pass around to the chair at the opposite side of the table."

"Huh!" he exclaimed, half jestingly. "How do I know that it isn't a trick-chair, and that it will fly through the ceiling or disappear through the floor the minute I touch it?"

"You don't know; that is the crux of all the mysteries of this house. You don't know them. I do."

"Mrs. Harvard," he said, "you're a wonder!" and he dropped upon the chair.

Katherine passed quickly to the opposite side of the table.

She pulled open a drawer in it, and closed it again. She moved some of the magazines and books that were upon it. She dropped her handkerchief to the floor and stooped to regain it, and as she straightened again she heard a sharp and angry expletive from Belknap; it was not really an oath, although very near to one.

Katherine was smiling when her eyes encountered Belknap's angry gaze.

"You are not uncomfortable, are you?" she asked. "That steel arm doesn't pinch too closely, does it? You see, I thought it wise to teach you a lesson. One of my workmen procured me the model of that chair in the ancient city of Nuremberg. History will tell you of others, somewhat like it, although this one is an improvement."

Katherine, in one of her motions at or behind the table, had loosened the mechanism of the Nuremburg chair. A steel arm which ordinarily looked to be merely a part of its back, had been released, and had swung around to the front, a foot above Belknap's waist, and had locked itself fast, with the result that while he was entirely free to use his arms and hands and legs and feet, he could not rise from the chair, or get out of it; and he had already made the discovery that he could not, for he had tried.

"Will you be good if I will release you?" she asked him.

"You'd better wait a little till I recover my temper," he said with a grim smile.

"When you wish to be freed, tell me."

"You should have lived in the middle ages," he said, half crossly, half admiringly.

"No; I would not then have had the aid of electricity and hydraulics."

"Well anyhow—"

"There is something that I want to ask you about, Mr. Belknap. Perhaps I had better keep you where you are until I do that. You may be more amenable."

"Possibly. What is it?"

"I want you to tell me everything that you know about my brother Roderick. That is why I have come to you to-day. Otherwise I should have left you entirely to yourself until to-morrow."

"H-m!" he said.

"Are you willing to tell me all that you can tell me?" she asked.

"I don't know, Mrs. Harvard. Possibly we can bargain about it."

"Bargain about it?" she asked.

"Exactly that," he rejoined.

"What is it that you would want me to do in return for such information as you can give me about my brother?"

Belknap hesitated a moment, in deep thought. Then he replied:

210

"To-day is Tuesday. I will want you, to-morrow night or the night following—and I will decide that point when I see you to-morrow—to come here to me, say a little before two o'clock in the morning. I will want you, then, to let me go outside. I will be prepared and ready to go as soon as you arrive. I will want you to remain here, waiting for me, until I return—which will be an hour; possibly two hours. If you will definitely agree to all of those stipulations, I will, right now, tell you all that I know about your brother."

"I wonder," she replied, musingly, "if you are in the habit of keeping your promises."

"No," he frankly admitted, "I am not. But I will keep that one."

"Would you also keep the other one—to return here within two hours?"

"I will do that, save in one event. You see, I am quite frank with you."

"You appear to be so."

"If that event occurs—and I believe it very likely that it will—I will not return; I will go elsewhere; disappear; will have ceased to annoy you by my presence at Myquest. Surely that would please you more than to have me back here, a burden on your hands."

She nodded without replying. He went on:

"If we agree to this bargain—if I do go outside to-morrow night or the one following, and have not returned by four o'clock, you will know that I will not come, and that you are well rid of me."

Katherine shook her head negatively.

"I don't think that I can agree to that, Mr. Belknap, even at the tempting price you offer—information about my brother," she said.

"Why not?"

"There are several reasons. For one thing, I am beginning to suspect that your knowledge of him doesn't amount to much; I have begun to doubt if there is anything that you can tell me about him that is worth while. Still, I might nevertheless bargain with you, and hear what you might tell me, if it were not for another consideration."

"Tell me what that one is," he asked her. "But first, let me out of this chair."

She nodded, and passed around behind him. Although he turned his head and tried his best to observe her every act, he had not the least notion when and how she again worked the mechanism of the Nuremberg chair. But the steel arm that held him fast was released; it flew back to its former position as if it were one of the braces at

211

the back of the chair, and as he got upon his feet, Katherine returned quickly to the opposite side of the table. From there she replied to his last question.

"The other consideration—and I have decided that I cannot believe any promise that you might make in the negative about it—is this: the use you would make of your two hours of liberty. You might seek my father and mother, and betray to them the fact that my brother lives—although I do not really think you would do that; you would have no good reason for doing it. You might help yourself to all the jewels of my guests while I waited here and passively permitted it. You might—"

"One moment, please," he interrupted.

"Well?"

"If I will tell you exactly what brought me to Myquest at this time, exactly why I am here at all—if I tell you precisely what my errand outside will be—will you give me your word (I know that you will keep it if you make the promise) that you will not speak or write or otherwise convey any warning whatsoever of my intention?"

"I will consider it," she replied with a slow smile. "You had better act upon that much of a promise from me, for otherwise you cannot get out until I choose to let you out."

"All right," he answered instantly. "I'll tell you."

CHAPTER XXXV

BELKNAP SHOWS HIS HAND

"Shall I tell you about your brother first?" Belknap began, "or shall I—"

"Yes, please," Katherine interrupted him.

With pronounced deliberation he selected another chair and drew it forward. Smilingly he seated himself upon it. In a mocking tone he said:

"But, no. That will keep. I perceive that you are more concerned with that subject than by the fear that some of your guests might be robbed. It is quite natural, I agree. But it is good bargaining when one holds back the highest price for the last bid."

Katherine shrugged, and did not reply.

"Now, listen, please," he went on, "for what I will tell you is the truth—and I have the feeling that you will believe me, in part, if not in whole."

Katherine made no response, even in gesture.

"I am a man of strange complexities," he continued. "Frequently the variety of them amazes me. I am a many-sided individual. I was born without compassion, without morals, and without physical fear. Also I inherited (I assume that I did) a passion for precious stones. As I grew older I began to make a collection of rare and priceless gems. I became, literally, a collector—in other words, a madman on that subject.

"I made one rule for myself when I began the collection, which, by the way now contains the pick and choice of the world. That rule was that I would never pay one dollar for a gem or jewel that I coveted."

"Do you mean," Katherine asked, "that unless the jewel came into your possession by theft it would have no value in your eyes?"

"Precisely, Mrs. Harvard." He bent forward in the chair and fixed his eyes upon hers. "Have you ever heard of a certain wonderful stone—two jewels in one, in fact—that is called 'Nadja's Eye'?" he asked her with an intensity of utterance that assured her of his entire earnestness.

"Yes," she replied calmly, although he could see that she gave an involuntary shudder. "I have seen it. It is a baleful thing."

"It is a ruby of the size and shape of a pigeon's egg," he went on, as if he had not heard her; only she was presently to know that he did. "Imbedded in the center of it is an emerald of two or three karats. It is claimed that nature could not have put it there; that the two jewels are too foreign to each other for such a thing to have resulted from natural causes; that the art of some ancient and skilled lapidary must have accomplished it. But the fact remains that it is there. Very well." He caught his breath sharply and was very pale. "You say that you have seen it?"

Katherine nodded.

"Then, in that case, you know that it is here, at Myquest, now, don't you?"

"No," she replied. "In fact I am almost sure that it is not."

"You know that it is the property of Mme. Savage, don't you?"

"Yes; but I also know that she keeps it in one of her safe deposit—"

"You are mistaken, Mrs. Harvard. She does not. It is never out of her possession. She carries it with her wherever she goes—just as she carries always with her that other rare gem that she owns which has so often been described in the newspapers. But for that, barring its value in cash, I would not give a flip of a coin."

He got up from the chair and began to pace the floor at the opposite side of the table from Katherine.

"Let me tell you, Lady Kate, that I would barter my soul—if I have one—to possess the 'Eye of Nadja,' as it is named in Hindustanee. Twice I have had her home in the city searched by men in my pay, and under my direction. Twice I have engaged women-crooks to drug Mme. Savage and search her. For more than a year I have kept at least one and sometimes three women in her home, as maids, to spy out the hiding place of the wonderful jewel. They have seen it, but they have never been able to discover where and how she hides it; but they have been able to convince me that she takes it with her wherever she goes, and that it is never far out of her reach. So I knew, when I discovered that she was coming down here, that she would bring it with her.

214

"Very well. I came to Myquest primarily to get the 'Eye of Nadja.' I believed that because of the threat I could hold over you, I could compel you to aid me in securing it; but I speedily changed my mind about that. But I came here also to keep an eye on the *Madame*—to be close to her where I could watch her—to study her, and to determine because of that close observation, what her method and means of concealing the jewel might be. I am an expert at that sort of thing. It has been a life-study. If a man who carries a large sum of money in one of his pockets is under my observation ten minutes, I can tell you in which pocket he carries it. It is a science that I have mastered.

"I know now, therefore—I am convinced that I know—where to find the 'Eye of Nadja'; I know what Mme. Savage does with it when she stays at a place like Myquest. I am sure that I can get my hands on it, and get away with it within two hours after you let me out of this place to-morrow night, or the following one.

"There you have it, Lady Kate—and I have your promise that you will impart no warning whatever of my purpose."

"Will you tell me," Katherine asked coolly, "why you have waited until now to take the jewel, if you have been so sure of how to take it?"

"I waited because I had to wait—because I was stupid—because it was not until you had succeeded in locking me fast in this chalet of yours, where I have been in absolute solitude, that I have had the sense and the wit to apply all of my brain power to the problem. It was not until after I was imprisoned by you that I was able to deduce the truth from my study of Mme. Savage."

"Are you satisfied, now, that you know how and where to find the ruby?"

"I am sure of it."

"If I should consent to grant you the two hours' liberty you desire, would the theft of the 'Eye of Nadja' be all that you would attempt—whether you succeed in securing it or should not succeed?"

"Yes. I will promise that—and I will keep the promise."

"I place little value upon your promises, Mr. Belknap; you have assured me that they are of little value."

"I will keep that one."

"Does Mme. Savage conceal the jewel on her person?"

"No. I don't think that she ever does that; nor in the room where she sleeps. I am so certain about that that I am willing to agree not to go to her room when you set me at liberty, unless you are considering the project of conveying some sort of message to her about it."

"I have already given my promise as to that, Mr. Belknap—in case I consent to your proposition. I will not even mention the name of the jewel to anybody in that case."

"Well, then?"

"Is your covetousness of 'Nadja's Eye' your only object in being at Myquest?"

"Yes."

"What about card-cheating, and your suggestions of blackmail?"

"Merely by-products, Lady Kate. Pastime."

"I can believe that. What is Señorita Cervantez to you?"

Belknap was startled by the sudden question, and showed it; but he replied without hesitation:

"She is—no; she was, once, my wife."

"Your—wife?"

It was Katherine's turn to be startled.

"Yes," he replied. "We were married ten years ago, when she was seventeen and I was twenty-four. She left me within two years—when she found out that I was a crook—and secured a divorce. I am telling you the literal truth, Lady Kate. It is my one weakness that she is the only woman I have ever—er—cared for. I succeeded in finding her again something less than three years ago. She had learned to love another man in the meantime—chiefly, I suppose, because she had never loved me, really. She had not married the other man, notwithstanding her divorce from me, because she believed that I would have procured his death if she did so—as I unquestionably would have done—as, without much doubt, I would have done anyhow, if I had been able, ever, to find him; to be sure of his identity. I have only known of him; I have never, knowingly, seen him. All that I know about him is his name—his real name, which he does not use."

"But—" Katherine hesitated, and then went on: "but she returned to you!"

"She returned with me; not to me, Mrs. Harvard. A moment ago I mentioned my one weakness. I was not accurate; I have another which I have had occasion, many times, greatly to regret. It is, doubtless inherited from my mother's side. I carry about with me, always, a compelling respect and sentinel-like regard for good womanhood. To my shame, in the light of my other characteristics, I admit it. I forced Roberta—that is her given name—to become a part of my life, but it was always an extrinsic part. I have made her condone my criminalities—even to play a part in them, at times. But she is as good and pure as I am—the opposite."

"But—"

"I have controlled her, up to a certain point, by holding a threat over her—and she has dreaded its fulfillment more than she has feared anything else in the world."

"A threat! You coerced her by the same method that you used to try to work your will with me."

"Precisely; and my threat against her had to do with the same person as with you."

"Why, what can you mean by that statement, Mr. Belknap?" Katherine demanded, puzzled.

"Lady Kate," Belknap said, evenly, "the name of the man whose life I threatened in Roberta's case, and whose liberty I threatened in yours, is the same. His name is Roderick Maxwilton."

CHAPTER XXXVI

THE JINEE ON GUARD

Katherine started to her feet, white to the lips.

"My brother!" she cried out, almost with a gasp.

"Yes, Mrs. Harvard; your brother," Belknap responded coolly.

"Where is he now?" she demanded.

"I don't know."

"You have admitted that you do not even know him by sight; that you would not recognize him if you should see him."

"I would not."

"Then your threats in regard to him were idle ones."

"In part—yes. I could have searched him out long ago if I had determined upon doing it. If I had done it, I would have killed him, or have had him killed. I tell you that frankly. I did not do it, or attempt it, simply because I knew that I would cut off the limb between me and the tree if I did so. If I had injured him, Roberta would have killed me—and she possessed the means to do it. She might even have gone to the length of sacrificing herself to me in order to secure the needed opportunity, had it become necessary. I have determined upon doing it a thousand times, and as often changed my mind. I have hoped against hope that Roderick Maxwilton might die a natural death; for, in that case, upon my promise to abandon my manner of life, Roberta might have turned to me again. Since an interview I had with her recently, in her room, here at Myquest, I have given up even that thought. He was here—your brother—that same night. She met him outside—"

"Then—I saw him!" Katherine exclaimed in a half whisper.

"Possibly," he rejoined coolly. "But you would not recognize him. He possesses a hundred disguises—so she has assured me, and I believe her. If I did not know the impossibility of his entering the secret service because of the crime that is charged against him (and

218

which I happen to know he did not commit) I would have thought that Carruthers, whom you heard me defy, might be he. But that is absurd. He could not get into that department without a clean record."

Belknap had been pacing up and down and stopping and pacing again. Katherine had resumed her chair. Now, she sat with clasped hands, staring straight in front of her. He noticed the fact and passed around to her side of the table until he stood beside her chair, within reach of her.

"You see," he said, "that I could seize you now, if I were so disposed. You have been off your guard."

She raised her eyes to his and smiled wanly, without changing her attitude.

"Possibly," she said; "but I do not think that you will attempt it."

He shrugged, with a measure of contempt in the gesture. He had taken that position with that very purpose in view in case she should deny his last plea—the one he was about to make. If she guessed his purpose, she gave no sign of the fact.

"Mrs. Harvard," he said, "I have thrown down every card I possess, face up, on the table. I would commit murder a dozen times over, with no regard for the victim, if by doing so I could possess the 'Eye of Nadja.' I would sacrifice Roberta for it; and I cannot make a stronger statement than that. Are you giving heed to what I say?"

"Yes. I might follow you better if you should stand a little farther away—say against the table behind you. You can as easily seize me from there as where you are, if you have the mind to do it."

He moved backward a step until his weight was against the big table, and stood with his hands resting lightly upon it at the sides. He said:

"The jewel is of no value to anybody save a collector. If it were stolen, nobody would dare to buy it. Mme. Savage does not appreciate it. It is a great care to her, and there is not a doubt that she would be glad to be well rid of it. If you will let me out of here to-morrow night at two, or the night following, at the same hour—I will decide upon which one to employ—and if you will, yourself, remain here, waiting, until four o'clock, I will promise you this: whether I succeed in obtaining the jewel or not, I will, after the attempt to get it, go away. I will disappear. I will not give up hope of securing the ruby, sometime, but I will never cross your path again—nor Roberta's. Nor you brother's. I will leave them free to marry when

219

they will. I will not put so much as a straw in their way, before or after it. I will do more. This: I will, within a few days, send you documentary proof of your brother's entire innocence of the charges that lie against him with the government. Such is the price that I am willing and eager to pay for the opportunity I seek. Will you pay it?"

"Wait a moment," she replied in a low tone, as if deeply impressed by what he had said; and as she spoke, she got slowly upon her feet.

Her entire manner was if she were utterly absorbed in the contemplation of his offer—and, as had been the case with her a moment before, Belknap was this time taken off his guard.

She arose directly in front of her chair and stood there with bowed head during a full minute while he watched her narrowly and expectantly.

His whole mind was centered upon the possession of the coveted ruby.

After another moment she moved slowly nearer to him, until, in fact, she stood nearly beside him; within, say, twice the length of his arm.

Then he heard a sharp click. He saw her leap backward, away from the table. The table itself dropped like a plummet through the floor, and, because he was leaning against it, carried him with it. An instant later he found himself in utter darkness, for the aperture above the table, in the floor over his head, had closed.

He cursed aloud; and then he ceased to swear. The floor above him slid open again.

"The jinee was on guard, Mr. Belknap," he heard Katherine say. "Stand still and I will bring you back. Then I will leave you. But I will tell you now that I have decided to accept your proposition, and your promises. You shall have your opportunity—and I will keep to my promise in regard to it."

* * * * * * *

Katherine went straightway in search of Roberta, and not discovering her among the guests who were scattered about the grounds, sought her in her room. The door was quickly opened in response to her summons, and she stepped inside, closed the door behind her, and turned the key.

"I have come," she said abruptly, "to ask you about my brother Roderick. You may speak out; there is no longer any necessity for voicelessness. I have known, almost since the hour of your arrival, that you are Roberta of the telephone talks with me."

Roberta gasped. Katherine continued:

"I know still more—no matter how; for example, that you were once the wife of Conrad Belknap; and that you are now willing and eager to become my sister-in-law; but—"

"A moment, please, Mrs. Harvard," Roberta said quickly when Katherine hesitated because she was suddenly conscious of the severity of her tone, and realized that she had not intended that it should be so.

"Well?" Katherine questioned her.

"I have never been the wife of Conrad Belknap," Roberta replied in her natural voice, and smiling, "because, as far as I know, there is no such person. The right name of the man I married ten years ago, and whom you know as Conrad Belknap, is one that is remembered in the neighborhood of your Kentucky home. I had supposed that Mr. Harvard would mention it when he told you the rest of my story, although he did say that he intended not to talk with you about it until after I had done so."

"Mr. Harvard has not talked with me about you at all," Katherine said.

"Then, how—"

"No matter how. We will leave discussion of your personal connection with things that have been happening at Myquest until later. Just now I want you to tell me, and at once, how I can communicate with my brother. I know that you can tell me; I know that you must tell me. I know that you met him in the middle of Saturday night, under the box-elder by the lake. I saw you there together. I saw his face, afterward, and did not recognize it. I assume that he was disguised."

"Mrs. Harvard, I—"

"Please reply to my question. Where is my brother, and how can I communicate with him?"

"He is not far away, Kat—Mrs. Harvard. He is, in a sense, watching over you, even now; but—I beg you to believe me when I state positively that I am acting under his positive and imperative instructions when I reply to the first part of your question by saying that I cannot tell you exactly where he may be found, without first obtaining his consent. You would not have me break my solemn word to him?"

"No, but—"

"But you can communicate with him, if you will. I can get any message to him that you wish."

"Thank you," Katherine replied, somewhat coldly. "Please inform him that he must make himself known to me, and let me speak with him, alone, at once; before the dinner hour to-morrow, certainly. Can you do that? Can you communicate with him before you sleep to-night?"

"I think so. I will try. He—he loves you very dearly, I know. He has only thought that for the sake of all concerned you should not know of his nearness until—until he believed the hour to be propitious."

Katherine melted.

Suddenly—without warning of her intention—she opened her arms and folded them around Roberta, who stared back; or would have done so if she could, because of her surprise; for Katherine, quite unintentionally, but because of the intensity of her feelings, had thus far spoken, and preserved a demeanor, of hauteur, reserve, and coldness.

"I know part of your story, Roberta," Katherine said in a more kindly tone, while she held her in that close embrace. "You shall tell me the rest of it—your own side of it—another time. But, I know that you love Roderick; I know that you have not hesitated to make great sacrifices to protect him from your common enemy. More still, although I have been aware from the beginning that you were associated with Conrad Belknap in some inexplicable way, I have been drawn to you, I have believed in you, and I have grown to love you."

Thus, we will leave them together; for Roberta would not have it that the story she had to tell should wait.

Everything that she had told to Bingham Harvard she repeated to Katherine in a much more intimate way—and she added much to it, of a personal nature, which there had been neither time, inclination, nor necessity to relate to him.

Katherine, in all respects save one, gave confidence for confidence. She admitted that the knowledge she already possessed of Roberta's past had been told to her by Belknap, and she confessed that she had assisted him to make his escape. But she went no farther than that. She said nothing about the Nest, nor did she admit that she knew aught of Belknap's intentions or plans after his departure.

* * * * * * *

At the Nest, Belknap had not entirely lost his equilibrium when the table against which he leaned, and the floor under it, sank beneath him! but it had happened so suddenly, and with such entire unexpectedness, that he had been obliged to clutch the edge of the table madly with his fingers, and so to steady himself, in order to keep his upright position.

One thinks quickly under such circumstances, and his first thought had been that Katherine had but played upon his rapt eagerness concerning the jewel, in order to get the best of him and then to repudiate his offer—and him.

His amazement when she called down to him that she would accept his proposition and would keep to her promises in regard to it, was intense.

He would have replied to her if she had given him time; but at once the table, and the two or three feet of flooring around it, began to rise toward its former position, so he decided to wait until he was once more face to face with her. When, however, his head was again above the level of the floor, he saw that she had gone, that the doorway to the outside world was closed, and that he was again alone.

"What a woman!" he muttered for perhaps the hundredth time since he had been in the chalet; and then again, "What a woman!"

How fervently he wished that he knew the secrets of that mysterious house—or some of them at least. But he had already convinced himself of the utter fruitlessness of searching for them.

He had passed hours and hours at that task, with absolutely no result; the mysteries of the marvelous mechanisms concealed within the Swiss chalet, defied him.

"But," he told himself, "I have her promise; and she will keep it."

He selected a book and tried to read, but having so recently dwelt at length, and in words, upon his passionate longing to possess the "Eye of Nadja," it absorbed him, and he could not take his mind off of it.

With a sudden loss of temper (which he sometimes indulged, when alone) he flung the book angrily from him without regard to where, or what, it might strike; and at the moment he bent forward and buried his face in his hands to think.

When, ten minutes later, he lifted his head, he uttered a sharp exclamation of astonishment, and sprang to his feet and stared.

Straight ahead of him, at the far end of the big room, and just above a platform that extended at the top of a short flight of steps, the afternoon sun was streaming into the chalet through a wide expanse of plate-glass window from over which the steel shutters had been magically withdrawn.

He knew what had happened. The book that he had thrown—and he had no idea where it had struck—had hit against and operated the mechanism of that shutter.

With an exclamation of joy he started toward the uncovered window.

CHAPTER XXXVII

THE WISDOM OF LADY KATE

The window out of which Belknap gazed when he had mounted to the platform, overlooked the lake, and was directly above it—in fact, projected over it. Beneath him to the surface of the water he judged the distance to be all of eighty feet or more.

The window, as it happened, was Katherine's favorite eery; she loved to sit there to read and enjoy the view.

But it was not the view that Belknap appreciated just then.

The entire shore of the lake was spread out before him. Across it he could see the boat- and bath-houses. Beyond them, through vistas which have already been described, the great house, much of its veranda, and many of the pathways that approached it, were visible.

While he looked he saw Carruthers step out upon the platform of the boat-house, and behind him came Harvard; and he also saw that Carruthers, as if he had already observed the unshuttered window of the chalet, made some remark to Harvard which called his attention to it.

Belknap dodged, and he harbored just a little doubt in his mind about having made the move quick enough to escape the sharp eyes of the secret service operative.

"Damn!" he exclaimed, as he descended the few steps to the floor of the chalet.

He heartily wished that his chance shot with the book had not found the mark it had—or that he had watched the flight of the book when he cast it from him so that he might search more understandingly for the hidden spring.

But, regrets were unavailing; they were bitter regrets, too, for he began to feel quite sure that he had been seen at the window—seen anyhow, whether he had been recognized or not.

Presently, after deep thought, he told himself, aloud:

"If a book, thrown in anger, can find out one of the secrets of this infernal nest of mysteries, I, with brains and forethought and system, and with care and coolness, must surely be able to find others."

He decided then and there that he would begin the search anew, and that he would not abandon it until he had made discoveries, or was interrupted; and he began by drawing plans of the interior of the room on paper; a plan of the floor, others for each wall-surface by which it was inclosed, and still another one to show the position of each article of furniture.

Those he divided into squares, and each one of the squares into smaller ones; and he systematically numbered each of the large squares, and lettered the small ones inside of them.

That done, he began the search, checking off each lettered square as he progressed, and obliterating each large square as he finished with it.

"It's some task," he told himself, "and it will take time; but I believe that it is bound to win."

Whether it did or not, remains to be seen.

* * * * * * *

Carruthers did catch a glimpse of a face at the window of the chalet, but he was unable to recognize it.

Like the other guests at Myquest, he was under the impression that the Swiss chalet at the top of the bluff was tightly closed and was rarely, if ever, used.

But he was a secret service operative, and he was hot on the trail of a man who, as he confidently believed, was in hiding somewhere near. The uncovered window—which he remembered had been shuttered closely the last time he saw it—interested him instantly.

"What better place," he asked himself, "could Belding find in which to hide, always provided that he could get inside of it." Carruthers had already investigated the surroundings and approaches and the exterior of the chalet sufficiently to convince him that it was practically inaccessible.

He had been discussing with Harvard the possible hiding places that Belknap might have found upon the estate, when he made the discovery of the open window. At once he called Bing's attention to it. But he said nothing about his momentary glimpse of a face beyond it.

226

"I was under the impression that the little building on the bluff was not in use," was what he said. "Somebody has been there since this morning, however. Look."

Harvard was already looking while Carruthers talked. He was also surprised to see the unshuttered window, for Katherine was always careful to keep everything tightly closed at the Nest, whenever there were guests at Myquest; and Katherine, as he happened to know, was not then at the Nest. He had seen her enter the house when she went to Roberta's room.

"Wait a moment. I will be back presently," he said to Carruthers; and he went into the boat-house, to one of the house-telephone extensions, where he asked that Mrs. Harvard be summoned to the phone at once.

Katherine had just left Roberta and gone into her own room when the telephone rang.

"Have you been at the Nest this afternoon?" Bing asked her.

"Yes. Why do you ask?" she answered.

"You have left a window uncovered. It is attracting attention. Carruthers has just seen it. You had better go back and close it. That is all," he told her, and hung up.

Katherine was just a trifle pale when she replaced the receiver.

She knew that she had not opened the shutter, and that therefore Belknap must have discovered the spring that operated it—wherefore, if he could do that much, it was possible, even probable, that he could accomplish still more.

Her first impulse was to return to the Nest at once; but she considered.

"Why do that?" she asked herself. "The window has already been seen. To close it again now would be to add more to the suspicion, if any, that has already been suggested."

Then it was that she made another decision: she would go back to Belknap in the evening, as soon as she could escape from her guests after dinner, and she would tell him that he should have his liberty to undertake the theft of the "Eye of Nadja"—and she smiled at the thought—that same night or not at all.

The decision made, she lost no time in seeking Mme. Savage, who, she knew, would have lately awakened from her daily afternoon nap.

Katherine had promised Belknap that she would give no sort of warning to anybody of his intentions, and also that she would not mention or write the name of the coveted jewel. But she formed a plan, nevertheless, before she gave her consent to his wild scheme,

227

by which she believed she could defeat him at his own game, and prevent the theft.

"*Madame*," she said, when she had been admitted to the old lady's room, "I read a story long ago that was called 'The Jewel Worshiper.' It has given me an idea for the entertainment of my guests. I want to reproduce the scheme of that story in a tableau, and I can do so if you will help me out—you, and Miriam Saulsbury, and two or three of the others. Will you do it?"

"Surely, my dear. What is it that you want?" *Madame* replied.

"I want your jewels—all of them. The most beautiful ones, and the rarest one you possess, particularly; and Mrs. Saulsbury's pear-shaped diamonds; and Betty Clancy's wonderful pearls; and—and all that I can get hold of."

"Why, of course. But what in the world are you going to do with them, my dear?"

"You won't tell?" Katherine asked, demurely.

"Certainly not."

"I will be the jewel-worshiper, myself. I will be seen in a cabinet that is lined with black velvet which will be ablaze with the jewels, on my knees, worshiping them. That is all I can tell you now. But I may have them?"

"Surely. Come and get them whenever you want them, dear."

"But I want them now. Let me see; there is the one you thought the burglars tried to get the other night; and there is—" She paused a moment, then added: "But I don't suppose you would care to let me use that one."

"Do you mean the—"

"Yes, yes," Katherine interrupted quickly. "We need not name it. It always gives me shudders whenever I think of it."

Mme. Savage laughed.

"Of course you can have that, too," she said. "Bend nearer, my dear, and let me whisper while I tell you where it is. You will be surprised, but I always hide it in outlandish places where nobody would ever think of looking for it. It is—" she whispered close to Katherine's ear—"inside of the scrubby old cane that I always carry when I go for a walk, and put away in the corner of the music-room behind the piano when I return. Bring the cane to me, dear, and I'll show you how to open it. What do you think of that for a hiding place? Eh, my dear?"

Katherine brought the cane hurriedly, with a large, round knob at its top.

Mme. Savage first loosened the ferrule of the cane by unscrewing it; then she turned it end for end and lifted off the knob which she opened by touching a spring at the bottom which had been concealed inside of the cane. From the hollow space she took an object that was wrapped in foil and tissue paper. That, she placed in Katherine's hand.

"There it is, dear," she said. "Take it. Keep it as long as you please, only be careful where you put it after you show it in the tableau. Stand the cane over there in the corner," she added as she readjusted it.

"Oh, no," Katherine replied, smiling. "I will put it back in the music-room where I found it."

CHAPTER XXXVIII

RODERICK AND JULIUS

Belknap's systematic effort to discover some of the secrets of the Nest was not without results. Many of the hidden buttons and concealed springs and levers, practicable screws, nail-heads, ornamental-work, and what-not of all descriptions, could not defy the inch-by-inch search for them that he made—and the very fact that Katherine delayed her visit to him after the discovery of the opened shutter afforded him opportunity. Also, he worked in haste, although thoroughly, fearing that the discovered window would bring her quickly to the Nest.

By the time that he was hungry, and felt the necessity of preparing something to eat, he had accomplished much—although it must be admitted that his discoveries did not take him as deeply into the mysteries of the strange house as he could have wished.

There were mechanisms that he sought which he could not find; and he found several that he had not sought. He was as much in the dark as ever concerning the openings in the floor, and the operation of the door of entrance; but he did know the secret of the Nuremberg chair.

He decided that, when she came to him again, if she were inclined to be fractious, as he expressed it to himself, he might induce her to sit upon the chair, or push her into it, and so catch her as he had been caught. Then—well, then he could make his own terms.

He was no wiser than before in regard to getting out of the house, unless, indeed, he should decide to smash the plate-glass observation window and make the leap of eighty feet or more to the water under it.

But that was a matter for future consideration—if it should become necessary.

Meantime, as soon as he had eaten, he returned to the search, hoping and believing that he would uncover more secrets before Katherine appeared.

* * * * * * *

Black Julius became more at ease after his talk with Katherine in the wood.

His discovery that she was not only cognizant of Belknap's escape from the house, but had actually given the man her personal assistance, had troubled him so profoundly that it had almost (though not quite) obliterated the immeasurable joy of another one (which had seemed unbelievable and impossible), that he had made that same night.

It was when he was brought face to face with Carruthers in Bingham Harvard's den at the time of the conference.

The instincts of the negro amounted to a sixth sense.

He might, from a little distance, have looked upon Carruthers's face, watched his motions, and otherwise have observed him, without interest; but, brought into actual contact with him, touching his hand, and thus the point where he could "feel" his presence, he had sensed rather than seen through the shell of disguise that Carruthers wore.

Black Julius's instinct was like the scent of a favorite dog. It knew.

He had "toted" Roderick Maxwilton, and petted him and played with him from the time he was born into the world, just as he had served Katherine; and he had been almost as devoted to him, until little Katherine came. His positive recognition of Roderick Maxwilton in the person of Carruthers of the secret service, was therefore instantaneous.

Nobody save Roderick himself had noticed the agitation of Julius at the time; but he had known—as he had also believed would be the case when they were brought face to face—that Julius recognized him.

Thus it happened that as soon as it was both possible and convenient, Roderick, otherwise Carruthers (and otherwise also, Brainard) went to Julius's cottage near the garage to see him and talk with him. That happened soon after his discovery of the unshuttered window of the chalet.

Julius did not return to his cottage at once to wait for Katherine, as she had directed. There were duties that he had to perform first,

231

and so it was a little more than an hour afterward when he entered it, and there discovered Roderick awaiting him.

Roderick (we will call him so for the purposes of this interview) left the chair whereon he had been seated and waiting, the instant Julius appeared.

For the moment he was the boy again; he was the lad, and Julius was the faithful servant of his house whom he loved and trusted. And to Black Julius the impulse was precisely the same, although reversed.

Roderick took a step forward and stretched out both hands. Julius grasped them with his own, and for a time the two were speechless before one another, and, oddly enough, it seemed as if Roderick was the more greatly moved of the two.

It was Julius who spoke first.

"Mr. Roddy! Mr. Roddy! Why, Mis-tuh Rod-dy, it don't seem mo'n the day befo' yesterday since I was totin' yo' 'roun' with these old han's uh mine; it suttinly don't, Mr. Roddy." Julius always lapsed into the soft dialect of his youth when he was greatly moved.

"Dear old Julius!" Roderick replied. "You knew me the moment you saw me last night, didn't you?"

"I suttinly did, Mr. Roddy."

"Then you never believed that I was dead and buried, did you?"

"I know'd you wasn't, suh. Mis' Kitten told me."

"But, Julius, even Mis' Kitten didn't know me. How was it that you did?"

"I dunno, suh. I reckon mebby I smelt you, jes' like a houn'-dog would do it. I didn't see no scar, or no growed-up man, when I looked at yo' las' night. I didn't see anything at all but jes' the little boy Roddy. Uhuh! 'Twouldn't made no difference about it, neither, if I hadn't been told that the scar wasn't real. If it had been real sure enough, I'd 'a' know'd you just the same."

He stopped, and when he spoke again his voice had a note of stern displeasure in it, as if he were, in reality, speaking to the lad of years agone, and chiding him.

"Why haven't you told Mis' Kitten about yourself, sir? Don't you know that she's been eatin' her poor little heart out for you all these yeahs? Why, sir, only just a little minute ago I was talkin' to her, and it was all I could do to keep myself from blurtin' it all out. Why ain't you done told her, Mr. Roddy, befo' now?"

"Never mind about that, Julius. I shall tell her very soon."

"Yes, sir."

"Now, Julius, I want to question you on another matter."

232

"Yes, sir." Julius was instantly on his guard, for he guessed what the next question might be, and he had no idea of betraying Katherine's confidence, even to her brother.

"That fellow Belknap must be hiding somewhere within the bounds of the estate," Roderick continued. "I know that he could not slip through the meshes of the net that I have spread for him, and escape. Therefore, he is somewhere near here. Now, you know the place probably as well as you know the old place at home, so I want you to think hard, and then tell me of all the possible hiding places near us that you can remember."

"Well, sir," Julius replied thoughtfully, and his face was like a mask, "I can't just say that I do know of a place where he could hide—an' keep hid. I suttinly don't."

"I have been searching, Julius, and my men have been searching, all day—all the time since Belknap disappeared. They have not been able to obtain a trace of the man."

"No, sir, I reckon they ain't."

"But—I think that I have."

"Yes, sir. Mebby so."

"I have got a notion, Julius, that he has found a way to get inside of that little house on the bluff at the end of the dam. What do you think about that?"

"I don't think anything about it, sir."

"Why not?"

"'Cause they can't nobody get inside of that house on the bluff 'lessen Mis' Kitten lets 'em in. That's her own 'special nest, Mr. Roddy, an' nobody ever goes into it but jest her own self. He couldn't get into it unless she let him in, an' Mis' Kitten wouldn't do that, would she—'specially when she wouldn't let me into it, or Phemie, or even Mr. Harvard himself? No, sir!"

"One of the windows has been uncovered within the last half hour, Julius, and I saw somebody peering out of it."

"Then you saw your own sister, Mr. Roddy."

"No, Julius, I know better than that. It's my profession to know things."

"Then you saw double, that's all. You just thought mebby he might be there, an' so you thought you saw him there," Julius insisted.

"Possibly," Roderick replied; but he was more than ever convinced that he was correct about it.

CHAPTER XXXIX

FULFILLING THE COMPACT

There was yet another person who was both puzzled and troubled in regard to the Nest, and that person was Bingham Harvard, one time alias the Night Wind.

For Bing had seen the face at the window the instant he stepped his foot upon the boat-house platform, and he knew that the face was not Katherine's.

True, he had not seen it plainly enough to recognize it, but there was nevertheless not the slightest doubt in his mind concerning the identity of it.

It had been Belknap's face, of course, and Belknap could not have found entry to the Nest without the personal assistance of Katherine, therefore she was hiding him.

It was with the greatest difficulty that he succeeded in controlling himself so that his companion, Carruthers, might not see the shock he had received, and he found that he faced even a greater difficulty when he attempted to reason out to his own satisfaction why Katherine should have consented to such an act.

Try as he might, he could find only one possible solution of the problem, and that was that Belknap had succeeded in so working upon Katherine's sympathies that she had been prevailed upon to help him to escape. That Katherine—his wife—Lady Kate of the Police—peerless and fearless Katherine—was afraid of the man, and had been forced through fear of him to do what she had done, Harvard did not for a moment believe. "And," he told himself, "in her own good time she will tell me all about it."

So, in a sense, he shrugged his shoulders and dismissed the thought of it; or tried to do so.

But, just the same, he did not intend that Conrad Belknap should get away, even if it were Katherine's wish that he should, and so he set himself to watch.

Not to watch Katherine! Do not for a moment suppose that! But to watch for Belknap's appearance when he should be let out of the Nest by Katherine, to make his getaway from the vicinity of Myquest; and to see to it that he did not make his escape. Not to lay hands upon the man himself, but to dog him, and follow him, and keep him within reach, until he should fall into the hands of one or more of the watching sleuths who were on his trail.

Katherine he would permit to go and come, as she pleased and he would not let her know what he knew until she got ready to tell him all about it; but all the same he would not stand passively near and permit that crook of a thousand crimes to impose upon her sympathies, and thus escape the consequences of his errors.

That being settled in his mind, he felt better; quite at ease, in fact.

Katherine was quite the life of the party at the dinner table that evening; so much so that her husband regarded her with well-concealed astonishment, and Carruthers, who had arrived at not unsimilar conclusions, with interest. Both men, husband and brother, were at fault in their reasonings—yet Katherine had her own reasons for her gaiety.

Why should she not have been gay?

She had obtained possession of the "Eye of Nadja," and had concealed it, without breaking any of her promises to Belknap in any sense of the word. She had restored the "scrubby old cane" to its accustomed place behind the piano in the music-room, and the bulb at its top was not empty, either; it contained a nice round pebble, wrapped in the same foil and tissue that had contained the wonderful ruby with an emerald buried in the middle of it. Belknap might find the cane if he chose, for she did not doubt that Belknap had worked out the secret of the ruby's hiding place by some mysterious process of his thieving intelligence—he might make his escape, if he could, and take the old and worthless cane with him. She would set him free that very night, and she would be well rid of him.

True, when he found that he had been fooled, he might forget his promise to send her the documentary evidence that would establish her brother's innocence, but, if such evidence was in existence, there would be other ways to find it. She would, later, consult Mr. Carruthers on the point, for she had taken a great and unaccountable liking to that same Carruthers who somehow reminded her of something, or somebody, or—she knew that she liked him, and believed that she could trust him; and he was an expert operative of the secret service who were the best detectives in the world.

* * * * * * *

That evening was not a pleasant one outside, after dinner. Fog had blown in from the ocean, and a gentle rain, without wind, was falling. The guests remained indoors. The absence of Belknap was commented on, and regretted. The atmosphere, even within the house, was surcharged with unrest, and the members of the party, one after another, discovered that they had letters to write, or books to read, or complained of headaches, or otherwise found excuses to seek their several rooms very early.

Bing was himself among the first to find one, and go, and he took Clancy with him. Carruthers disappeared soon after dinner. Betty yawned several times without concealment, and departed, and so on, until Katherine, a little past ten, found herself alone with Roberta—and the trouble was that Roberta seemed inclined to more confidences; seemed eager for another heart-to-heart talk with Katherine. But Katherine found a way to avoid even that.

"Roberta," she said, when they were alone, "I wish very much that you would take the daguerreotype of Mrs. Clancy's great-grandmother that you still have in your possession, to my father. You will find him in the library, reading. I want you to ask him to help you to work out the puzzle of your likeness to her. He can do it."

Thus Katherine was free to go to the Nest whenever she chose—and she decided to go at once.

Would she have been disturbed, do you suppose, if she had guessed that her husband, having taken Tom Clancy into his confidence and secured his aid, had taken Tom with him, and gone already to a post of observation from whence any person who entered or departed from the Nest could be seen?

Would she have been disturbed if she had known that Carruthers and several of his men had drawn a cordon around the house and grounds of Myquest through which, as they confidently believed, no person could penetrate?

It is to be doubted if she would have cared a hang about them if she had known both circumstances. They were not there because of any betrayal by her. It could not matter, and she did not care, what might happen to Belknap after he left the Nest. That was up to him.

More than likely she would have gone on her way unconcerned even if a thousand pairs of eyes had been watching, and she had known the fact.

It has been said that because of the opened shutter at the Nest, Katherine was on her guard lest Belknap, having discovered that secret, had likewise uncovered others; so, when she did approach the chalet, she was ready for any emergency—for there were some appliances there which she knew he could not find.

But she was in no wise prepared for what she saw when she got there. Her extreme caution in approaching and entering had been entirely unnecessary; and, after she was safely inside and the door was closed, she may be forgiven for laughter.

Belknap had discovered another one of the mysteries of the Nest, for, over against the great stone fireplace, within a network of steel wires that extended from beneath the granite shelf straight out over him and down in front of, and at either side of him, he was as securely caged and helpless as ever any wild beast in a menagerie has been.

And the joke of it was, the steel network of wires had never been intended for a trap! It was no more and no less than a fire-screen; but, like almost every mechanical contrivance in the chalet, it was operated by touching a button. And that particular button could be easily found, for it was exactly like the one that Katherine had shown to him at the opposite end of the shelf beneath the little idol.

Belknap was more crestfallen than angry. He was too glad of Katherine's arrival to be angry.

"You have got yourself into a nice fix," she told him. "You should have stood beyond the end of the shelf when you touched the button which lowers the screen; not at the middle of it. Did it hit you on the head and hurt you when it shot out and dropped into place?"

"It did," he replied. "Will you kindly let me out?"

"In a moment. I have something to propose to you first."

"I think that I'll agree to almost anything after this experience," he said with a grin. "Anything save abandoning 'Nadja's Eye.'"

"Will you accept your liberty to-night, instead of waiting longer?"

"Yes."

"It is storming outside, and everybody at the house has retired. Will you go earlier than two o'clock?"

"I will go now, if you like, if it is true that all the guests have gone to their rooms," he replied.

Katherine was thoughtful for a moment, then she said:

"It is only fair that I should warn you of something, Mr. Belknap. I am convinced that Myquest is watched."

"As to that"—he snapped his fingers—"so am I. I will take care of that part of it."

"Very good." She stepped to the end of the shelf and released him.

As he stepped free she moved swiftly across the room, and, as if by magic, the door swung open while she walked, and he was not able to see how she did it. At the opposite side of the room she stopped and faced him.

"Go," she said. "The way is open. I have kept all of my promises to you; I expect that you are still man enough to keep yours to me."

"I will," he said. "May I—"

"No. You may do nothing more. You may not address me again; otherwise, I will relent. Go."

He went.

Katherine relapsed upon a chair as soon as the doorway had closed after him.

CHAPTER XL

BELKNAP'S PREPARED GETAWAY

It was exactly twelve minutes, according to Bingham Harvard's watch, after Katherine entered the Nest, when Conrad Belknap came out of it.

He descended the first steps swiftly, was lost sight of along the winding path among the boulders, could be seen again in his descent of the second stairs, and then—to the astonishment of those who watched—he started rapidly toward the house.

They followed—and therefore they did not see Katherine when she came out from the Nest ten minutes later, and at the bottom of the stairs directed her course through the wood toward Julius's cottage. She knew that Julius would be awaiting her, because she had told him to wait.

Belknap ascended the steps to the veranda boldly. The hour was still early. If he should encounter one of the guests—well, he had just returned; that would be all. He knew the methods of secret service men, and did not believe that Carruthers's errand at Myquest was generally known.

He encountered nobody. The house had not been closed up, nor the lights extinguished. He entered the music-room at one of the windows.

As directly as the needle of a compass points north, he went to the corner behind the piano and secured the "scrubby old cane."

He lifted it, examined it attentively, worked at the knob on top, found it secure, tried the ferrule, and loosened it as far as it would unscrew. Then he tried the knob again, and opened it.

He turned white to the lips when he discovered the object wrapped in foil and tissue inside. He extracted it. He held it worshipfully in the hollow of one hand and stared at it. His other hand moved as if to unwind the wrappings, and stopped. He put the object that was wrapped in foil and tissue into his pocket.

After that he appeared to be considering his next move; he was, if the watchers had but known it. He was thinking that he would like to have one more interview with Roberta before he went away; but he decided against it.

He went out of the music-room like a flash. It was wonderful how quickly he could move when he wanted to—like a cat, or any other predatory animal—naturally.

The two watchers lost sight of him then, and could not follow. They had thought that he would leave the house by the way he entered it—but Cranshaw Belding, otherwise Conrad Belknap, was far too wise for that sort of thing.

"We have lost him," Tom Clancy said.

"Go around to the rear, Tom," Bing replied, and darted away without imparting his own intention.

Harvard, as it happened, having so often been in the position of fugitive himself, presaged Belknap's movements by what he would have done himself under like circumstances, and his ideas were well assumed. He went to the rose bower, from which he could watch the side entrance.

Belknap appeared at last, moving cautiously. He darted among the shrubbery, and kept himself amid the deepest shadows; but Harvard had seen him lift his head and point, as a hunting-dog points, in the direction of his course.

Harvard caught sight of him again as he went out upon the platform at the boat-house.

Belknap secured a paddle and lifted a canoe into the water. He got into it and paddled out upon the lake, making his way directly toward the dam. If it had been possible to approach the Nest by that route, Harvard would have thought that he was returning to the chalet.

He was not. He paddled directly to the dam at the opposite end from the Nest, and Harvard, running like a hare, followed along the shore of the lake. But when Bing Harvard got near enough to the dam he could see only an empty canoe that was hugged against it.

"What the dickens—" he began to ask himself, but before he completed the self-asked question he had thrown off his coat, vest, and shoes, and was in the water.

He swam quickly to the canoe where it was hugged against the dam—and then he discovered that three big spikes had been driven securely into a block of wood which, in its turn, had been ingen-

240

iously wedged into the masonry of the dam itself; and that a hemp rope no larger than a clothes-line was knotted around the spikes—a knotted rope, to facilitate descent, Bing had no doubt.

It was Belknap's prepared getaway, made on the sly; but it was a daring method. The fall from the top of the dam to the jagged rocks below was sixty feet, as Harvard well knew.

"By Jove," Bing muttered to himself, "the fellow deserves to get away! And he will, if he reaches the bottom in—"

He stopped, fascinated by what he saw.

The block of wood into which the spikes had been driven, that had been wedged into the masonry of the dam, trembled; it was coming loose.

Harvard reached out for it frantically. He would have grasped and held it if he could, and saved the life of the man he had been pursuing.

But he was not quick enough.

The block of wood came entirely loose before he could seize upon it, and disappeared across the top of the dam. During an instant, which seemed an eternity, Harvard listened; but no cry came up to him from the depths below; only a dull thud, a subdued crash, and silence.

They found Belknap half an hour later. It was apparent that he had been killed instantly. His neck was broken, and there was a jagged wound above his right temple besides. While…

Unmindful of what was going on, the guests at Myquest slept peacefully.

Within the larger garage, to which the body of Belknap was carried, a group of people was gathered. There were several strangers there who went outside, presently, at the request of Carruthers, for they were the men who had been assisting him. Rodney Rushton was there, and Tom Clancy, and Julius. Roberta was there, clinging close to Katherine. Senator Maxwilton was there, he having still been deep in the discussion of genealogy with Roberta when Katherine summoned her. Bing Harvard was there, very silent and very still.

When Carruthers sent his men away, he closed the door and turned to face those who remained; but—

As he made the turn he swept one hand across his face.

As if by magic the hideous scar that had so distorted and changed his every feature, was torn away, and he stood revealed to all as Roderick Maxwilton.

Katherine, who had been a long time in consultation with Julius, was, in a half measure, prepared for it; nevertheless she started forward with a quick cry of joy and threw her arms around her brother's neck, to the utter amazement of Bing.

It was the Senator (who, oddly, seemed not surprised at all) who stepped to Bing's side quickly and uttered the three words that explained the situation.

"It is Roderick," he said; then, after a moment, he added: "I knew yesterday, Bingham. He took me aside and told me. Then, tonight, after dinner, we went together to his mother; and—Bingham—she is as happy now as she was on that day, years ago, when she brought him into the world."

"Roberta," the Senator went on, "come here." Then: "Katherine, Roberta is a Maxwilton. She is a cousin, many times removed. She is even closer kin to your wife, Tom," he added, turning to Clancy. "They had the same great-grandmother. She is, I am proud to state, a Maxwilton."

"You bet she is!" Roderick announced, reaching out and clasping one of her hands. "And she is going to be a Maxwilton by name as well as by nativity."

"This is not a moment nor a place for rejoicing," Katherine announced, "so, although it is late, I want you all to come with me to the library. I have something of interest to tell."

"One moment," said Roderick. "Before we leave the silent member of this party, I have something to tell. He has been as bad as bad could be, but there was an explanation for it, if not an excuse. He is dead, now. In his possession, when his clothing was searched, we found quite an assortment of papers. Some of them related to the hiding places of certain engraved plates which the United States government will now secure, and destroy. Others referred to matters connected with me, and are proof sufficient of my innocence of certain acts with which I was once charged, if, happily, it were not the fact that I have already been acquitted of it by my own department. So I shall suggest that no further reference be made to his misdeeds, and in making that proposal I know that I will have the approval of my chief. He is dead. Let him rest."

"And he died without knowing that he did not possess the 'Eye of Nadja,'" Katherine exclaimed. "I am very glad of that. Yes, I am glad of it."

And, until she told her story in the library, they did not know what she meant.

www.ingramcontent.com/pod-product-compliance
Lightning Source LLC
Chambersburg PA
CBHW031950240626
47153CB00003B/923